SWANN DIVES IN

A HENRY SWANN NOVEL

SWANN DIVES IN

CHARLES SALZBERG

FIVE STAR

A part of Gale, Cengage Learning

GALE
CENGAGE Learning·

Detroit • New York • San Francisco • New Haven, Conn • Waterville, Maine • London

GALE
CENGAGE Learning®

LIBRARY OF CONGRESS CATALOGING-IN-PUBLICATION DATA

Salzberg, Charles.
    Swann dives in : a Henry Swann novel / Charles Salzberg. — 1st ed.
        p. cm.
        ISBN 978-1-4328-2622-2 (hardcover) — ISBN 1-4328-2622-0 (hardcover)
        1. Private investigators—New York (State) —New York—Fiction. I. Title.
PS3619.A443S92 2012
813'.6—dc23   2012018081

First Edition. First Printing: October 2012.
Published in conjunction with Tekno Books and Ed Gorman.
Find us on Facebook– https://www.facebook.com/FiveStarCengage
Visit our website– http://www.gale.cengage.com/fivestar/
Contact Five Star™ Publishing at FiveStar@cengage.com

Printed in Mexico
1 2 3 4 5 6 7 16 15 14 13 12

ACKNOWLEDGMENTS

I'd like to thank my good friends, Elliot Ravetz and Sharyn Wolf, for their unending support of my work. I'd also like to thank Darren Winston for his extremely helpful crash course in the world of rare books. I just hope I got most of it right, Darren. Thanks to the real-life embodiments of Ross Klavan, Richard Dubin, Jonathan Kravetz, and Mark Goldblatt, for allowing me to attach their names to characters who might or might not be anything like them. I hope they're still speaking to me once this book hits the shelves. Thanks to D.B. for engaging me in a contest of words and pages, which spurred me on to finish this book.

To my agent, Alex Glass, thank you for handling all the minutiae that comes with being published, always with good humor. Thanks to Alice Duncan, my editor; Marty and Roz Greenberg; and to all my friends, colleagues, students and strangers who purchased *Swann's Last Song* and urged me to write another. I hope I haven't disappointed (or embarrassed) you.

"If a man indulges himself in murder, very soon he comes to think of robbing, and from robbing he comes to drinking and Sabbath breaking; and from that to incivility and procrastination."
—Thomas de Quincy, "On Murder . . ."

"This taught me a lesson, but I'm not sure what it is."
—John McEnroe

★ ★ ★ ★ ★

PART 1
NEW YORK CITY

★ ★ ★ ★ ★

"Whatever liberates our spirit without giving us
self-control is disastrous."
—Johann Wolfgang decibels Goethe

1
BAD RECEPTION

One flight of stairs too many. That was the straw that broke this camel's back.

Not lunging dizzily over the sides of roofs searching for faulty cable connections. Not day after dreary day of lugging heavy loads of equipment—cable boxes, cable wires, signal power checkers, not to mention my sorry ass—in all kinds of god-awful weather. Not the clients—yes, we were supposed to call them clients, as opposed to what they actually were: royal pains in the ass, angry at having to carve out huge chunks of their day to stay home and wait for me, their media savior.

Just those damned, interminable flights of stairs; stairs that sent waves of lactic acid shooting through my calves, straight up into my thighs, causing my legs to metamorphose not into fragile fluttering butterflies, but thick redwood stumps.

What was it, two, three years I'd been working for the cable company? I'd lost track. Ever since my last case as a skip tracer, a nightmarish experience that sucked the wind out of my sails almost effectively as a five-story walk-up, my life was pretty much a blur, as out of focus as a cableless TV. At the age of forty-six, I was trying to find myself instead of finding other people. Only I wasn't doing a very good job of it.

Casting about for some new way to make a semi-honest living, I reckoned communications was the way to go. As television signals bounced from skyscraper to skyscraper, like so many steel pellets in a giant pinball machine, the airwaves were left saturated with ghosts that haunted the unconnected. Cable companies, the true ghostbusters of the last half of the twentieth century, were ready at the rescue. Add to this the fact that HBO, Showtime and their rival pay TV stations were thriving, not to mention that untested force called Web TV, and it was inevitable that cable was in everybody's future, mine included.

So, I did what everyone else does when they're looking for a job in New York City, I answered an ad in the *New York Times.* After two weeks of technical training, which included a crash course in customer relations—something I was sorely in need of, as my dislike of everyone, yes, even myself, has been well documented—I was issued my official New York City Community Cable Company credentials, including the bright blue and red identifying logo patch, which I convinced one of my former skip trace clients to sew on my work shirt at no cost. After all, it was the least she could do. Two years earlier I'd located her husband and, using the friendliest persuasion I could muster, made sure he ponied up the long-past-due child support payments, which allowed her, for the time being at least, to extricate herself from the welfare rolls.

So here I was, a foot-soldier in the war against double and triple image ghosts and out of season, nonmeteorological snowstorms. In the beginning, it was refreshing to enter someone's apartment as a welcome guest, rather than an intruder looking to nail them for some unpaid bill or other transgression against the economic system of this fair land of ours. Instead, I was there to improve the quality of their couch-potato lives; to see to it that their otherwise dull, colorless evenings were filled with fun and frolic; to ensure that they would not miss their favorite soap opera, game show, reality show, sit-com, quiz show, sporting event, drama or late-night gab fest, due to the ubiquitous urban bugaboo of bad reception. Instead of an ogre, there to bring home the harsh reality of a cash-and-carry society, I was the prodigal son, a white knight returning to them the gift of fantasy. I was there to brighten their dull, ever-so-ordinary, hum-drum lives. I was Santa Claus, the Tooth Fairy, the Easter Bunny, Thomas Edison and Bill Sarnoff all rolled up into one. It was as if I had undergone a miraculous religious awakening. Did I go so far as to think of myself as a messiah of the airwaves? The truth? Yeah, damn it, sometimes I did. Delusions of grandeur? Not if your reception was nonexistent.

It was another typical cable day. I was answering a call on West 58th Street, about as close to the river as you can get without getting your feet wet. A walk-up, nestled among used-car lots and empty buildings waiting to be rehabbed to accommodate those who now think of Hell's Kitchen as chic. Fifth floor, naturally. It was early July and very hot. And humid. The novelty, joy and pseudo-religious aspects of the job had long since vanished, and I was wondering how much longer I could keep this up.

Sweat dribbling down the back of my neck, I stepped into the vestibule and pressed the buzzer. No answer. I glanced at my watch and noted it was only 11:30. The rules, as decreed by the high command of Community Cable Company, aka CCC, stated I could be at a customer's abode anywhere from eight in the morning till one in the afternoon. I was well within the guidelines. I'd done my part. So where was the client?

I flirted with the idea of blowing off the rest of the day, but before I took a step backward out the door, I buzzed again. Why? Because I'm persistent. It's a trait that's gotten me in plenty of trouble before and will again, I'm sure. I'm trying to learn how to take no for an answer, but it hasn't sunk in yet. Still no answer. I tried the super. Nada. I buzzed a couple other apartments. No answer from any of them, either. I pulled out my wallet, grabbed the only credit card I had left, shoved it in the space in the door between the lock and the doorjamb and, just like that, I was in.

I trudged up the particularly steep set of stairs and when I finally reached the fifth floor, leaving my breath somewhere around the third, I vigorously knocked on 5B.

"Yeah?" a froggy voice from inside answered.

"Cable."

"Just a second."

More than a few seconds passed, while I tried in vain to get back breath that was probably lost forever, and when the door finally opened I was faced by an old geezer with white hair that looked as if an electrical charge had been applied, scrawny, frail-looking, unshaven. He was wearing baggy trousers that hung well below his waist, even though they were ostensibly held up by suspenders, and a Hard Rock Café T-shirt stained with God only knows what.

"I been waitin' since eight o'clock. Been up since six," he whined in a voice that was like fingernails on a blackboard. Only worse.

"I buzzed. No answer."

"Buzzer's broke."

"You could have left a note or something. How'd you expect me to know you were here?"

"Not my problem, bud." He pointed to a clock on the wall. "You're late."

I tapped my watched. "Ten and one. Didn't they tell you?"

"Get told a lot of things. Most of 'em don't mean a damn thing." He looked over to a clock radio resting on a table next to a couch that had obviously been rescued from the street. "Dammit, I'm missin' my programs. Why's it gotta be closer to one?"

"Why don't they just sew up the ozone hole and put an end

14

to global warming? Why are you on the fifth floor? Why not the first? Just another one of a series of life's irritating little mysteries. Part of God's infernal plan," I said. "So, what's the problem?"

"How the fuck do I know? You're the cable guy. You tell me."

"Mister, it's gotta be eighty-five degrees out there and the humidity's off the chart, so cut me some slack, will you? Describe the problem and I can get on with it."

"Ain't got no cable, that's the problem. No cable, no TV reception. No TV reception, I don't get my programs. I don't get my programs, I'm pissed and I call the cable company and they send a wise guy like you out to fix it. It's as simple as that."

"Yes," I allowed. "I guess it is. If only the rest of life were that simple."

"You the cable guy or some kind of goddamn philosopher?"

I pointed to the telltale insignia on my shirt, which, I noticed, was beginning to fray and come off at one corner. I'd have to have that taken care of before the next inspection. CCC frowns on sloppy dress, which they equated with sloppy service. That you could dress like Cary Grant and still give bad service didn't seem to occur to them.

He squinted at my name tag over the cable logo. *H. Swann.* "That you?"

"Yeah."

"Swann? What kinda name is that?"

"Mine."

"Like the song," he said, as he grimaced and scratched his crotch.

"How's that?"

"You know, the river song . . ."

As if I hadn't heard that one before.

He started to sing, "Way down along the Swannee River . . ."

"Oh, yeah . . ." I said, rolling my eyes.

15

"So, what's the *H.* for?" he asked.

Harried. Homesick. Heart-broken. Hellacious. Helpless. Homeless. Hash browns. Hostile. Hapless. Handicapped. Hamstrung. Hopeless. The possibilities were endless. But I gave him the truth: "Henry. Now, why don't you show me where the damn set is."

He scratched under his arm, coughed, grimaced, then he showed me. I turned the set on and got nothing but a January snowstorm. "Is there access to the roof?"

"How the hell should I know? You think I go up to the roof? To what? Sunbathe?" He waved his pale arms in my face, one of them half-covered with a tattoo of an American eagle in faded blue and white. "This look like I get out much? Besides, I'm afraid a heights, bub."

I hitched my bag over my shoulder and started toward the door.

"Where the hell you going?"

"To the roof. To check the connection. Got a problem with that?"

"So whaddya think it is?" he asked, following close behind me.

"I think you've got no cable, that's what I think."

"Wise guy," he said as he went at his crotch again. I wanted to warn him that too much of that and his nuts might fall off, but in the name of good customer relations, I kept my mouth shut. Working with the public takes discipline and patience, both of which for me are in short supply.

I climbed yet one more flight of stairs, stepped out onto yet one more barren rooftop and checked yet one more set of connections. They seemed okay. I came back downstairs. He was waiting for me at the door, his pale-ass, veiny white arms folded menacingly across his chest. "Well?" he said.

"It's gotta be a problem with the block."

"That's just what I told 'em. When I called the other day, I said it had to be out there on the street. So why'd they waste my time sendin' you?"

"Sadism."

"Huh?"

"Never mind. Can I use your phone?" I had a cell in my pocket, but I'd be damned if I was going to use up my minutes on this guy. Or any other client, for that matter.

"What makes you think I got one?"

"A man's got cable, he's got a phone."

"What're you, Sherlock Holmes?"

"Never was, never will be."

He cleared his throat, which by now sounded like a garbage truck pick-up. I backed away. "Had to give up a goddamn morning just so you could tell me the block's out," he grumbled as he showed me to the phone. I called in and spoke to my supervisor, dutifully reporting the problem. After I finished, he told me I had a message from someone named Jake, and then reamed me out for getting personal messages at the office. The only Jake I knew was a bail bondsman I used to do some work for once in a while, in a former life.

After reassuring the old man that his cable would be fixed by the end of the day—an out-and-out lie; I just don't know what got into me—I went downstairs, pulled out my cell and called the number. Sure enough, it was my Jake, the bail bondsman.

"What's the deal, Jake?"

"Got a job for you."

"No personal house calls, Jake. You gotta go through the company."

"Not that kind of job."

"You know I'm not in the business anymore."

"For old time's sake."

"I buy you a beer, you buy me one, that's old time's sake.

17

But this is a business I'm not in anymore."

"Come on, Swann, I'm not askin' for the moon here. I'm in a tight spot. Help me out, just this once, pal 'o mine. Come on down to my office when you get off work and I'll clue you in. It's a no-brainer case, pal. Your specialty. Besides, I'm sure you could use a few extra bucks. Whadaya say?"

"I don't know . . ."

"Henry, I don't want to have to call in old markers, you know . . ."

"I wasn't aware you had any, Jake."

"Give me some time. I'll think of something."

I paused a moment. Oh, what the hell. A few bucks were a few bucks. Besides, I hadn't seen Jake in a while, and I didn't have all that many friends that I could afford to alienate someone who considered himself in that small group.

"Okay. I'll be there around seven."

Jake's office was in downtown Manhattan, not far from the courthouse, from whence he got most of his business. When I arrived, Jake was alone, his feet propped up on his desk, watching a small black-and-white TV.

"I think this is the same position I left you in the last time I was here," I said. I couldn't see the TV, but I heard the unmistakable sound of a sit-com laugh track.

"It's comfortable," said Jake. "So why not?"

I came around to his side of the desk, pulled up a chair and sat down beside him. "You like this piece of crap?" I asked, gesturing toward the TV.

"The Cos? He's the best. Even in reruns."

"If you say so. You know, Jake, they invented color TV a few years back. Things can't be so bad that you can't afford to buy one for yourself."

There was a roar of fake laughter, and Jake's eyes were pulled back to the screen, as if they were magnetized.

"I like black and white," he said. "Reminds me of my child-hood."

"That's something most of us would like to forget . . ."

"Not me. It was what they call idyllic."

"You been reading the dictionary again, Jake?"

"Fuck you. You know, Swann, while you're here, I been havin' some trouble with the reception. Wavy lines, double images, like that." He pointed to the screen. "See what I mean."

"Call the cable company."

"I don't got to. I already got you here."

"But that's not why, is it?"

"No, but I thought maybe I could get me some free advice. You're the expert now, aren't you?"

"Jake, I hate to break it to you, but you call the cable company and they send some jerk like me out here, no charge."

"Yeah, well, what are friends for?"

"What are they for, Jake?"

He reached over and flicked off the TV, just as Cosby was about to set one of his kids straight on the awesome yet reward-ing responsibilities of life on the planet. He pulled a file from a drawer and slapped it on his desk. "Got me an Olympian here, Swann. A runner and a jumper. I need you to find him and bring him back."

"There are plenty of guys could do that for you, Jake. I'm out of the business. You know that."

"I need you on this one, Swann."

"Why's that?"

"Because you're still the best."

"Cut the crap, Jake. I was never the best. I was cheap. I was relatively honest and sometimes, when things were really bad, I'd handle the shit-ass little jobs you offered because I needed the money. Come to think of it, I always needed the money."

"You could probably still use the money."

I didn't say anything because the obvious rarely has to be stated.

"I never did know why you quit."

"Because life wasn't what I thought it should be."

"Tell me something I don't already know. When you find out what it is, let me know."

"You'll be the first."

"You still a Met fan?"

"I'm still a masochist, so you tell me."

"I think they're going all the way this year. Valentine actually knows what the hell he's doing. That Ordonez kid, no stick, but he can really pick 'em. And Piazza, Ventura . . . so their pitchin' ain't quite up to snuff, they can still cop the wild card. Take it from me, two thousand's their year. Been to any games lately?"

"Nope."

"That's a shame. Maybe I can do something for you."

"You can, Jake. I'm hungry. I'm tired. I've been on my feet all day. Lay it out for me, so I can turn you down the nicest way I know how and you can get back to the Cos."

"Burglary. Twenty grand shot to shit if you don't get him back."

"That's kind of high for a simple breaking and entering, isn't it?"

"Priors. He gets nailed on this one, he goes down for a long time."

"What about the collateral?"

Jake made a passing sign with his hand.

"You asshole."

"I got a heart, okay?"

"And look where it got you."

"I can't afford to eat twenty big ones, Swann. You find the dude, I'll make it worth your while."

"You never did before."

"Very funny."

"Yeah, well, I'm in the entertainment business now."

"Name's Carlos Robles. From uptown, near where you used to have your office. But I don't have a good address on him. He's a family man. Find them, you'll find him."

"You make it sound easy."

"For you, it will be."

"Why not just do it yourself, or get one of your regular flunkies?"

"Because I don't want it to get around I was made a fool of, okay? Besides, I feel sorry for you, Swann. You're a shadow of your former self, and I want to show you what you been missing."

"You're a saint, Jake."

"Ain't that the truth."

"It's against my better judgment—not that I have any—but okay, for old time's sake. And for the money, naturally. How much are we talking about?"

"Two-fifty."

I flicked the TV back on. The cutest little Huxtable was in the midst of wrapping dad around her little finger. "Enjoy the Cos," I said, as I made a dramatic move toward the door.

"Okay, okay. Five hundred. Jesus, why not just rip my heart out?"

"Because first I'd have to find it, and I haven't got that much time. Besides, I think you ought to hang onto it, Jake. It reminds those of us who know you that you are, on occasion, capable of human emotions."

He frowned. "Thanks a lot, pal."

I smiled, scooped up the file, tucked it into my jacket pocket, and headed for the door.

"When will I hear from you?" Jake asked, his feet recapturing their former position on his desk.

"Tomorrow, maybe. I can't afford to waste a lot of time for a measly five bills."

"Yeah," said Jake, "and just think of all those sets waitin' to be fixed."

2
SWITCHING CHANNELS

You may not be able to teach an old dog new tricks, but we don't forget the ones we've already learned. Call it muscle memory, if you will. I figured since Señor Robles was purported to be a family man in the tradition of Robert Young, Tim Allen and Bill Cosby, the best way to trace him was through his family. Jake knew that too, which is why all the pertinent information was in the file. I figured the best place to start was with the local elementary school.

I awarded myself a well-deserved day off by calling in sick. Nevertheless, I still wore my snappy, ever-in-style, blue-gray cable outfit because I thought it might come in handy as a disguise. I'm not big on changing appearances, but you can often make people's misperception of you work in your favor. I've spent a good part of my life being underestimated, and I like keeping it that way.

First stop was P.S. 171 on Amsterdam. After sweet-talking the guard at the front door—is this what the world has come to?—I went directly to the principal's office where I asked the school secretary if the Robles kid was registered. He was. In fact, eight of them were. From reading the file, I knew the one I was looking for was named Roberto and he was nine years old, which put him in the fourth grade. Yes, there was a Roberto Robles in the fourth grade. Could I have his address? No way. Could I speak to the little fella. No, no, no, no. Absolutely not. Could I leave a note for him to bring home to his mother? A couple of hems, a couple of haws, and then it seemed as if that would be all right. I said I'd be back in a few minutes with a note for Roberto to take home.

I found a Duane Reade down the block, picked up a package of colored construction paper, a magic marker, and a roll of scotch tape. I chose the most brightly colored sheet in the package—cherry red—threw the rest away, drew a few squiggly lines on it. I folded the paper in half and taped the sides together. On the front, in large, thickly drawn letters, I wrote, "Mrs. Carlos Robles."

I went back to the principal's office and handed the secretary the note, impressing upon her how important it was to make sure little Roberto got it and took it home to mom.

A few minutes before three, I stationed myself at the front exit to the school. I figured classes would be dismissed in order of grade, lowest first, and I was right. Five to three the nine-year-olds came tumbling out of the building, boys first, their testosterone propelling them out onto the sidewalk like marbles shot out of a cannon. The kid holding onto a bright red folded piece of construction paper, which he had pressed tightly against his notebook, had to be Roberto Robles. As soon as he hit the pavement, he stopped and jammed the note into his backpack, then headed north, up the avenue.

I followed the kid home, which turned out to be a rundown tenement on 152nd Street, just off Broadway. The kid pushed open the door and went inside. I was right behind him. Maintaining a flight between us, not that he was paying attention to anything other than the Gameboy he was fiddling with, I followed him up to the third floor and watched from the staircase as he knocked twice on the door of an apartment. Seconds passed, then the door opened a crack. A man wearing a wife-beater stuck his head out, looked around, then let the kid in. I went downstairs and called Jake.

"Can of corn," I said.

"You found him?"

"Yeah."

"I knew I could count on you, Swann. Now reel him in."

"Jesus, Jake."

"It's part of the package, Swann. You know that."

"Can't you send someone else down here to take care of that? I'm out of practice and besides, his kid's in there with him. What the hell am I going to do with him?"

"My heart bleeds. You got the cuffs, don't you?"

"Yeah."

"Use 'em."

"What if he's got firepower? You know I hate that shit. That's why I quit doing business with you. Bill skippers, wife deserters, that was my game. Cons, that's something else."

"He's just a B and E man. No physical shit on his record. Chill out, Swann."

"It's a new America, Jake. Eight-year-old kids carry Uzis. They make bombs and blow up schools. They shoot their parents, their schoolteachers, their friends."

"So frisk the damn kid. See ya in about an hour. If you run into any trouble, dial nine-one-one."

"Thanks for nothing."

I hung up the phone and fingered the cold metal pair of cuffs that bulged in my back pocket—I'd brought them out of habit, not because I expected to use them.

I climbed those damned stairs again and pressed my ear up against the front door of 3-D. I could hear the TV blasting. It was Judge Judy reaming someone out. I rapped on the front door. Nothing. I rapped again. A man's heavily Spanish-accented voice called out, "Yeah, who the fuck is it?"

"Community Cable."

"I didn't call no fuckin' cable, man."

"There's a problem in the building and I need to check your reception."

"Reception's fine, man. Get lost."

"You don't let me check it, I got to turn it off in the entire building."

"Shit."

I heard footsteps. The voice, directly behind the door now, said, "How I know you the cable guy?"

"Look out the peephole," I said, stopping just short of adding, "asshole."

His eye blocked the light coming from inside. I pointed to the insignia on my shirt.

"You dressed like cable, man, but that don't mean you cable."

Carlos had just summed up one of the more important lessons of life, one I'd learned the hard way: appearances are often deceiving. Never completely trust your eyes, ears or sense of smell. Most people don't understand that, and that very elemental misunderstanding, that basic miscomprehension of life, is something I have always relied on. That cynicism is, I'm afraid, what makes it virtually impossible to be around me for any length of time. "Here, take a look at this," I said, holding my ID card up to the peephole with one hand while I gripped the cuffs in my back pocket with the other.

He unlocked the door, opened it, and there, standing in his boxers, holding a bottle of Corona and reeking of weed, was Señor Carlos Robles, in the flesh.

"Mr. Robles," I said, moving my shoulder forward and sticking my foot in the door so he couldn't close it on me, "I'm afraid we've got another, non-related cable problem. Seems you stiffed a friend of mine . . ." Before he could react, I yanked the cuffs out of my pocket and, in a move I could still perform in my sleep, slapped one cuff on his right wrist.

"Hey, man . . ."

I whipped his other arm around behind his back and lifted up. "I don't want any trouble, especially with your kid in the other room, so why don't you just cooperate and we can resolve this thing. All you've got to do is let Jake turn you in and you're home free."

While I was in the midst of giving this little speech an odd thing was happening. I was getting an adrenaline rush, a rush I hadn't had in over three years. It was introduced as a tingling sensation that coursed through my body, not unlike the lactic acid that attacked me when I climbed stairs, but much more pleasant. I wondered, did I really miss all this? The thrill of the hunt, the ecstasy of the capture? Was this possible? Please, God, no . . . I did not want to be drawn back into a life of uncertainty, a life that too often made no sense. And so, instead of enjoying the feeling, I fought it. I told myself that the rush was no rush at all, simply a combination of nerves and fear.

"You hurtin' me, man!" he moaned.

"Stop fighting me and it won't hurt."

"All right, man, all right. But my kid. I can't leave him here alone. He's only nine, man. My wife'll fuckin' kill me."

"Okay, here's what we'll do. You tell him to come out here with a pair of your pants, a shirt, and your shoes, and we'll take him with us. When we get down there, we'll call your wife and she can pick him up."

"Fuck, man . . ."

"This is non-negotiable, Carlos," I said, hoping he knew what the word meant.

Fifteen minutes later, Carlos, his son, Roberto—clutching his father's clothes to his chest—and I got into a cab and headed downtown.

"I know you from somewheres, man?" he asked as we headed down Broadway.

"Don't think so."

"You ever a cop?"

"No."

"You live 'round here?"

"No."

He shook his head. "I know I know you, man."

"I've got that kind of face."

Throughout the cab ride downtown, he didn't take his eyes off me, which gave me the willies. Finally, as we were crossing 14th Street, his face lit up. "Hey, I knew I knowed you, man. Paradise Bar and Grill, right? You a friend of the owner, Joe Bailey. And Manny, the bartender. Ain't that right? That's where I seen you. You used to hang out there, always saying, you know, that stuff. Po-it-tree, man. That was you. The Po-it-tree man. I used to hang out there, too. You was pretty good, man. You still talkin' that shit?"

"I think you've got the wrong guy."

"I ain't wrong, man. You worked as a dick, right?"

"No."

"Well, I mean, they didn't call you no dick. They called you somethin' else. Skip man. Something like that."

I sighed. He had me nailed. "That was then, this is now."

"How'd you get that cable suit, man?"

"It's mine. It's what I do . . ."

"You shittin' me . . . oh, man." He started to laugh. "I got fuckin' hooked by the cable guy. Shit, can you beat that?"

"No, Carlos, my friend, I guess you can't. But if I were you, I'd keep that little piece of information under your hat, because it won't do much for your street cred."

That didn't stop him from laughing. I would have laughed with him, but I didn't think it was all that funny.

I deposited Carlos, the kid and the clothes with Jake, who

welcomed me with his typical annoying as hell shit-eating grin.

"Okay, finito," I said, as one of Jake's mangy assistants called the kid's mom. "We're even. Pay time." I stuck out my hand.

"Check's in the mail."

"You gotta be kidding."

"You don't trust me?"

"Jake, I trust my mother, but I still cut the cards."

"Nice attitude, Swann."

"It's the only one I've got. And don't forget to add twenty-five bucks for the cab down here."

"Who the hell told you to take a cab?"

"Don't give me any shit. I've had more than enough for one day."

"Okay, okay." He went to his desk and removed his checkbook. He took a pen from his pocket, which, from the way he hesitated before writing, must have been filled with his own blood. "Here," he said, "enjoy it in good health. And since you done such a good job, and since you're an old friend of mine, I got a bonus for you."

"What's that?" I asked suspiciously.

"Here," he said, pulling an envelope from his shirt pocket. "Don't open it till you get home. I want it to be a surprise."

"Thanks, Jake," I said, slipping my "bonus" into my pants pocket, "but do me a favor, will you? Next time you call me, make it just to tell me how much you miss me."

3
TAKE ME OUT TO THE
BALL GAME

I hardly ever do what I'm told. It's probably genetic. My father never did anything he was told either—until, that is, my mother told him to take a hike, which is what he did. Haven't heard from him since. Do I miss him? Nope. He's one person I wouldn't find, even if I could.

As soon as I got outside I opened the envelope—I don't delay gratification well, probably because I get so little of it—and found a note. When I unfolded it, a ticket dropped out. I picked it up and saw it was for a Met game against the Braves the next afternoon. I read the note.

Swann, appreciate what you did for me. Thought you might like to take in a game with me tomorrow afternoon. Be there or be square.

Jake

I smiled, stuck the ticket in my pocket, balled up the envelope and note and swished it into the nearest trash can. I hadn't been to a game in a couple of years and, since the Mets were hot, breathing down the Braves' necks (okay, it was early; plenty of time for them to fold in the stretch), it didn't seem like a bad way to spend a Wednesday afternoon in July.

The next day, I called in sick and, under bright blue, nearly cloudless skies, I hopped the number seven out to Flushing Meadow. I was perfectly capable of finding my own way to my seat, but I couldn't seem to shake the usher, an old-timer who

30

must have wiped the seat vigorously half a dozen times while I fumbled in my pocket for some loose change.

The seats were great, near the dugout on the first-base line. There was a plaque in front of me announcing the box as the property of Shields, Phillips, Kelly and Levine. I was in a corporate box. I assumed somebody owed Jake a favor and he was passing it on to me.

It was approaching game time and the Mets and Braves had finished batting practice and were getting ready to trot back out for the one-thirty start, but there was still no sign of Jake. I assumed he'd gotten stuck at the office and would be along as soon as he could. It was a beautiful day: blue sky, low humidity, bright sunshine, temperature in the mid-eighties. Perfect baseball weather. The stadium was beginning to fill up, mostly with teenagers, large groups of T-shirted kids on camp outings, and a smattering of retirees or those intrepid baseball fans willing to skip a day of work. About one-ten, just as we were rising to sing the National Anthem, sung by two jokers in suits who billed themselves as "The Singing Lawyers," I began to get a little antsy. I considered giving Jake a call on his cell phone, but once the last note ended, a cheer went up, the Mets took the field, and I thought, the hell with it. If he didn't make it, he didn't make it. I certainly didn't need him to enjoy the game.

Al Leiter was in good form and the Braves went down in order in the first. Painting the corners like Picasso resulted in two strikeouts and a dribbler to Ventura at third. In the bottom of the first, the Mets took an early lead. Henderson singled, then went to second on Alfonso's single. Olerud stroked a double into the right-field corner and suddenly the home team was ahead two-zip. The sun was shining. God was in heaven and all was well in Metland.

By the top of the third, Jake still hadn't showed. Just as I was about to get up and grab myself a beer and a hotdog, a well-dressed man in a dark, pin-striped suit and rep tie made a move to sit down next to me.

"Sorry," I said, "I think you've got the wrong seat."

"I don't think so," he said with that imperious voice that in my experience only men of power and wealth have mastered.

"I'm expecting a friend," I pressed, "and I'm pretty sure he's got the seat next to me."

"These are my seats," he said authoritatively. And you know what, I believed him. In fact, I believed him so much I didn't even ask to see his ticket stub. Instead, I glanced at the plaque on the rail in front of me and wondered whether I was going to be seated next to Shields, Phillips, Kelly or Levine.

A collective groan went up, and I turned my attention to the field, where the Braves were nibbling at Leiter. He'd given up two scratch hits, and once the batters got on, they were running wild on the bases, obviously frustrating Piazza, who'd tossed his mask to the ground angrily. The Braves managed to tie the score and, with only one out, they were still threatening.

Chipper Jones was up and the count was full when the guy turned to me and said, "I've heard a lot about you, Mr. Swann."

"What's that?"

"I apologize," he said. "I should have introduced myself. My name is Carlton Phillips." He extended his hand and I couldn't help noticing the expensive Rolex strapped to his wrist. I had the distinct feeling that Mr. Phillips was not used to apologizing for anything. I gestured toward the plaque. He smiled. "Corporate seats. They're not used all that often by any of the partners. We work much too hard to take time off, especially during the day. Mostly, they are made available to clients."

"I guess it must be me who's in the wrong seat."

"No. You aren't. But you are a little confused, aren't you?" Pronouncing each syllable separately, he seemed to be using twice as many words as he actually was.

"Do I look confused?"

He smiled in a way that informed me that he knew I was. "Are you enjoying the game?"

"Which game is that?" I asked, but he didn't seem to hear me. He glanced at his watch. "I'll let you get back to the game on the field again soon. I promise. I know this isn't exactly an orthodox place in which to conduct business but . . ."

"Business?"

"Yes, Mr. Swann. I'm here to speak to you in a professional capacity. I'm a friend . . . well, really a business acquaintance of Mr. Stein."

I may have been confused, but I wasn't stupid. It was clear I'd been set up. The whole shebang, right down to finding Carlos Robles, was just an elaborate charade engineered by my good friend and Mr. Phillips's business acquaintance, Jake Stein.

"That son of a bitch . . ." I muttered, while in my mind I thought of all the ways I could get back at Jake.

"He was merely doing me a personal favor, although I don't necessarily disagree with your personal analysis of him."

"A favor, huh? For you. But what's in it for me? Other than these seats, I mean."

"That's something you might find out, if you give me five minutes of your time."

"I'm a little busy right now," I said, turning my attention back to what was happening on the field. I was pissed at Jake, using me to look good to some big-time lawyer.

"I can wait till the inning's over, if you prefer."

I turned and stared at Phillips. Despite the heat, he was unruffled. I don't know why, but that irritated the hell out of me. He just sat there, hands folded across his chest, smiling back at me, so damned confident, so damned sure of himself. He never once looked out onto the field. "You're not going to leave me alone until you say what you want to say, are you?"

He smiled. "I'm afraid not."

"Shit. Okay. Go ahead. But you'll have to forgive me if you don't have my full attention. There's a game going on out there. So do me a favor, will ya? Make it short and sweet."

"I'll do what I can," he said, and shot me a look that let me know he wasn't used to giving the condensed version of anything, much less being dictated to. This was a man who demanded attention and, despite the fact that it seemed as if he needed me for something, he didn't disguise the fact that he didn't like me one bit. But that was okay. I wasn't crazy about him either.

"I'd like to engage you to find someone for me. It's my daughter. I believe she may be in a bit of trouble, which, to be frank, isn't an unusual state of affairs for Marcy. I'd like to help her. You see, I'm an attorney and if she has gotten herself into a jam, I believe I can do something for her."

"What kind of jam might she be in?" I asked as the word "drugs" immediately pole-vaulted into my head. That's usually the case with the spoiled kids of arrogant, know-it-all fathers.

"I'm not quite sure. It's the people she hangs out with. You see, Marcy has suffered some emotional problems over the years. She has a tendency to look for love in all the wrong places. If backed against a wall, I'd be forced to admit that this is, in large part, my fault . . ."

"That so?"

"Yes. I'm afraid, by nature I'm a rather distant person. Some might even consider me cold, unemotional, remote." He smiled. "At least those are the words one of my ex-wives used in her divorce petition. As a result, I believe Marcy is rather closed off from her feelings."

"Shrink-talk."

"Pardon me?"

"You've been to a shrink, haven't you?"

34

"Is it that obvious?"

"You talk the talk. Either that or you've been watching too much Dr. Phil."

"It's helped me come to grips with a lot of my, uh, problems. The shrink, I mean. I don't have time to watch television during the day, when I presume the person you mention is on."

"So now that you've come to grips with your problems you'd like to help your daughter with hers. Is that it?"

"Is there anything wrong with that?"

I shook my head. "Sounds very fatherly to me. Kinda makes me wish I had a dad like you."

He cocked his head to one side, as if evading my shot at him. "Let me tell you something, Mr. Swann. I couldn't care less if people like me. In fact, in my business it's sometimes a plus. But what I do demand, and what I almost always get, is respect. So you can take all the shots at me you like, believe me, I've heard worse, but if you work for me, and I'm confident you will, you will have to respect me."

"Let me tell you something, Mr. Phillips. I don't care if people like me, either. So we've got that much in common. But whether they like me or not, they have to understand that although I will willingly, even eagerly, take their money, they don't own me. Which means I don't have to respect them and I don't have to take shit from them. All I have to do is get them what they want."

"I suppose I can live with that. Are you married, Mr. Swann?"

"Used to be."

"Divorced?"

I shook my head.

"Separated?"

"Death. Hers, not mine."

"I'm sorry." He hesitated a moment, as if weighing the value of his next question. "Do you mind if I ask how it happened?"

I knew he couldn't care less. Why should he? He was only interested in getting me to work for him. I knew what he was doing. He was trying to bond with me, make me like him, which would result in my taking his case. What a waste of time. I don't have to like someone to work for them. They just have to pay me. On time. Copiously. Or not. I answered him anyway.

"Freak accident. She was walking down the street. A manhole cover blew. It hit her and practically sliced her in half."

"Horrible." He shook his head back and forth, like one of those dashboard bobble-head dolls. I knew what he was thinking. He was a lawyer. He was wondering how much I got. He would have been disappointed. Suing the city or Con Ed isn't easy. Besides, I didn't have the heart for it. By the time my wife's death sank in, I was well past caring. I didn't want a three- or four-year lawsuit hanging over my head, reminding me every day what happened. I just wanted to let it go. Fortunately, he didn't ask me to elaborate. Not so much out of concern for my feelings, I was sure, but rather because I meant nothing to him other than the job he wanted to hire me to do.

He touched his hand to his mouth, dragging his fingers slowly down his chin. "Children?"

"One."

"Girl?"

"Boy."

"How old?"

I knew the answer. I really did. But there was something going on on the field, and I couldn't put my finger on the precise figure at that particular moment. So I said the first number that popped into my head, which was thirteen. Upon further reflection, the answer was fourteen, because he'd just had a birthday a couple of months earlier. But what did it matter? One of us didn't really care.

"He lives with you?"

"With his grandparents in the Midwest. Missouri. Someplace like that." I knew the answer to that question, too, but I didn't want him to think he knew me or anything about me, which would enable him to work me. I know the drill. It's what I use to get information I need. The less you look like you care, the more people tell you. Sometimes, if you handle it right, if you're good at what you do, and I am, the problem isn't getting people to talk, it's getting them to shut up. The smarter they are, the more they want to impress you, the more they want to talk. It's amazing how much information you can get by asking the right questions and then keeping your mouth shut.

At the same time, you can't underestimate people. You're much better off thinking everyone's smarter than you are, even if it's not true. It wasn't difficult with Phillips because I was pretty sure he was smarter than me, knew more than I did, but the fact that he did, and he knew it, could work to my advantage. The smarter he thought he was, the smarter I'd turn out to be.

"I'm sorry," he said.

"Don't be. It's the best thing for him."

"How often do you see him?"

"Often enough," I snapped. He was beginning to cross the line, a line I didn't want to cross myself.

He shrugged. "Of course, it's none of my business."

Leiter was delivering a pitch, a high, hard one. Javy Lopez swung and missed. Strike three. The crowd roared. In the bleachers a fifth K appeared, hanging over the stands.

I turned to Phillips as the Mets disappeared into the dugout. "So how old's this daughter of yours?"

"Twenty-two."

"Seems old enough to take care of herself."

"Wish that she were. She's with a man who can only get her in trouble. She met him at school last year. She was a junior.

37

He was a graduate student. What they refer to as a perpetual student. He's thirty-two, I believe. She took up with him seriously nine months ago. Three months ago both of them disappeared, and I haven't heard from her since."

"I hate to be the one to break it to you, Mr. Phillips, but this is not an unusual a story. Rebellious daughter takes up with a man she knows her family won't approve of, then runs off with him. It's a way to stick it to the old man. Sooner or later you'll hear from her, and you'll find out she's no worse off than when she left. Only somewhat poorer, I suspect."

"You might be right, Mr. Swann, but I fear that's not the case. I'm very anxious to find her, and as soon as possible. That's why I'd like to engage you. Jake says you're one of the best at finding lost people."

"In case Jake didn't tell you, I'm in communications now."

He laughed. "That's a quaint way of putting it, isn't it? He claimed you were on"—he paused—"sabbatical."

"I prefer to think of it more like permanent retirement."

"May I ask why?"

"Because I got tired of knocking my head against a wall. Because certain long and closely held personal and professional values that were the cornerstone of my existence suddenly went up in smoke. Because the world isn't rational, Mr. Phillips. It's chaotic and hostile and illogical and messy and downright confusing. And when you get right down to it, nothing matters very much but the here and now. I found that sometimes it's better to let what's lost stay lost. Just replace it and get on with life. In the long run, it simplifies things."

"I can't very well replace my daughter, can I, Mr. Swann?" he said, his eyes glued to mine. If he was trying to make me feel guilty, it wasn't going to work. I didn't need him to do that job. I could take care of it plenty well myself.

"No, I don't suppose you can," I said, though I had a sneaking suspicion that if he could, he would. In a heartbeat.

"I don't see how working for me would entail too much of a compromise to your new set of, shall we say, dubious values. Let me put it to you in a way you might understand, a way that might fit in with your newfound philosophy of the here and now. I would be willing to make it well worth your while. With your ability, I don't think it would be more than a week's worth of work. For that week's labor I would be willing to pay you, oh, let's say ten thousand dollars, plus expenses, of course. And for any week or part thereof that it takes you beyond that, I will pay you another ten thousand dollars. That's the kind of here and now I'm talking about. How does that strike you?"

"Ten grand?"

"That's right. And a bonus if you find her quickly and bring her back safely. A very generous bonus."

Now this is precisely the moment when those extra flights of stairs began to make their way into the picture. Ten thousand plus, well, that might hold me a fair amount of time while I pondered the possibilities of another mid-life career change that didn't include any form of climbing. But before I committed to anything, I thought I might like to see if I could jack up the stakes a might. Solely on principle, you understand.

"You've certainly caught my attention, but the truth is, I already have a job, which I'd probably lose if I went to work for you. I'm not sure the money you're talking about would be sufficient incentive . . ."

He smiled. He knew just what I was about. "Everything is negotiable, Mr. Swann. But in this case, I think I'll stick with my first offer, which is my best offer. Besides, I see the game is getting a little more interesting now—it seems the opposition has tied the score—so why don't I give you my card and you can call my secretary and make an appointment to come in and see me. Then we can discuss the financial arrangements and I can provide you with all the information I have. How does that sound?"

"It sounds . . . doable, Mr. Phillips. Very doable." He took his wallet from his inside jacket pocket, removed a card, handed it to me and stood up. "Enjoy the game, Mr. Swann. And thank you very much for your time. Oh, and by the way, I love the sneakers," he said, looking down at the pair of red Converse I was wearing.

"Thanks."

"They bring back memories."

"Good ones, I hope."

"Some good, some bad. But that's the way life is, isn't it, Mr. Swann?"

"I guess it is. And by the way, thanks for the tickets," I added, but by the time I got the words out, he was halfway up the steps. He didn't look back. Ladies and gentlemen, Carlton Phillips had left the building.

I did enjoy the game. The Mets wound up coming from behind in the eighth inning, when Ventura poked a double to the alley in right and Piazza smacked a home run over the left-field fence.

That evening, when I got home, I called Jake. After cursing him out for playing me for a fool, I asked, "So, what's the scoop?"

"He's rich, he's powerful, and he needs help. I help him by getting you to help him. He helps me some time in the future. You help him find his daughter, he owes you a favor. Then you owe me a favor. That's the way it works, pal. And we all need friends, Swann, even you."

"I've gotten this far with acquaintances, not friends. Besides, I don't think the concept of friends is something Carlton Phillips has quite grasped. But if you want to believe that bullshit, that's fine with me. And that favor stuff, well, in theory maybe it works, but in practice favors are rarely paid back."

"Cynic."

"You bet."

"Well, in any case, I'll bet the money probably ain't half bad. How much did he offer you?"

"Five grand a week," I lied.

"I think you can do better."

"I know I can."

"Does that mean you're taking the case?"

"Like everything else in life, pal, it's negotiable."

And I left it at that.

4
Money Talks and Bullshit Walks

I didn't get much sleep that night. I didn't even try. Instead, I sat in a chair facing the window looking out onto the brick wall of the now empty, adjacent building. Living in the East Village, I was in the midst of a gentrification nightmare. In the not-so-distant future, I was sure the building would be gone, demolished to make way for a large co-op. Where would I go? What would I do? I tried not to think about it. Something would turn up. It always has.

In the meantime, kids from Brooklyn—Williamsburg and Greenpoint—spilled into the streets from the L train onto 14th Street, then headed south, packing the bars and restaurants along First and Second Avenues, then headed West, to Alphabet City, Avenues A, B, and C, an area that used to be drug havens, where you took your life in your hands if you dared to venture over there, where junkies and dealers reigned. But there was something about the old, wild west atmosphere I missed. It wasn't the danger, but the sense that I belonged amongst the low-lifes and hustlers. I was them and they were me. Maybe it's a holdover from the days when my office was in Spanish Harlem, amongst con men, drug dealers, and petty criminals. Now, amidst this migration, I felt like an outsider. I had nothing in common with these intruders, and it made me uncomfortable. But, since my rent was remarkably low, not uncomfortable enough to move. I would adapt. I had to. At least until my landlord sold the building out from under me and I would have to move, like so many others had before me.

I tried to talk myself out of my new job. But it wasn't working. Finding people, finding answers, solving mysteries, bringing order to chaos, was in my blood. That rush I experienced in Robles's apartment was no aberration. Though I tried to suppress it, I realized the adrenaline that pumped through my body that afternoon was what had kept me in the business as long as I was in it. It made me feel alive. It gave meaning to my life, something missing since my wife died and I banished my son, Noah, to the Midwest. For three years, I'd been "dead," though I didn't know it. Now I had the opportunity to be reborn. I didn't want to get mystical about it—the lure of the mysterious, the need to tidy up—but, under the circumstances, how could I turn Phillips down? I had no choice. This job was my fate.

One job, that's all it was. In and out. Just a little jump-start to the old lifeline. Get the ticker ticking. Maybe communications wasn't the way. If it wasn't, then this little job, this digression, would cleanse the palette, perhaps leading me in the direction of my true calling. Whatever the hell that was.

And then, okay, let's not kid ourselves, there was the money. Ah, yes, the money. They say money can't buy happiness. Truth is, money can buy just about anything, or at least a close facsimile. That's why they call it money. Money makes the head spin and the world go round. That's not so bad, so long as you get them spinning in the same direction. Besides, fake happiness is almost as good as the real thing. A minimum of ten grand for a week's work, well, that was mighty sweet. Too sweet to turn down.

Yet I knew if I took the job, I'd be opening up a can of worms I wasn't sure I wanted open. My last case left me an emotional and physical wreck. It toyed with me, then destroyed my basic presumptions of life, of the world, of the universe, and left me doubting myself and my place in the cosmos. I'd done all the right things. I'd followed all the clues, one by one. I'd followed the true and righteous path, only to find that it wasn't very true and it certainly wasn't very righteous. I woke up one morning to find that the sun was rising in the west and setting in the east. Is that logical? Is that the way life is supposed to be?

Of course not. But that's the way it was . . . and in order to accept it, I was the one who had to change. If the universe couldn't be reordered, maybe I could be. Maybe.

But if the world wasn't ruled by reason, what was ruling it? If life was totally random and unpredictable, chaotic and messy, how could anyone set a course of action, follow a blueprint for living? I read somewhere once about the universe being like a box of scrambled letters. Shake the box up and you'll mostly get gibberish. But every once in a while, a word is formed. But the chance of duplicating that feat is astronomical. Was it possible, Einstein aside, that God does, indeed, play dice with the universe?

Cable was so much simpler. Make the right connections and the reception will come in bright and clear. You see what you see. You get what you get. And that's the way I liked it. That was my new job. Making connections . . . and making them stick. Making the world safe for video broadcasts. No more mysteries. No more heartbreak. No more double images.

Obviously I needed more than that. I needed to test the universe one more time.

And so, I would roll the dice and see what came up.

The next morning, just before ten o'clock, I was seated in the reception area outside Carlton Phillips's office. Very corporate. Very uptight. Just the kind of environment that makes me itchy. But I suppose to the kinds of clients who hired the firm, it was reassuring. They're not looking for warmth and a sense of spiritual well-being. They're looking for cold, hard cash—much like me—and the office décor was a very effective signal that that's just what they were going to get.

After announcing my arrival, the receptionist ran down a menu of items I could choose from to satisfy my thirst. I declined them all. Just as I was making myself comfortable, sinking back into the soft, chocolate brown leather couch, leafing through the latest issue of *Forbes*, looking for advice as to where to put my money, assuming I ever had any, the receptionist motioned to me and in a voice devoid of any real sincerity or feeling, announced, "Mr. Phillips can see you now."

Phillips was dressed a little less formally than he'd been the day before at the ballpark. He'd shed his jacket to reveal a pair of Tweetie and Sylvester suspenders, he was tieless, and the sleeves of his white, pin-striped shirt were rolled halfway up his arms.

He stood up from behind his desk to greet me. "I'm glad you decided to come, Mr. Swann. But I would think for a business meeting like this, you might have taken the time to dress appropriately."

"Isn't it casual Friday?"

"It's Thursday."

"Jeez, woke up this morning and it just seemed like a Friday. Guess I'm going to have to get myself a calendar."

He made a derisive face and looked at his watch. "Yes. Well, in order to save us both a lot of time, what say we get right down to business."

"That's why I'm here," I said as I took a seat opposite his desk without it being offered. I thought he'd sit too, but instead he began pacing back and forth across the expanse of his office. His wasn't a nervous pace, but one meant to keep me in a subordinate position. I would have to follow him around the room with my eyes, thereby ceding control to him. I could imagine him in a courtroom, pacing in front of the witness stand, trying to intimidate the poor witness sitting there. He was probably very good. But there wasn't a chance that would work on me.

"You're making me nervous," I said, indicating with my finger his moving around the room.

"I'm not here to make you comfortable, Mr. Swann."

I wanted to tell him he was an asshole, which he was, but the fact that he was going to pay me ten grand a week helped me to keep my mouth shut.

"I haven't heard from Marcy in almost six months. I've left messages for her on her cell, but she doesn't answer them. I have no idea where she is, but I know she's with him. His name's Sean Loomis. He's a worm, and everything you need to know about him is contained in this file." He moved to his desk, opened a drawer and took out two manila envelopes, which he tossed on my lap. Then he resumed his route around his office, his hands jammed into his pockets, never once looking in my direction. "I've also included the most recent photo I have of Marcy. It's a year or two old. Her hairstyle has changed . . . it's darker, and I believe it's longer. She tends to change her looks quite often. One day, she actually came home with her hair streaked green, just to piss me off, I'm sure. What this won't tell you about Sean is that he's devious, cunning, dishonest and totally amoral. A sociopath in the truest sense of the word. Which is probably why Marcy was attracted to him in the first place."

"Have you actually met him?"

"I don't have to. I know the type. He's a leech. He doesn't care about my daughter, only what she can do for him."

"What's that?"

He looked around, extending his hands, palms up. "What do you think?"

"So you think he's after your daughter's money? Her connections?"

"The thought crossed my mind."

"You don't think very much of your daughter, do you?"

"What's that supposed to mean?"

"It's possible he just likes her, that he's attracted to her, that they're in love."

He laughed.

"You find that amusing?"

"I do. I know my daughter's history with men, and it isn't good. I would be shocked, pleasantly so, if your suggestion were the case. But it's not. Trust me, if I had any faith in my daughter's choice in men, I wouldn't be sitting here with you now. But she's still my daughter, and I'd rather extricate her from this relationship before she gets in so deep she'll be lost to me . . . and herself . . . forever."

The phone rang. We both glanced at it. "I told my secretary to hold my calls. Whatever it is, it can wait." The phone rang twice more, then stopped.

"Let's move forward. As I mentioned yesterday, they met at school, Syracuse University. She was a junior in communications—the Newhouse School—I did tell you that at least academically she's very bright, didn't I?"

"It must have slipped your mind."

"Well, she is. Not that she's ever lived up to her potential."

"Most of us don't."

He glared at me. I didn't care. I liked pissing him off. I don't know why. I just did.

"Loomis was a graduate student in American literature. He also fancied himself a writer. Marcy told me he was working on a novel of some sort, though I have my doubts. I wouldn't be surprised if he used that simply as a pick-up line to impress girls, especially ones with money . . ."

"Saul Bellow claims writing is an aphrodisiac," I said as I cracked open the first file. The photo of his daughter was on top. She was cute, but nothing special. Very little makeup, wearing jeans, a white T-shirt and over that, a light green v-neck sweater. She could have been in an ad for the Gap. I looked closer. There was something about her eyes. They didn't seem focused on anything. It was as if they were aimed inside, not out, giving her a kind of creepy look. I tried to look for some resemblance to her father, but I couldn't spot any.

"Pretty girl."

He seemed surprised. "Yes. I suppose she is."

"Looks like her mother?"

"I hope not."

"I'm sensing you've got a problem with your wife."

"Ex-wife. But we're not here to discuss my domestic situation. So, let's get back to business. Marcy took up with this Loomis character and, by the middle of the semester, they were living together off-campus. Though I never visited, I'm told they lived exceedingly well. He drove an expensive motorcycle and always seemed to have plenty of money."

"Maybe he has an indulgent family . . ."

"I hardly think so. His father disappeared years ago, and his mother works as a waitress in a diner," he said, his voice dripping with disdain. Yet one more reason to dislike him, dumping on people who work hard for their money.

"So, you're suggesting Loomis makes his living in some non-legitimate way."

"I don't know of any university that remunerates even their finest students enough to pay for the kind of lifestyle he's become accustomed to."

"Maybe your daughter's financing his fancy lifestyle."

"She's on a very short leash when it comes to money. She's proven before that she doesn't know how to handle it. I pay her tuition and the rest is up to her. I'm trying to teach her that there are no free rides in life. Just because she was born into money doesn't mean she's rich."

"You think this Loomis guy is into drugs? Using? Selling?"

"The fact is, Mr. Swann, I don't care how he makes his money. I'm not hiring you to check on his background. Or to bring him to justice. I'm simply hiring you to find my daughter, to make sure she's all right. Several months ago both Marcy and Loomis dropped out of sight. They vacated their apartment in Syracuse and left no forwarding address. I haven't heard from her since."

"What about her mother?"

"She passed away three years ago."

"I'm sorry."

"No need to be. We'd been divorced for half a dozen years before that. She was a bitch."

"Does Marcy have any siblings?"

"I have a three-year-old from my second marriage. So, effectively, Marcy is an only child."

"What about her friends?"

"Ever since she met Sean, she's cut herself off from anyone who was ever close to her. The names of her friends, at least the ones I know about, are included in that second file. But I doubt you'll find anything out from them. I've already pursued that avenue."

"Who put together the file?"

"My associates."

"Why couldn't they go find her?"

"It's not what they're trained to do."

"So you just want me to find your daughter, determine she's all right, then report back to you?"

"That's correct. You don't have to put her in shackles and drag her back here, if that's what you're worried about. Once I know where she is, that she's all right, I'll rest easier."

"Fair enough. That was twelve thousand a week, right?"

He smiled. "Nice try, Mr. Swann."

"It was, wasn't it? Okay ten grand, plus expenses."

He nodded.

"Then I guess we've got a deal."

"Not so fast. First, I'd like to know a little about your methods."

"What do you care how I work, so long as I get results?"

"I didn't get where I am"—he waved his hands around—"by not being thorough, Mr. Swann. I'm not a micro-manager, but I like to know what I can expect from my employees."

"If you're expecting Sherlock Holmes, you've got the wrong guy. I'm not one of those guys on TV or in the movies who looks at the scene of the crime and knows who did it. I'm strictly blue collar. I talk to people. I get their stories. I use their stories to find what I'm looking for. There's no magic, no sleight of hand. Think of me as a reporter. I follow one lead to another. It usually gets me where I want to go."

"I certainly hope so, because that's what I'm paying you for. We've got a deal." He shook my hand, hard, holding it a beat or two longer than he had to. It was a power thing. I knew that. But I didn't care. I didn't have to like him. I just had to work for him.

"On your way out, my secretary will have you sign a work-for-hire agreement and then give you a check for the first week. She will also provide you with a company credit card, which you may use for any reasonable expenses you might incur. The only thing I ask is that you confer with me on anything over five hundred dollars—not that I don't trust you, of course."

"You trust your mother, but you still cut the cards."

"Yes. Good advice. I would also ask that you inform me of any progress you've made. A call every so often would suffice."

He took a business card from his desk, turned it over and wrote something on the back, then handed it to me. "This is my cell. I presume I can rely on your keeping this confidential."

"The number?"

He smiled again. "Yes, as well as all the rest of this. And, Mr. Swann, I take it for granted, though perhaps I shouldn't, that this transaction between us, and any information you may obtain during your investigation, will not go any farther than this room. This is, after all, a family situation, nothing more."

I nodded, though something told me it would turn out to be more than just a simple "family situation," as he put it.

"Of course. Then I will be hearing from you soon, I trust?"

"As soon as I find something to report, you'll be the first to know."

"I'd like your cell number, please."

I gave it to him.

"If you have any questions after going through these files, feel free to call."

"I will. But there is one more thing . . ."

"Yes . . ."

"If you had to guess, what would you say that your daughter's state of mind might be?"

He was silent for a moment. "That's a good question, Mr. Swann. And I'm afraid that only one word comes to mind."

"And that is?"

"Confusion."

No problem there. It was a state I was very familiar with.

5
A MOTHER'S KISSES

Sean Loomis's mother worked in Queens, which, as it happens, was one of the last boroughs of New York City to be outfitted with cable. As one of those responsible for hooking it up, I was far too familiar with this exotic land east of Manhattan. Only a short hop over the Queensborough Bridge, yet it was eons away from the wealth and glitz of Manhattan, its sister borough. A polyglot of ethnic neighborhoods—Greek, Italian, Indian, Pakistani—which, along with parts of Brooklyn, like hipster haunts such as Williamsburg and Greenpoint, was beginning to get the spillover from Manhattan; kids who wanted to be near the excitement of the city but weren't yet making the bucks to sustain that lavish lifestyle. And many of them wound up in my neighborhood.

Sandy Loomis, who'd reverted to her maiden name of Brennan, worked the dayshift in a nondescript, greasy spoon diner in Astoria, only a few stops out of Manhattan on the R train. I arrived just before three in the afternoon, when I figured I'd pretty much have the place to myself. I helped myself to a seat at a back booth, opened up a newspaper and checked out the box scores while I waited to be served. I'd made it to the Western Division standings when she approached the table and gave me the once-over. Barely looking up from the paper (a skill I'd acquired in a former life casing cars waiting to be repoed), I returned the favor.

"Can I help you?" she asked in a voice that was surprisingly sexy, maybe because of what I detected to be the remnants of a slight Texas twang.

She wasn't what I'd expected. Maybe because she didn't look like anyone's mother. She appeared to be in her late thirties, though she was, according to the information I had, forty-seven. She wore a little too much makeup and her curly, shoulder-length strawberry blond hair was tied back into a ponytail. Her off-white waitress uniform with blue piping, which ended abruptly just above her knees, hugged a body that looked like it had logged plenty of gym time. Instead of comfortable, sensible work shoes, she was wearing a pair of sexy, tan, heeled, open-toed sandals, which accentuated a very shapely pair of legs. From a distance, she could easily have been mistaken for a woman with a few ticks left on the biological clock. Her nails were painted bright red, and were surprisingly long for someone who made a living carrying around plates most of the day. I suspected a good part of each week's salary never made it past the Korean nail salon across the street.

"Late lunch," I said.

She eyeballed me a moment before she gestured toward the plasticized menu propped up between a ketchup bottle and sugar dispenser. "Just let me know when you're ready to order, sugar," she said.

I glanced at the menu, covered with photos of the possible meals I could choose from, none of them particularly appetizing.

"Any suggestions?"

She leaned in a little. "That would be to eat somewheres else, honey. But since you're already here, you might as well order something relatively harmless, like a BLT. Cook hasn't learned how to screw that one up yet." She leaned in closer. "But give him time."

"Thanks for the heads-up. How about a Coke to go with that."

"What do you want that on?" she said, pulling out a small pad from her pocket and a pencil from behind her ear.

"Depends on what you have."

"White, whole wheat and rye," she said in a way that made me believe she really cared which one I chose. I knew the healthier choice and yet, in the hedonistic, semi-self-destructive way in which I've always led my life, I chose white. The more white, unorganic, processed, preservative-filled food I can cram in me, the better. She frowned; at least I thought it was a frown, though in truth I couldn't be sure, then turned on her heels and headed back toward the kitchen.

I had no intention of telling her who I was and what I was after. People tend to open up more readily if they don't feel threatened. Connect with them first. Create a bond, no matter how phony it might be, and then you'd be surprised how much they open up. In the end, for most people, it's not a matter of getting them to talk, but to shut up. Rarely do people have anyone who actually listens to them. And so, when someone does, they take full advantage of the opportunity to unload. You'd be amazed the kind of stuff you can get from people once they think you give a damn. Do I give a damn? Rarely. Not unless there's a payday involved.

She brought over my order, set it down in front of me, then headed back to the counter. I let her go. There'd be plenty of time for questions later.

I ate slowly, one eye glued to the sports pages in front of me, the other on Brennan. I wanted to see the way she moved, the way she held herself when she didn't think anyone was watching her. I'm Sneaky Pete and Peeping Tom, rolled into one.

There were only a couple of other people in the place, so Brennan spent most of her time behind the counter, her pug,

Irish nose jammed in an oversized paperback novel. Every so often, she'd lift her head, cast an eye in my direction, as any well-trained waitress would, just to see if I needed anything. I did, but it wasn't on the menu. And since she couldn't possibly read my mind, she invariably returned her attention to her book. Finally, after maybe twenty minutes, she looked my way again and I motioned for the check with an imaginary pen stroke.

She nodded and came out from behind the counter, sashaying over to my booth. When she handed it to me, I asked if she owned a piece of the place.

"Are you kidding, honey?" she said with a deep, throaty laugh that rocked the joint. "Do I look like an owner?"

"You sure don't look like a waitress."

Her faced reddened. "So," she said, suddenly flirtatious, striking a pose, "what do I look like?"

"Like someone who wandered in here by mistake, like off the set of a movie."

"You're fulla shit," she said with that same throaty laugh.

"You think so?"

"Yeah. I think so."

"Maybe I am."

She smiled. "You wouldn't be trying to pick me up, would you, sweetie?"

"And if I were? Would that be bad enough to get me tossed out on my ass?"

She put her hands on her hips, thrusting them forward in a way that told me everything I needed to know. "It depends."

"I'd ask on what, but I don't think I want to know."

"You're pretty fresh, aren't you?"

"Look at me, honey, do I look fresh to you?"

"I guess not . . ."

I knew I could straight out ask about her son, or I could wheedle it out of her slowly, without her even being aware of

55

what was going on. I figured if I did the former, I'd get nothing. This was a tough chick who wasn't about to give up her son to some stranger. I had a feeling she knew he was trouble, and maybe in trouble, too. But he was still her son.

"Why don't you sit down for a while and we can get to know each other," I said, patting the bench beside me.

"Are you kidding? Can't you see I'm working?"

"Gee," I said, looking around, "you coulda fooled me."

Her eyes mimicked my tour around the place. "Okay, but just for a minute or two. The boss comes back and finds me takin' a load off, talking to the customers, I'm out on my ass. I need this job, as sucky as it might seem." She leaned in and mock-whispered, "You don't think I'm doing this for my health, do you?"

"If you are, it's working wonders."

"I'm gonna call you Slick," she said as she slid into the seat across from me, making sure to sit on the edge, ready for a quick getaway.

"So what's your name?" I asked.

"Sandy."

"Sandy what?"

"You writin' a book or something?"

"I'm not smart enough to do that."

"You look smart enough to me. Brennan. What's yours?"

"Swann."

"First or last?"

"If we get to know each other better, you'll find out."

"What makes you think that's ever going to happen?"

"You never know."

"You're intriguing me, Swann."

"I'm a very intriguing guy, Sandy. Worked here long?"

"Long enough."

"You don't look like a waitress."

"Oh yeah? What do I look like?"

"Like someone biding your time till something better comes along."

"And what, pray tell, might that be?" she said, crinkling her eyes mischievously.

"You tell me."

She smiled. "Yeah, well, I got bigger fish to fry, that's for damn sure."

"What kind of fish are we talking about?"

"I done a little acting in my time. Nothing big, you understand. I was on a soap once, though."

"That doesn't surprise me. You've got . . . presence," I said.

"Really?" She blushed slightly. I could see I had her on the ropes. No time to let up.

"Yeah. You got that and more."

"Presence, huh? I like that."

"So, what kind of part did you play? Sexy vixen, breaking up the marriage of the town mayor, I'd guess."

She laughed. "It was an under-five. You know what that means?"

"Not a clue."

"It's when you've got under five lines. It's a step above being an extra. But it's more money and sometimes, if you're lucky and they like what they see, you might get bumped up to a recurring role. That didn't happen to me, but I've got a tape of it."

"I'd like to see that some time."

"It's not that kind of tape."

"What kind of tape might it not be?"

"You know, one of those tapes they put up on the Internet."

"No matter what kind of tape it is, I'm sure you're the star."

"You are so full of shit."

"We only know each other five minutes and already you've

got me figured out. So, you live around here or what?"

"Not too far. You?"

"Manhattan. But not the good part."

"What part would that be?"

"East Village."

"You one of those squatters?"

"Sandy, look at me," I said, patting my slight but growing paunch. "Don't I look like my squatting days are long over?"

She laughed. "So what are you doing out here in the boon-docks?"

"Business."

"What kind of business?"

"I'm in communications."

"Really? That sounds kinda important . . . and mysterious."

"Yeah, I'm a very mysterious guy."

"Women like guys that are mysterious."

"So I've heard. You married or what?"

She twisted in her seat. "Not really."

"I guess I know what that means. Kids?"

"Aren't you the nosy one? You're not a cop, are you?"

"Do I look like a cop?"

"Maybe. Maybe not."

"I'm just a curious guy with time to kill before I've got to be somewhere. Any kids?"

"Two. Girl and boy. She's married. Lives in California. Don't see her much. We don't get along all that good."

"You don't look old enough to have a married daughter."

"Look closer, honey."

"I can see pretty good from where I am. What about the other one?"

"Sean. He's the brains in the family. Still in school. Grad school," she added proudly.

"How old is he?"

"Thirty-two."

"A little old to still be hitting the books, isn't he?"

"He's what you call one of those perpetual students."

"That must cost you a bundle."

"You think this place looks like I make enough in tips to pay for something like that? He's on his own."

"How's he manage it?"

"I'm not sure, but he always seems to have enough dough. He's an enterprising kid. Not like his father, but you don't want to get me started on that sonuvabitch."

"So where's he at now? Your son, not your husband."

"Upstate."

"It's a big state, Sandy."

Her eyes shrank and she gave me a look that let me know she could be a real ball-buster when she wanted to. "Why are you so interested in my son?"

"I got a kid, too. He's in school. Upstate, just like yours. SU."

"You're kidding! That's where my kid's at."

"Small world, after all. Your kid live on campus?"

"He lives close by, I think. Yours?"

"He's in one of the dorms, though he keeps bugging me to live off-campus. I don't really trust him. Kid'd go wild if there weren't any rules. What about yours?"

"He was wild way before he got up there. But I think he's settled down a little. He's got himself a girlfriend."

"They live together?"

"They rent a house, I think."

"How long's it been since you've seen him?"

"Six months. Maybe more. We aren't that close. Every once in a while he comes down to the city on business and he'll give me a call."

"What kind of business is that?"

"I don't ask and he don't tell."

I snapped my fingers. "You know, I just thought of something. I'm going up there next week to visit my kid. I could drop by and see how your son's doing. You got an address for him?"

"You don't have to do that."

"If the shoe were on the other foot, I wouldn't mind you looking in on my kid."

"I don't actually have an address for him. He moves around a lot."

"Just give me his number. I'll give him a call and take him and his girlfriend out for dinner. I'll even drag my kid along."

"I had one, but he changed carriers and got a new number and he hasn't gotten around to giving it to me yet."

"How would you reach him if you had to?"

"Why would I have to?"

"You know, like an emergency or something?"

"I don't think he'd care if I needed him, and I can't imagine a circumstance when he'd need me," she said, and I could detect a hint of sadness in her voice.

To someone else, what she was saying might sound odd, but not me. I see it all the time. People drift apart. They lose touch. They become disconnected. That's usually where I come in, and if that weren't the case, I'd probably be working some mind-numbing civil service job. Or someplace like Community Cable.

"Life's complicated, Sandy."

She was quiet. I thought maybe she was going to cry. I wouldn't have liked that. Tears make me uncomfortable. But I was safe when the door opened and a customer walked in. Sandy looked up. "Look, I gotta get back to work."

"Sure thing."

She stood up and ironed her skirt with her hands. "I'll get your check."

She returned to the counter. I followed her. I handed her a

twenty. "Hey, why don't you give me your number? Maybe you'd like to go out to dinner some time."

"Or a show?"

"Yeah," I said, not feeling particularly proud of myself because, in the end, I'm afraid I'll do just about anything to get what I want. "That might be nice. In fact, why don't we set something up now? What're you doing Friday night?"

"Working."

"How about Saturday?"

"It's a date."

"Give me your number and I'll give you a call."

She tore off a blank check, scribbled down her number and handed it to me. "Pick someplace nice," she said. "I like to be swept off my feet."

6
A SHOCK TO THE SYSTEM

As soon I emerged from the subway, my phone started vibrating in my back pocket. It was Carlton Phillips.

"Any progress?" he asked without bothering to say hello.

"It's been less than a day, hardly enough time for your check to clear."

"I thought you were good at this, Mr. Swann."

"I'm not a magician. These things take time. And by the way, I don't like people looking over my shoulder. It annoys me. I don't work well when I'm annoyed. Why don't you back off and wait for me to call you."

"That's not the way I operate, Mr. Swann. I'm paying you excellent money, and I need to know you're earning it."

"When people don't want to be found, like your daughter, they don't leave a trail of bread crumbs."

"It's necessary that I be informed of your progress."

I wanted to say fuck you, asshole, but instead I tried to be as diplomatic as I could, which wasn't very, I know. "Do me a favor. Don't call me. If you do, you'll be wasting my time. You don't want to do that, do you?"

"That would be the last thing I'd want," he said sharply, and hung up before I could say goodbye. What a shame.

Usually, I would have just headed home after work, maybe stopped in at a local bar for a beer, but I was too keyed up for that. I needed to be on the move. I didn't have any particular destination in mind. I don't know why, but I had an urge to reconnect with my past by paying a visit to the Paradise Bar & Grill.

When I emerged from the subway at 145th and Broadway, I hardly recognized the place. It still had that Latin feel to it, but it was fading. Fast. In the two years since I'd been gone, the Trumpers, as I called them, had gotten their greedy little hands on some of the real estate, and gentrification seemed to be in full swing. Now, instead of bodegas and bars and cuchifrito stands, the avenue was punctuated by several high-rises in various states of completion. The prevalent language used to be Spanish. Now it was English. Money seeks out real estate, and that was what was happening here. It wouldn't be long before Spanish Harlem went the way of the East Village, and then where would guys like me end up?

I walked slowly north, toward 148th Street, hoping the building that housed my old office wasn't one sacrificed for urban renewal. Reaching 147th, I spotted the building where I'd had my second-floor office, but the windows were boarded up and the grimy little all-night bodega downstairs was dark. It was only a matter of time before the building would be demolished. I stood there a moment, trying to imprint a mental image of the place the way it used to be in my mind. I took my cell out of my pocket and found the camera function. I aimed the phone at the building, snapped a photo, then tucked it back in my pocket and crossed the Avenue.

The Paradise Bar & Grill was no more. In its place was a restaurant called Mo and Larry's. A menu in the window announced unrecognizable dishes with mysterious ingredients like fennel, leeks and chipotle. I looked inside to find the place packed with well-dressed yuppies, not one of them over the age of forty. No Manny. No Joe Bailey. No Billy D. And now no me.

I don't know why I missed it. It was just another grungy, dive bar, but I felt like another piece of me had been chipped away. I walked to the corner and looked up the side street where a small crowd was gathered around a couple of guys playing dominoes on a folding table. I spotted a familiar face. Hector, a middle-aged hustler who was a regular at the Paradise B & G.

"Hey, Hector," I called out as I moved closer.

He looked up and I could see the fear in his eyes, as if one of his marks had tracked him down and come to exact revenge. Or, even worse, that the cops were coming to bust him.

"It's me. Swann."

He squinted and pushed his head forward, like a turtle emerging from its shell.

"You remember. Swann. From the P B & G."

"Swannnnn," he rolled the name over on his tongue, and probably his head, too, trying to figure out where he knew me from.

"The dick," I said the word feeling particularly good as it crossed my tongue.

"Oh, yeah, man. I think I remembers you now. Been a while, ain't it?"

"Yeah. Almost two years. The neighborhood's changed, hasn't it?"

"You gots that straight. Where you been, man?"

"Around. How about you?"

"I been around, too, man."

"Funny we didn't run into each other before this."

"Huh?"

"I don't want to interrupt your game."

"No, man, it's okay. This here's Geraldo. We call him Jerry. Jerry, this here's Swann. He used to have his office down the block. What was it they called you?"

"I'm sure they called me a lot of things, but you're probably referring to skip tracer."

"Yeah. That's it. So, what you been tracin' lately?"

"Airwaves."

"Huh? You mean you be tracin' air what?"

"A little joke."

"I don't get it."

"That's okay. Most times neither do I. Let's just say I'm doing a little of this and a little of that."

"Yeah, I know what that's like, man," he said, though to him a little of this and a little of that probably meant panhandling on the subway, chiseling women out of their welfare checks, and hustling dominoes. Hector was an operator—at least he was, back when I knew him. I doubt he ever did an honest day's work in his life, somehow eking out a living from no particular marketable skills.

"Listen," I said, "it's been a while since I've been up this way, and I see the neighborhood's changed a lot . . ."

"No shit, man. I ain't gonna be 'round here much longer."

"And the 'hood would be the lesser for it, Hector."

"Huh?"

"What happened to the P B & G?"

"Bailey closed the joint."

"How long ago?"

" 'Bout a year, I guess."

"Why?"

"Raised the rent like three, four times what he was paying. Couldn't handle it with the business he was doing. I told him to run the numbers in the back, or deal some dope, but he wouldn't listen to me." He shook his head. "Motherfuckah had principles."

"Who the fuck does he think he is?" I said.

"Yeah. Who the fuck."

"Where is he now?"

"Damned if I know."

"And Manny?"

"I heard he wents back to P.R. I thinks his dad kicked the bucket and left him a few bucks. I thinks maybe I heard he opened up his own bar down there."

"Billy D?"

He laughed. "Upstate, man."

"Pinched?"

He nodded. "Tried to stick up a Duane Reade, and there were two off-duty cops there. He was lucky they didn't blow his fuckin' head off." He tapped his head with two fingers. "Never did have much up here, if you knows what I mean."

"You're the only one left."

"That's me, man. Last of the moccasins. But the pickin's are slim, so's I don't think I'll be around here much longer. Maybe I'll move back up to the South Bronx. Got me some family up there, you know. And the boys I grew up with. Maybe even upstate. I got some bros up near Albany."

The dude Hector was playing with was starting to get restless. I could see it was time to move on.

"Thanks for the update, Hector."

"No problemo. Listen, you sticks around a little, till I finishes here, and maybe I'll let you buys me a drink. I gots this business proposition you might be interested in."

"I'm afraid I've got all the business I can handle right now, so I'll take a rain check."

"Okay, man, another time. When it rains." He laughed heartily at his own joke, waved me off and went back to his game as I slunk away, into the darkness, headed back to the subway, which would take me back downtown, where I belonged.

7
WILL YOU STILL LOVE ME TOMORROW?

The aim was to collect as much information as I could about Sean Loomis before I hit the trail to look for him and Marcy. If that meant spending some money wining and dining Sandy Brennan, okay by me. Money was no object, because it wasn't mine. I had an American Express card now. Like everyone else in America, I was living *la vida loca* on credit. Only I didn't have to pay the bill. This is only one of the things that makes America great.

I made a reservation for eight o'clock at Dos Caminos, on Third Avenue and Fiftieth street, a far cry from the Paradise Bar & Grill, but a place I was familiar with. I managed to dig up a clean, button-down shirt, a pair of moderately pressed pants and a sport jacket that wasn't too rumpled. Tie? Not a chance. I even chucked the Chuck Taylors for a pair of beaten-up brown loafers I found semi-hidden in the back of my closet.

I like being early. Not only because I can scope out the place and the situation, but because it puts the other guy on the defensive. This gives me an edge that can make a difference.

The weather was good, so I chose an outside table and was already sipping a prickly pear margarita when Sandy Brennan strolled over. She was all dolled up, wearing a short black skirt, low-cut, pale blue blouse that hugged her ample chest, and a pair of black stiletto heels that accentuated her long, tan legs. She was wearing a wrist full of silver bracelets and a small silver crucifix dangled from a silver chain around neck. When I stood to greet her, she startled me by leaning forward and giving me a kiss on the cheek. It was obvious we were there for different reasons. She was on a date. I was working.

"This is very nice," she said as she sat down opposite me. She unfolded her napkin daintily and put it on her lap, her bracelets tinkling against each other as she lifted her hands back up to the table. "I see you've started before me."

"Got here a little early."

"That's okay."

"Something to drink?"

"Why not," she said, sweeping her hair out of her eyes with her fingertips. "What you're drinking looks pretty good."

I motioned to the waiter, pointing to my drink and indicating the same for Sandy.

"You must do pretty well to afford a place like this," she said.

"Not exactly. I've got a confession to make," I said.

"That sounds ominous. You're not going to tell me you're gay, are you?"

"I don't dress well enough to be gay," I said.

She laughed. "So, what is it?"

The waiter, Dan, arrived with Sandy's margarita. She picked it up and said, "Cheers."

"This is delicious. Good choice." She took another sip. "So what's this deep, dark secret you're about to divulge?" she asked, putting her glass down. "And by the way, I love secrets."

"Maybe we ought to order first."

"What's your rush?"

"I want to make sure there are no misunderstandings here."

"What do you mean?"

"This is business, Sandy."

"What's business?"

"This dinner."

"I don't get you."

"You're a nice woman, Sandy . . ."

A hardness crept over her face. "You don't know me very well, honey. I'm not so nice."

"Neither am I. This isn't social. I'm on a case."

"What do you mean, a case? You're not some sleazy lawyer sent by that son of a bitch ex-husband of mine, are you?"

"No. I'm looking for information about your son. I've been hired by Marcy Phillips's father."

"Who the fuck is she?"

"You don't know?"

"I haven't the foggiest idea."

"She's your son's girlfriend."

" 'Fraid not, sugar. He's dating some girl named Shelly."

"You've met her?" I asked, getting a sinking feeling that if it were true, I'd have to start all over again.

"I spoke to her on the phone."

"Seen a picture?"

"No."

"You're sure her name's not Marcy?"

"I'm sure. So if that's all this is about, we're cool," she said, picking up the menu.

I didn't think she was lying. And if she were, she was a damn better actress than I gave her credit for. Were there two girls involved? Maybe. Was Marcy using another name? Possible. Whatever it was, I was pretty sure Sandy was out of the loop. That didn't surprise me. Men don't confide in their mothers, unless, of course, their name's Norman Bates. I still thought I might get some clues from Sandy as to her son's whereabouts. Besides, the truth is, I was kind of enjoying her company.

"I was thinking of going vegan, but I think I'll put a hold on that and have this steak thingy," she said, a mischievous glint in her eyes.

"Whatever you want, sweetheart. The sky's the limit."

As we waited for our food to arrive—I ordered some shrimp dish—I pumped her for information.

"Tell me something about your son."

"Why? I already told you he doesn't know this Marcy whatever her name is," she said, finishing off her margarita.

"Maybe he does, maybe he doesn't. But I need to speak to him anyway."

"Why should I help you?"

"Look, this guy Phillips is a complete asshole. To make it worse, he's a lawyer. I don't like lawyers. Never have, never will. But he's a father and he's worried about his daughter. You worry about your kids. I worry about mine. He thinks she's with your son. Maybe he's right, maybe he's wrong. But it's my job to check it out. I'm just interested in the girl."

"How do I know you're for real? You've already lied to me. At least once." Our waiter passed by. She raised her glass slightly, tilted it toward him, and smiled. He nodded.

"I haven't lied to you. I just didn't tell you everything."

"So, who the hell are you? Really."

"Henry Swann. I'm a skip tracer, which is . . ."

"I know what the fuck a skip tracer does. I had a deadbeat husband." Dan set down another margarita and removed the empty glass.

"Thank you," she said. She turned to me. "So, Sean's not in any trouble?"

"Not with me."

"What do you want to know?"

"What kind of kid is he?"

"He's smart. And since the time he was a kid, he knew how to make a buck."

"What do you mean?"

"When he was twelve, he decided to clean out his room of all the stuff he didn't want anymore. But instead of throwing it out, he set up a table outside the building and tried to sell it all. You know what? He sold every single thing he put out there. Most of it was junk, but I think he pulled in something like twenty-eight dollars. It's not that people needed what he was selling. They just liked him, is all. They thought he was cute and wanted to help him out. And you know what? He was a helluva talker. Got that from his father. He made up a story about every toy or piece of clothing he was trying to sell. He was very entertaining.

"Then he was hooked. He had nothing else to sell, but he was passing the neighborhood library one day and they were throwing out a bunch of books. He got himself a wagon, loaded it up with the books, then the next Sunday he went to the local flea market and sold them for five dollars apiece. He made over a hundred bucks. That's a lot of money for a twelve-year-old. And you know what? I think that's when he fell in love with books and reading. Before that, he couldn't've cared less about books. But after that, when he got bored he'd pick up one of those books and read. After that, he always had his head in a book. He didn't care about sports. He didn't have many friends. He was either selling books or reading one of them. Sometimes, if he really liked the book, he refused to sell it. He had a roomful of books, and he wouldn't let me get near them."

"What'd he do with the money?"

"Spent it on more books and record albums and then, when he got old enough to date, he used it to impress girls. For his junior prom, he used his own money to rent a tux and then, when it was over, he took his date over to Central Park, and he hired one of those horse and buggies to ride him around for an hour. It must have cost him a fortune, but he didn't care. He just sold more books."

Dan appeared with our food.

"Looks delicious," she said.

"Dig in. How about friends?"

She chewed a moment, then answered. "He didn't have many growing up, and once he left for college, I didn't see him much. But he's a very private kid. Always was. When he got old enough, he actually bought a lock and put it on his bedroom door. Even if he were living next door, I know I wouldn't see him much and he certainly wouldn't confide in me."

"But you know his girlfriend's named Shelly."

"Only because he let it slip one day, during a phone conversation."

"And as far as you know, he's up in Syracuse now?"

"Far as I know. You going to track him down, Sheriff?"

"I'm gonna try."

"How will you do it?"

"It just comes to me, Sandy," I said as I downed the last of my prickly pear margarita and turned my attention to the shrimp. "Like magic."

I don't know what got into me. Maybe it was the margaritas. Three of them, by the time we finished. Or the good food. Or that I hadn't been with anyone in a while. Or that I couldn't let Sandy Brennan take the subway home alone. Or that it was a very long ride back into the city.

Whatever it was, when she asked me to spend the night, I didn't think twice.

When we were lying there together, naked, after having made love, I wanted to sleep, but she wanted to talk. I don't want to talk even when I don't want to sleep.

"You know," she said, "it's not like I hop into bed with every guy I meet."

"Me neither," I said, my eyes half closed.

"Usually, I have to know a guy pretty good before something like this happens."

"Me, too," I said.

"So, I'm feeling a little strange about this."

"Why's that?"

"Because I don't really know you. Like now, what are you thinking about?"

There are many answers to that question, but only one that any man ought to give.

"You."

She punched my arm lightly. "You're smooth, Swann. But how do I know you're not full of shit, like every other man I've ever met?"

"You don't. But maybe it's true." A poem by e.e. cummings popped into my head and I started reciting it. I don't know why, I just did.

> " 'mr youse needn't be so spry
> concernin questions arty
>
> each has his tastes but as for i
> i likes a certain party
>
> gimme the he-man's solid bliss
> for youse ideas i'll match youse
>
> a pretty girl who naked is
> is worth a million statues.' "

She laughed. She kissed me. We made love again. And then she let me go to sleep. At least I didn't have to take that long ride home till morning.

★ ★ ★ ★ ★

PART 2
SYRACUSE, NEW YORK

★ ★ ★ ★ ★

"That" comes out of "this" and "this" depends on "that."
—Chuang Chou, *Chuant Tzu*

8
NORTHERN EXPOSURE

When I arrived at Syracuse's Hancock Field, a cozy little airport that seemed like a throwback to earlier days of aviation, I hailed a cab and asked to be taken to Syracuse University.

"It's a big school, mister. Any idea where you want to be dropped off?" asked the driver, who looked to be in his early to late sixties. It was warm, but he was wearing a jacket and tie, which seemed to be a little out of place, considering he was driving a cab.

"Let's try the registrar's office."

He shook his head. "No friggin' idea where that is. How about I just drop you off at University Avenue. It's by the quad and near the Sheraton, in case you're looking for someplace to stay."

"Let's do it."

"You don't mind me asking, what kind of business you got at the university?" he asked as we pulled onto the highway.

"I'm looking for somebody."

"I'll bet there's a story behind that."

"Just a father looking for his missing kid."

"You the father?"

"No. He hired me to find her."

"You some kind of detective or something?"

"Just a guy who's pretty good at finding things, then getting them back to their owners."

"Too bad. Woulda been something to tell the wife. You been

married as long as me, forty-two years, you're always looking for something to say other than 'please pass the salt.' "

"Nowhere to go from there but the pepper."

He laughed. "Been to Syracuse before?"

"First time. You from around here?"

He shook his head. "Came here from Detroit over thirty years ago. Supposed to be a temporary thing, but I been here ever since. Just be glad you ain't here in the winter. Man, it's a bitch. They call it 'lake effect' snow, and it comes in hard and fast. All the moisture in the lake is lifted up, changed into snow, then dumped on the city. First year I moved here, a storm dumped eighty, ninety inches in the space of a couple of days. Snow drifts over your friggin' head. Even had to close the friggin' city for a while. No one seemed to care. They're used to it. Don't call it the Salt City for nothing. I see a warm climate in my future, soon as I can convince the wife."

"I'm guessing you didn't always drive a cab."

"What gave you that idea?"

"The jacket and tie."

He turned and smiled. "You're pretty good, mister. Yeah, I wear that to remind myself I ain't just a cabbie. Just doing this 'cause I'm between jobs. It's rough up here. Upstate New York is dyin', and I'm dyin' with it."

"What kind of work did you do?"

"A little of everything. Worked on the line when I was in Detroit. Then the docks for a while. That got old real fast. Drove a truck when I got here. I was a cut man for a while. Boxed a little when I was young, so I knew the drill. Ever heard'a Carmen Basilio?"

"Sure have. Terrific welterweight."

"That's him. He came from around here. Canastota. Had his first fight in Binghamton. Hell of a puncher. Knocked the sucker out in three rounds. Next guy, one round. Took the middleweight crown from Sugar Ray, who was, the way I see it, pound for pound the best boxer ever. Carmen took a lot of punches, which is why he needed guys like me. Still lives up here. You ever box?"

"I've made it my life's work to avoid pain any way I can. Boxing's just asking for it."

"I'll take that as a no."

"How about you?"

"Did my share of fighting growing up. Had to. Never looked for a fight, though. But I ain't never backed down from one neither. I took a few turns in the ring, too. Just to see what it was like. But I had to be a lot better than I was to do it for a living. It only took a few shots to the head before I realized it wasn't for me. But I made some friends working out in the gym. That's how I learned to be a cut man and how I got connected to Carmen."

We passed the outskirts of an enormous mall on our right. "That's the Carousel," he said, motioning with his head. "Biggest mall in the country, after the Mall of America in Minneapolis. People come down from Canada to shop here. They think it'll save the city, and it did get us a bunch of jobs. But it ain't gonna do the trick. Unless you're working at the university or over at the casino, Turning Stone, jobs are damn hard to come by. I'm lucky to have this one, and this ain't no gem. Most of the time, I'm sittin' around listening to some asshole on the radio, like Rush Limbaugh, telling me something I already know, that the country's goin' to hell in a hand basket, while I wait for a fare."

We pulled off the highway and within a few blocks I could see the first signs of the university.

"I'm gonna leave you off at the hotel. That way, you can get yourself a room, then hop over to the campus and start looking for your girl. And if you need any help, here's how to reach me," he said, twisting in his seat to hand me a business card. "Name's Fred Gasper."

"Thanks," I said. I stuffed the card in my wallet. Who knew? Without wheels, I might need to take him up on his offer.

I scored a room on the eighth floor, overlooking Newhouse, the journalism school. I asked the kid at the desk, a perky blonde named Jacqueline, for a map of the campus, which she happily provided—she was, as it turned out, a junior who was spending the summer in town, picking up a few extra credits and a few extra dollars.

The registrar's office was only a few blocks away, and there I was greeted by a gray-haired, matronly woman who looked at me as if I'd set down from another planet.

"May I help you?" she asked, peering over a pair of large, sequin-framed eyeglasses.

"I hope so. I'm looking for a student. He's a grad student, actually. I'm a friend of the family, happened to be up here on a sales call, and promised his mom I'd look in on him, maybe take him to dinner. But damned if I didn't lose the address, and his mom just left the city for a weekend in Vermont and she's out of cell phone range—somewhere in the woods camping."

"What's his name?"

"Sean Loomis."

She hit a couple of keys on the computer, then looked up. "What school did you say he was in?"

"English Department."

"I see a Sean Loomis, but he's not a current student."

"That's odd. Maybe he's not taking the summer session."

"Wasn't here in the spring, either."

"I wonder if his mom knows about this. You wouldn't happen to have contact information for him, would you?"

She looked back to the screen, then up. "If I did, I couldn't give it to you."

"But you don't?"

She remained stone-faced. No way I was going to get any help from her.

"What about his girlfriend, Marcy Phillips? She's a student here."

"That would be the same thing."

"Ma'am, I'm just hoping you can help me out because I'm really up the creek here. I made a promise, you know, and I feel like a real idiot not being able to make good on it because I did something stupid."

She looked at me like I was, in fact, stupid, and then pounded a few keys. "I don't have anything for her either."

"Well, this is pretty mysterious, isn't it?" I paused for a moment. "How about this. Sean was getting his master's or Ph.D., or something like that, in English, so maybe I should speak to the head of the department. Who would that be and where would I find him . . . or her?"

"That would be Professor Richard Dubin. Hall of Languages. Room 203."

I walked along the quad, where on the grass a few students, probably taking summer classes, were sunbathing, playing guitars, tossing Frisbees. I couldn't help but think of my son, Noah. Fourteen. In a few years he might be one of these kids. It made me sad. I don't know why. I didn't spend much time trying to figure it out. I slammed the door on those thoughts and refocused on the case.

I knocked on the door of 203 and a husky voice boomed, "Come in."

The small office was a mess. Books and papers piled on the floor, on the shelves and perched precariously on the large wooden desk, behind which sat the man I presumed was Professor Richard Dubin. His feet were propped up on his desk and he was reading a newspaper, which hid everything but the top of his clean-shaven head. "Don't just stand there. Take a seat," he said without bothering to look up.

I sat and he continued reading.

"Don't worry, I've got all day," I said.

He peeked over his newspaper to check me out while I did the same with him. He looked to be in his mid-fifties, had a goatee and was wearing a bright yellow T-shirt that read, "What if the hokey-pokey is what it's all about?" There was a cigar burning in an ashtray.

"Funny, because that's what I've got, too. Let me guess," he said, "you're not a student." He folded the newspaper and flung it to the far reaches of his desk.

"Right."

"And you don't look like any student's father either," he added, picking up the cigar.

"Right again," I said.

"So why are you darkening my doorstep on this beautiful July . . ."—he checked his watch—"late morning?" He waved the stogie in the air.

"I was hoping you might be able to help me."

He brought the cigar to his lips, took a drag and exhaled slowly. "I'm the one who needs help, my friend. But alas, these are my required office hours, and since there aren't any students banging down my door looking to profit from my enormous fount of wisdom, I might as well try helping you. So, enlighten me. I'm all ears."

"I'm looking for someone."

"Ever hear of Google, my friend?" he said, placing the cigar back in the ashtray and leaning back in his chair.

"Sounds familiar."

"Students want to know something, they don't come to me anymore, they go straight to Google. Sometimes they get the right answer, sometimes they don't. But either way, I'm cool with it because they leave me the hell alone. So, naturally, I'm curious as to why you're not doing the same thing."

"Using Google or leaving you the hell alone?"

"Both."

"The kind of information I'm looking for Google doesn't provide."

He bent forward, picked up his cigar again, took a long drag, stared at it lovingly, then exhaled slowly. "You know, it's true, sometimes a cigar is just a cigar."

"You allowed to smoke in here?" I asked, waving away the fumes wafting in my direction.

"I've got tenure. I can do any damned thing I want, short of shagging a student. Dean had a big meeting last fall. Evidently, that's a deal-breaker, not that it stops a lot of people around here. Bunch of perverts. But that's the pool of available hook-ups, so who am I to judge? I guess I should stop. Smoking, that is. Not shagging. But I love a good stogie every once in a while. If it kills me, it kills me. It's gonna happen sometime, so it might as well be from something I enjoy. So, what's your name and what's your story? And you don't have to make it short. I've got another hour to go before I can disappear into the ether, and believe me, on a beautiful day like this no one's going to show up. They hardly ever do, unless they're begging me to change a grade or sucking up to me. I don't mind the sucking up. In fact, I thrive on it, but begging for grades is a real drag. I've got a rule. You don't like your grade and you come in here to complain, I automatically lower it. It discourages even the most dogged grade hounds. I'm bored. Entertain me."

I looked around at all the books piled on the shelves and stacked up on the floor. "Looks to me like you've set the bar pretty high."

"They're mostly for show. They impress the hell out of the

students. They think I've actually read them all. And what they think can't hurt me. The fact that they're impressed is fine with the administration. The students are impressed, Admin. can raise tuition. They raise tuition, I get a pay raise. It's a win–win situation. I love academia."

"Some racket."

"Don't tell the civilians, or else everyone and their mother will be looking to get a Ph.D. As it is, we're seeing all those ridiculous MFA mills sprout up all over the country. Especially those low-residency scams. It's like printing money for the universities, and I guess it puts some dough into the pockets of a lot of out-of-work teachers and writers. But it's just another con. Before long your butcher, baker and candlestick maker will have one. But I'm sure you didn't come here to listen to me spout off about the great educational system of this country. Or to put the cuffs on me for printing money, seeing what they pay me to do the amount of work I actually do. But let that dirty little secret lie dormant for a while, like the moth on Frost's tablecloth. Let's start at the beginning. Your name?"

"Henry Swann."

"How Proustian. So, Henry Swann, what do you do for a living? Wait. Let me guess. From the way you're dressed, I seriously doubt you're a car or insurance salesman. I don't see you as a prospective grad student, either. And I doubt you're a process server, although I wouldn't be surprised to see one show up in my office one day."

"I've done a bit of that at certain low points of my life, but that's not what I do now."

"So I'm getting closer. The smart guess would be lawyer, but you've got much too good a sense of humor for that. And you don't dress well enough. No offense, of course, because take a look at me." He looked at me closer, squinting a bit. "You know what? You've got an aura coming off you. And a certain odor."

"I thought the shower this morning would have taken care of that."

"It's the kind of aroma no shower can eradicate. I sniff Raymond Chandler and Dashiell Hammett, with a dash of Ross MacDonald."

I smiled.

"I'm right, huh? A private dick."

"I don't know how private I am, or how much of a dick I am, either—I'll leave that up to others to decide—but I am looking for someone, someone you know."

"Who might that be?"

"Sean Loomis."

He picked up the cigar again, holding it front of his face as if it were a weapon he might use to defend himself. "So you're looking for Sean. I guess the next thing for me to do is ask why. So I will. Why?"

"Because he may have information as to the whereabouts of Marcy Phillips."

"And she would be?"

"His girlfriend. You know him or not?"

"I run the department, Swann. I know all my students, especially Sean."

"Why 'especially Sean'?"

"Sean's a bit of a legend around here."

"Enlighten me."

"He's been up here for several years, but for much of that time it's been in name only. He's kind of like the man who wasn't here. Or there. Or anywhere. Like the Scarlet Pimpernel. 'They seek him here, they seek him there, they seek him almost everywhere . . .' "

"He's registered but he doesn't attend classes?"

"You got it. Or at least he was registered. It seems he's taking a self-imposed sabbatical."

"Where would he be when he's not here?"

"It's not part of my job description to keep track of students. In fact, it's their job to keep track of me."

"Maybe you can point me in the direction of someone who can find him?"

He puffed on his stogie. "You might try his faculty advisor."

"Who would that be?"

"Dana Simmons."

"Where would I find her?"

"She's off for the summer and, unlike some others, me for instance, she doesn't teach. She actually has a life that takes her away from the beautiful city of Syracuse, New York. I can give you an email address and phone number and you can probably track her down that way. If you're lucky, she hasn't wandered too far afield."

"Thanks. While I'm here and you've got nothing better to do, how about telling me what you know about Sean."

"You ask the questions, gumshoe, and I'll provide what answers I can."

He was obviously enjoying himself, which was fine with me.

"When did you first come in contact with him?"

"Three or four years ago, when he was accepted into the program. Brilliant kid. Knew as much about literature as anyone I know, and that includes most of the lit professors up here. I'm probably the only one who knows more than he does, but you might chalk that up to the extremely high opinion I hold of myself. Sean has an encyclopedic knowledge of writers and books. He impressed me from the get-go—and I'm not easily impressed. But he was a bit of a scoundrel."

"What do you mean?"

"He refused to conform to the norm. He'd regularly hand in assignments a day late. Not two days late, not a week late. Precisely one day late. It was as if he were testing his professors, daring them to fail him. But the maddening thing was that his papers were so brilliant, they couldn't possibly do that. Maybe that's why he did it—just to show he was special, that he was better than they were. And shit, he probably is. That was the damned frustrating thing about it. He knew how to push our buttons and he wasn't above doing it.

"About a year ago, he upped the ante. He handed in a research paper to his professor, who happened to be his advisor, Dana Simmons, and when she read it she immediately recognized large chunks of it as being plagiarized."

"I suppose that's not so uncommon."

"More common than I'd like to think. But the bizarre thing was that it was plagiarized from her."

"You're kidding."

He raised his hand. "God's honest. It's not as if he thought she wouldn't recognize her own work. And it's not as if he needed to do it. Like I told you, the kid is brilliant. All I can think of was that he was just sticking it to her. And me."

"Why?"

"That's the sixty-four-thousand-dollar question. Maybe he was testing us, to see what we would do."

"What did you do?"

"The normal thing would have been to expel him on the spot, and it was seriously discussed. But instead we decided to suspend him for a semester."

"Why not expel him?"

"Dana and I—we decided to keep everyone else out of it— were baffled as to why he would do something so stupid, which we soon realized wasn't stupid at all, but totally calculated. He knew, of course, that she couldn't help but recognize her own work."

"Maybe he thought the paper would be read by a T.A."

"He knew Dana didn't work that way. He had an agenda, but

we just couldn't figure out what it was. We called him in and asked him about it, but he just smiled and refused to answer. It was a scene straight out of Bartleby. When we told him there were consequences, all he said was, 'Do what you have to do.' Like he was daring us to expel him. I figured that's what he wanted, for whatever reason, and damned if I was going to give him what he wanted. I preferred having him around, because otherwise there was no way I was going to know why he did it."

"He didn't deny it?"

"How could he?"

"He didn't explain it?"

He shook his head.

"When did this happen?"

"Last year."

"Has he been back since then?"

"Sporadically during the fall semester, but not this past spring."

"You haven't heard from him since?" I asked.

He shook his head. "Maybe Dana has. They were kind of close."

"Do you think there was something between them?"

"Something?"

"Sexual."

"I doubt it."

"Why's that?"

"Because I believe she's of the lesbian persuasion."

"Sounds to me, Professor, that this kid's trouble."

"Yeah, but he's also something very special."

"How about that contact information for Dana Simmons?"

"Sure," he said. Reaching for a pad on the far corner of his desk, he scribbled down the information, tore off the page and handed it to me. "Anything else I can help you with, Swann?"

"Not at the moment, but if anything occurs to you, I'm staying over at the Sheraton."

"I'd stand up and show you out, but I've got a bum knee and I think you can manage that yourself. Somehow, I don't think I've seen the last of you."

9
THE LOVELY LADIES OF
ALPHA CHI OMEGA

"I'm looking for someone who used to be a student here. Got any suggestions how I might find her?" I asked Jacqueline, who was still on desk duty when I returned to the hotel.

"Registrar's office, maybe," she said as the obviously multi-talented Jackie filed her nails and sucked on a Tootsie Pop at the same time.

"She's not enrolled anymore, so they can't help me."

"What's her name?"

"Marcy Phillips."

She shrugged. "Don't know her. My guess is she belonged to a sorority. If you find out which one, they might be able to help you."

"How would I do that?"

She took the pop out of her mouth and waved it around. "She's probably on MySpace or Facebook. She'd probably put it up there. If not, you could probably Google her name along with Syracuse University, and something would come up."

"You have a business center here?"

"Sure thing. Make a left and another left. Your room card will get you in."

After I got to the business center, I logged on and sent Dana Simmons an email, introducing myself, asking where she was and if I could talk to her. Next, I Googled Marcy Phillips and found she was or had been a member of Alpha Chi Omega. While I was at it, I thought about checking on Phillips, Sean and Dubin as well, but I was getting a little restless so I decided to take care of that when I got back from checking out the sorority house, which was only a few blocks away.

The Victorian building on Walnut Avenue, set back behind an immaculately kept lawn, looked like it came straight from a Hollywood set. Their motto, as I read in the literature I'd picked up at the University Student Union, was "Real. Strong. Women," which frankly I found rather disturbing. Does the world really need more Real. Strong. Women? Aren't they real and strong enough? Reading further, I found this news, "Along with our national philanthropy and domestic violence awareness, we are extremely fortunate to be supporting Heather House. The Lambda Chapter has organized Frisbee Fling, a traditional ultimate Frisbee tournament that involves all Greek life and other student organizations, in an attempt to raise domestic violence awareness on campus in an entertaining and informative manner. This year, our Frisbee Fling event will be September 26, in Walnut Park, along with the Alpha Epsilon Pi fraternity and their Wiffles, Waffles and Falafels event. Please join us and help stomp out domestic violence."

Too bad I wouldn't be around to participate.

As any red-blooded American male, I had visions of young women in sexy lingerie lounging around the living room dancing through my head, but when I knocked at the door it was opened by a smiling, slightly overweight co-ed, with stringy, dirty blond hair and dressed in baggy jeans and an oversized Syracuse T-shirt.

"May I help you?" she said sweetly, which gave me the distinct feeling that she was under the impression I was someone's father.

"I'm wondering if there might be anyone around who would know Marcy Phillips. She's one of your sisters."

91

"It's July, you know, so there really aren't many of us here. Just the ones taking summer classes."

"Yeah, sweetie, but you're here so there might be others around who know her."

"I've just finished my sophomore year, and I don't remember her being one of us. Are you sure you've got the right house?"

"I'm hardly ever sure of anything, but the information I got is that she was a member of your fine sorority a year or so ago. Is there anyone around who's a little more senior than you?"

She turned and looked inside, then back at me.

"Why are you looking for this Marcy Phillips person?"

I put my finger to my lips. "Need-to-know basis."

"Huh?"

"Privileged information."

"Are you for real?"

"Sometimes I ask myself that very same question, honey. And you know, all too often I don't know the answer. But I'm a lot more harmless than I look. If you don't believe me, you can check with Professor Richard Dubin, over at the English Department. He's a good friend of mine."

"He is?"

"Swear on the Alpha Chi Omega logo."

"It's just Greek letters."

" 'Real. Strong. Women,' " I said, holding up my fist in a black power salute.

"Huh?"

"Isn't that your motto?"

"I guess."

"You're not sure? Hmm. Perhaps I ought to report you to the Lambda headquarters."

"You're kidding, right?" she said with a hint of fear in her voice.

"You never know. What's your name?"

"Kelly," she stuttered.

"Well, Kelly, is there anyone else in the house right now who might be able to give me a hand here?"

She stepped out onto the porch and closed the door behind her.

"Madeleine, she's the vice president. But she's upstairs and I'm not supposed to bother her."

"Why don't you tell her there's a gentleman down here from Lambda headquarters who needs to talk to her."

"But that's not true, is it?"

"No, it's not. But Madeleine won't know that. If she asks you why I want to see her, just tell her it's about some possible violations of the chapter charter. That should get her lazy ass down here pretty quick."

"But she'll blame me and I'll get in trouble for lying," she said, close to tears.

"Don't worry, honey, I'll take the fall," I said, trying hard to keep a straight face.

"Okay."

"How about letting me inside, to wait?"

"I don't know . . ."

"It's what a true real, strong Lambda Chi woman would do."

She opened the front door, and I followed her in. When she disappeared upstairs, I headed to the couch, which was covered with clothing. I tossed some of it aside and sat down. These girls were living like pigs . . . which made me feel right at home. The place smelled like a combination of cheap perfume, sweat, and beer, all of which was heightened by the fact that the windows were closed and there was no air-conditioning. While I waited, I picked up a copy of *People* and thumbed through it.

Before I could get to the latest news about the Brad Pitt/ Jennifer Aniston nuptials, I heard thundering footsteps coming down the stairs. An instant later, faster than I thought possible, a young woman, barefoot, dressed in jeans and an inside-out SU T-shirt, her long, blond hair in complete disarray, was standing in front of me.

"Kelly . . . said . . . you . . . were . . . from . . . chapter . . . headquarters . . . and . . ." she said, trying desperately to catch her breath while she picked up the items of clothing I'd moved to the side of the couch.

"Relax," I said. I patted the cushion of the couch. "Have a seat, Maddy."

She stopped, put her hands on her hips, and gave me a look that probably sent chills up the spines of pledges, but did nothing for me.

"My name's Madeleine."

"I'm more comfortable with Maddy, so I think that's what I'll call you. Sit down, Maddy," I said, patting the couch, "and we'll talk. But you know, it's damned hot out there, and I could use something to drink."

"This isn't a coffee shop, you know."

"What about that Lambda Chi hospitality I've heard so much about?"

"Kelly!" she yelled. "Can you come down here, please? And bring a couple of glasses of diet soda. With ice." She turned back to me. "You're not from the Lambda, are you?"

"Nope."

She eyed me suspiciously. "Who are you?"

"I'm working for Marcy Phillips's father."

"How do I know you're not lying about this, too?"

"You don't. But you will," I said as I pulled my cell phone out of my pocket, "if you call Mr. Phillips yourself." I highlighted his number.

"Well, I guess if you've got his number you're really who you say you are. What's your name?"

"Henry Swann."

She smiled.

"Something funny?"

"Not really. It's just kind of coincidental, that's all."

"What's that?"

"Well, your name is Swann, like in Proust, and my name is Madeleine, like in the cookie that makes him remember his childhood."

"I'm impressed. English major?"

"Kind of."

"What's that mean?"

"I started out that way, but I changed."

"To what?"

"Psychology."

"That's just what we need in the world, more shrinks. I'm looking forward to the time when there are enough shrinks in the world so we can each have our own personal one who follows us around night and day, judging and interpreting everything we do. You look like you're having a hard time keeping your eyes open, Maddy. Did I interrupt your afternoon nap?"

"We were out drinking last night. I turned twenty-one."

"Congratulations."

"I tried to make it to twenty-one shots, but I think I pretty much passed out at around twelve."

"Your parents must be very proud, Maddy. Maybe you should get yourself a cup of coffee."

"Maybe you're right." She turned and yelled, "Kelly! Make mine coffee!"

"Is that some kind of sorority hazing thing?"

"What?"

"Ordering her around like she's the help."

"She's only a sophomore, and I'm like a senior."

"Long live the chain of command. Let's get down to business. You knew Marcy Phillips?"

"Yes."

"So?"

"So?"

"Tell me about her."

"She was a bitch."

"Is that your opinion or everyone's?"

She shrugged. "Some people probably thought she was okay, but I thought she was a bitch."

"Why's that?"

"Because she thought she was better than everybody else. Because she thought she was smarter than everyone else. Because she had attitude."

"Maybe she was."

"Was what?"

"Better and smarter than everyone else."

"Yeah, right."

"Did the other girls think the same way about her?"

"I can't speak for the other girls."

"So you had personal problems with her?"

Kelly came in with a cup of coffee and a diet soda and set them on the table in front of us.

"Thanks, Kelly," I said.

"This is much better than the last time, Kelly," said Madeleine as she sipped and then put the cup down.

"I added a little more coffee, to make it stronger."

"You ought to write down how much, so you don't screw it up next time."

I got the picture. I didn't know how much stock I could put in anything Madeleine told me about Marcy, since she might have looked at her the same way she was looking at Kelly: as a servant. And perhaps Marcy, who was probably used to being served, wasn't quite as submissive as Kelly. I learned a long time ago, there is no truth, only versions of it. If you understand that, you can get a lot closer to the truth you need, the one that gets you closer to what you're looking for.

Kelly made her exit, and I turned back to Madeleine. "You come from a wealthy family, don't you?" Self-control isn't one of my strong points. It's gotten me in a lot of trouble over the years, but it's also helped me find what I'm looking for. I'm willing to make the trade-off.

"What do you mean?"

"Seems to me like you're used to handling servants."

"You mean Kelly?"

"Yes."

"She's not a servant."

"Could've fooled me."

"You don't know anything about sorority life, do you?"

"Do I look like I've spent much time in sorority houses?"

"Well, it's part of the experience. Kelly knows what to expect."

"Was it part of the experience for Marcy?"

"If she'd have let it be, yes. But she didn't."

"That why you didn't like her?"

"I didn't like her because she was a bitch, not because she wouldn't serve me coffee."

"What did you know about her social life?"

"I didn't really pay much attention to her social life. I have better things to do than keep tabs on pledges. She was only a pledge for like a couple of months. Then she quit."

"Why?"

"Because sorority life wasn't for her?"

"You're asking me?"

"I'm saying she never sat down with me or anybody else and gave an explanation. She just up and quit. And you know what? I didn't shed even one, tiny, little tear. I don't think anyone else did, either. She never really fit in. And the day after she was gone, it was as if she'd never been here at all. That's how much she was missed."

"That's very cold, Maddy."

"I'm just telling the truth."

"You knew she had a boyfriend?"

"Yes. His name was Sean."

"Ever meet him?"

"Not technically."

"What does that mean?"

"It means we weren't like introduced. But I saw him with her a couple of times."

"Did you dislike him, too?"

"As a matter of fact, I didn't. He was very cool. And smart. I was surprised because I didn't think Marcy would go for that type. He rode a motorcycle. He was wearing a leather jacket and jeans when he came over to pick her up one night."

"Any idea where she might be now?"

"Not the slightest."

"Know who might?"

She frowned. "Maybe that dyke professor she was always talking about."

"Dana Simmons?"

"Yeah. That's her."

"What do you know about Dana Simmons?"

"Nothing."

"Then why the edge in your voice when you mention her name?"

"I told you. I'm a little hungover, so you haven't caught me at my best. I'm sorry if I seem a little bitchy. I'm really not so bad. I didn't even know her. I just saw them together a few times walking on the quad. Marcy was always saying what a great teacher she was. She's probably very nice and she's probably a very good teacher."

"Ever see Simmons, Sean and Marcy together?"

"No."

"And you can't give me any help in finding Marcy or Sean."

"That's right."

"Is there anyone else around who might?"

"It's the summer semester. Anyone who might be able to help you isn't here. But honestly, there wasn't anyone here who was close to Marcy."

"How'd she get in? Don't you have to pass some kind of test or something? Or at least have someone sponsor you?"

"She was a legacy. Her mother was a Lambda somewhere or other. And I think her father donated a lot of money to our chapter."

"So she bought her way in."

"She's not the only one."

"You're telling me, honey. Money talks and when it does, a lot of us listen. Was she close to anyone in the house?"

She thought a moment. "Maybe Jen."

"Where's she?"

"She's not in Lambda anymore, either."

"How can I find her?"

"She works at Cosmo's, on Marshall Street. At least she did. But I don't know if she's still here."

"Well then, I'll just have to find out, won't I?"

10
A FRIEND IN NEED

The aroma of pizza and grease smacked me in the face before I even reached the door of Cosmo's Pizza. It held the odd combination of repulsion and attraction, and I think if I were neither hungry nor in pursuit of information about Marcy Phillips I still would have gone in, if only simply to investigate what kind of establishment could successfully combine both these elements.

Inside, it could have been 1955 instead of 2001. I hadn't been in college in well over twenty years, but the feel of this place was not so different from the West End, the bar where we used to hang out in my short stint at Columbia University.

I took a seat at an empty table near the back and waited to be served. A young girl handed me a single sheet of paper, which served as a menu. I didn't bother looking at it. I wasn't there for the cuisine.

"What's good here?" I asked.

"Not much," she said, loud enough to be heard several tables away.

"What am I most likely to eat now and not puke up later?"

She shrugged. "The pizza. But I'd get it plain, if I were you."

"How about a beer to go with it?"

"Sure thing," she said, grabbing the menu from my hand. "What kind?"

"What kind you got?"

She gestured toward a row of four bottles lined up behind

the counter.

"Not much of a choice."

She shrugged.

"Miller."

Before she could scoot away, I asked, "Is Jen working to-night?"

"Yeah. That's her, over there," she said, pointing to a short, pudgy, dark-haired girl standing by the counter.

"Can you ask her to come over here when she has a chance?"

"Sure thing," she said. She turned and headed toward the counter, and as she passed Jen, she whispered in her ear and pointed in my direction. Jen looked over, tucked a pencil and pad in her apron and headed my way.

"You wanted to see me?"

"I did. My name's Henry Swann, and I'd like to ask you a few questions about your friend, Marcy Phillips."

"Why's that?"

"I'm looking for her and thought you might be able to point me in the right direction."

"That's the owner, Rose, at the cash register. If she sees me talking with the customers, she'll go ballistic."

An elderly woman with frizzy, dyed red hair was perched on a high stool behind the register, her evil-looking eyes scanning the room. "If she asks, just tell her I'm asking you a few questions about the menu."

"So what do you want to know? But you'd better make it quick."

"Did you meet her at Lambda?"

"I knew her before we pledged. We were in a class together. Art in the Machine Age. We sat next to each other. At first she didn't say much, but one day we were watching this slide show and she said, 'My dad owns that one.' I thought she was kidding. We kinda got friendly after that. She was very smart. She took great notes and she'd lend them to me if I missed class or something. When she decided to pledge Lambda, she asked if I wanted to, too. I told her I was pretty sure they wouldn't take someone like me, but she said not to worry. She had some pull. Her mother was in a Lambda chapter somewhere."

"Do you know where she is now?"

"I haven't seen or heard from her in maybe six months."

"What about her boyfriend?"

"Sean?"

"That's him."

"I don't know where he is either."

"Tell me what you know about him."

"I met him a few times, but we didn't socialize or anything. Once she met him, our friendship kinda like changed." A bell rang. She looked over her shoulder nervously. "I gotta pick up an order."

"Come back when you're done."

A few minutes later, my pizza and beer arrived. I was halfway through it when Jen reappeared at my table.

"So what else did you want to know?"

"How did she change, once she met Sean."

"For one thing, she quit the sorority."

"Why?"

"She just thought it was a crock, a waste of time. Once she quit, she got kind of an attitude."

"What kind of attitude?"

"Like she didn't care about anything that had to do with school anymore."

"Did you know she was going to quit?"

"It didn't surprise me."

"You think Sean had something to do with her quitting?"

"It's not like she said he did, but she quit not long after they got together, so you figure it out."

"You were angry with her, weren't you?"

She fiddled with her pad. "Kinda."

"Because she dumped you?"

"We were friends. I didn't have many friends. So, yeah, I was angry. I kinda felt like she abandoned me."

"You quit Lambda soon after she did."

"They treated me like shit once Marcy left. It wasn't so bad while she was there, because she kind of protected me. But once she was gone, it was like it was open season on me, because I wasn't one of the 'pretty ones,' " she air quoted. "So why should I stay?"

"Did you ever see Marcy with anyone else? Any other friends she hung out with?"

"She was friendly with a couple of her professors."

"Like who?"

"Dana Simmons."

"Who else?"

"Some older guy I didn't recognize. I assumed he was one of her profs."

"What'd he look like?"

"It was winter. Everyone up here looks alike in winter. You know, with those big, heavy coats and hats."

"Did she talk about either of them?"

"Like I said, once she and Sean started hanging out, I didn't see much of her."

"Did you know Loomis very well?"

"Not really. We all went out drinking one night. He picked up the check. I remember that." She smiled.

"Have you seen him lately?"

"A few months ago, near spring break, he stopped by for lunch, without Marcy. I asked him if he was graduating and he laughed."

"Anything else?"

"It was pretty busy around here and Rose"—she gestured back toward the counter with her head—"was in one of her moods."

"Where did Marcy live once she left the house?"

"She and Sean moved into some house off-campus they rented. I'm not sure where it was and I assume since I haven't seen either of them in months, they're not here anymore."

"You know, Jen, I'm kinda stumped here. I was hoping you might be able to point me in the right direction."

"I'd like to help . . ."

I believed she would. But that's all I got, which wasn't very much. But you know, in the end, the pizza wasn't half bad. But maybe that's because I wasn't paying attention.

11

No One in the Place, Just You and Me

Back at the hotel, there was a voicemail waiting for me from Richard Dubin. He wanted to meet me for a drink in the hotel bar at nine. It was only seven. Enough time to shower and take a short nap. I was curious as to what he wanted. It made me wonder if he knew more about Sean and Marcy than he'd let on earlier. When someone invites you to meet with them, it's almost never about you but about them, about what they want from you.

When I got to the hotel bar a few minutes before nine, Dubin was sitting on a bar stool, wearing faded jeans and a brightly colored Hawaiian shirt, sipping a beer. I stood in the doorway a moment, trying to figure out how I was going to play it.

Dubin spotted me. "Hey, Swann," he said, waving his hand, "get your ass over here."

I slid onto the stool beside him. He patted me on the back and said, "Glad you could make it, my friend. I'm a little early. I had nothing better to do, so I figured I might as well do it watching the Yankees." He gestured toward the large-screen TV over the bar.

"How'd you know I'd show?"

"It's Syracuse, man. In the middle of the summer. What else would you have to do at nine o'clock at night?" He looked up at the screen. "It's top of the sixth. They're up by two. Yankee fan?"

"Nope."

"Aren't you a New Yorker?"

"Yeah."

"Not a Yankee fan?"

"I prefer losers."

"Funny, you don't look like a loser to me."

"I guess you overestimated me."

"I doubt it. But I suspect you're very good at getting people to underestimate you. Listen, why don't we move the show over to one of the booths, where we can talk without being distracted by the game. What are you drinking?"

"What you're having is fine."

"Hey, Mike," he said to the bartender, "my friend here will have a Samuel Adams, and I'll have another one. We're going to that table over there. Mind bringing it over?"

He rose from the stool, downed what was left of his beer, then slammed the mug down on the bar dramatically. With Dubin's arm around my shoulder, as if I needed his help finding my way, we headed to the booth.

"Kid took a class with me last year, Twentieth-Century American Fiction," he half-whispered, gesturing back to Mike. "Not particularly bright, but a hard worker. I admire kids who work hard. The talented ones sometimes dog it. Kids like Mike work their asses off, and as a teacher, you really feel as if you're making a difference. The jury's still out as far as I'm concerned as to who comes out better in the end. Got any thoughts on that one, Swann?"

"Hard work over brains any time."

We sat across from each other.

"What category do you fall in?" he asked as he shuffled his formidable ass to a more comfortable position.

"Dumb and lazy."

"That's what you'd like people to think, but I ain't buyin' it. My guess is you're one of the rare ones who's smart and works hard. And I think you're smart enough not to man up to it. So, you're probably wondering why the invite."

"I'm a little curious. But not enough to let it bother me."

Mike arrived with the drinks and set them down. "Thanks, kiddo," Dubin said. "When are you taking another class with me?"

"I'm finished taking classes with you, Professor Dubin. You're a fun guy and all, but there's way too much reading for me. I'm taking a semester off and applying to business school."

"Good for you. The last thing the world needs is another lit major loose on the streets. They're way too dangerous. And not only to themselves," Dubin said, casting a glance at me. "By the way, this is Henry Swann. He's up here visiting from New York City. He's a private dick."

I winced at the description, but I could see Dubin was very pleased and amused, as if hanging out with someone like me gave him street cred. Or maybe he was just trying to get under my skin.

"Nice to meet you," I said, extending my hand.

"Name mean anything to you, Mike?"

He had a blank look on his face.

"Swann?"

Still blank.

"The name of a character in a book? Ring a bell?"

"Not really."

"We in the English Department applaud your good sense getting out of the lit world." He raised his glass in salute and took a swig.

"Thanks," Mike said with a confused look on his face as he headed back to the bar.

"The state of higher education couldn't be lower. There is absolutely no curiosity. These kids just want to learn enough to get a passing grade. Sometimes I just think I'm wasting my time. But then when I think about going back out into the world and getting a real job, I go have a few beers and wait for my paycheck to clear. At least I don't have to deal with any of that post-modern crap. You know about that stuff?"

"I tried reading it once. Got a bad headache."

He laughed. "Why shouldn't you? If the reader puts all the meaning in, then what's left for the writer, I ask you? Just another way for critics and academics to justify themselves. Blame it on the goddamn French." He took another swig, half-emptying his glass. "So, where were we? Oh, yeah, the reason I asked you to have a drink with me. Truth is, I'm tired of hanging out with the academic losers they have up here and I thought it might be interesting to get to know someone like you."

"That so?"

"You think I have some ulterior motive?"

"In my experience, that's usually the case."

"I guess that comes with your territory, but not this time. You're a new face, and you seem to be an interesting fellow."

"Am I?"

"Yes. And the fact that you deny it makes you even more interesting."

"I don't deny it. In fact, I revel in it. I'm so damn interesting that when it's slow, I rent myself out for parties. Tonight, I guess I'm the entertainment for the evening."

"I think of myself as an entertaining sort, too, Swann, so you might get at least as much out of this evening as me. Especially with a few more of these in me. Besides, I figured you're here alone and this has got to be better than spending the evening all by yourself in your room, whacking off."

"I guess we'll find out. But I still don't quite understand your spirit of generosity. I'm sure you've got better things to do with your time than spend it with me."

"I wish to hell I did. Ever read Bruce Jay Friedman's *Lonely Guy* stuff?"

"I have."

"That's me. Brilliant writer. Of course, no one knows who he is now, but he wrote some classics. *Stern, A Mother's Kisses.* Met him once. Poor guy. I met him a while ago and we got to be friends. He told me he can't even get people to return his phone calls, even *Esquire,* where he set the record for stories sold. Most of the money he makes now comes from that silly movie he wrote, *Stir Crazy.* I teach him, when I can, but it's an uphill battle. Anyway, that's me. A Lonely Guy. Divorced. Kids on their own. Both in college. The only time I hear from them is when they need dough. The pickings are slim up here—at least the ones over twenty-one—and I've got very little to do with myself for at least another month or so . . ."

" 'The show is not the show/ But they that go./ Menagerie to me, my neighbor be./ Fair play./ Both came to see.' "

"Dickinson. I'm impressed. A man quotes poetry to me, I don't mind admitting it, I get wet."

I picked up a napkin and tossed it to him. "Here. Dry off."

The napkin fluttered in midair a moment, then settled in front of him. He picked it up and laughed. "Seriously, Swann, it's possible I can help you with what you're looking for. But first, I'm kind of fascinated by your lifestyle. To a guy like me, who spends most of his time now in a city known primarily for its use of enormous quantities of salt, you are what passes for an evening of live entertainment. Tell me something about yourself. How'd you get into this business?"

"Purely accidental."

"You were hit by a car and when you woke up you were a private eye."

"Close." I took a sip of my drink. It tasted good. I knew I'd have another. "When I quit college I had a number of remarkably uninteresting jobs. One of them was working for a detective agency. It seemed like a pretty good idea, snooping on people. It was a good excuse not to think too much about my own life, and it gave me an opportunity to live vicariously through other people. I could visit the dark side without having to live there."

"Why'd you quit?"

"The detective agency?"

"College."

"I thought I could learn more on my own, so I decided to leave before they got rid of me."

"What school?"

"Columbia."

"I knew you were a smart guy, Swann."

"Getting into Columbia doesn't mean you're smarter than anyone else, it just means they had a quota to fill and I qualified."

"And what quota would that be?"

"Assholes."

"You must have been pretty good at it, since there are more than enough to go around."

"It was my major."

"And have you?"

"Have I what?"

"Learned more on your own?"

"Maybe. Maybe not."

"What'd you major in?"

"Your racket."

"Literature?"

"Yeah. I liked reading, so I thought it would be easy. I always look for the easy way out."

"Was it?"

"The reading part was. The regurgitating what the professors wanted to hear wasn't. I figured I could read just as well on my own, without the bullshit that went with it. Not to mention all the dough I was pissing away."

"You realized you've just maligned my entire *raison d'etre.*"

"For some people it works. For me, it didn't."

"You know studying literature, at least good literature, is not so different from what you do."

"How's that?"

"In literature and in detecting, you're looking for the truth. It was Raymond Chandler who probably said it best. 'There are two kinds of truth: the truth that lights the way and the truth that warms the heart. The first of these is science, and the second is art . . . The truth of art keeps science from becoming inhuman, and the truth of science keeps art from becoming ridiculous.' "

"I'm impressed."

"I've taught it enough times so it would be sad if I didn't know it by heart. You teach long enough, it all becomes part of the litany. I'm a minister in the church of American Literature."

"I'm no Raymond Chandler and I'm no Sam Spade."

"So what are you, Swann?"

"You'd need a team of shrinks to find that out, Dubin."

"Well, whatever you are, what you do is important."

"How's that?"

"You create order out of chaos. You make sense out of nonsense. That's why people like to read detective novels. They're reassuring. They have a beginning, a middle and an end. The bad guy always gets caught. The good guy always triumphs in the end. The social order is set right. Messes are cleaned up. You're doing God's work, Swann."

"Yeah. Right. What about you?"

"I'm just a simple teacher of literature. I do my best to clean up the mess, but all too often I'm the one creating chaos."

"You weren't always a professor, though, were you?"

"I've been around the block a few times. Born and raised in Brooklyn. Went to City College. When I finished I wasn't smart enough, or devious enough, to avoid the draft, so I spent a couple of years in the army. Fortunately, I never made it over to 'Nam because I was able to convince them I'd be more of a threat to our army than the Viet Cong. I could type, so they put me to work on the newspaper. I got out in one piece and was horny as hell, so I decided to take some acting classes, because that's where the women were."

"Did it work?"

"That's how I met my wife, so you tell me."

"I'm guessing that didn't turn out well."

"About as well as the acting career. We lasted long enough to have a couple of kids, one of each, both of whom are grown now. She was far more interested in her career than helping support me through grad school. But I managed to make it, working part time for a literary agency, while I got my Ph.D. Now she's married to some no-account actor who can't get himself arrested."

"She ever make it?"

"A few parts in soaps, if you call that making it. Now, like me, she's old, but unlike me, she doesn't have tenure. You ready for another one, because I sure as hell am."

I looked at my glass. It was empty. "Sure."

Dubin motioned to Mike, who was leaning against the bar, watching the game. When Dubin didn't get his attention, he looked at me. "You know how to whistle, don't you, Swann?"

" 'Just put your lips together and blow.' "

"Thanks," he said, and he did just that.

"I taught writing for a while, but I gave that up pretty quick."

"Why's that?"

"I met Saul Bellow once. A real son of a bitch, but one hell of a writer. He asked me what I did for a living, and I told him I taught writing. He said, 'There are enough goddamn writers in the world. Maybe you ought to teach a class on how not to write.' I never taught another one after that."

Our refills arrived and I decided to ease back into business. "So," I said as Dubin stared up at the screen, trying to catch sight of the score. "You said you might be able to give me a little more help with why I'm here."

"We weren't quite finished with you."

"I thought we were."

"Almost. You married?"

"Was."

"Divorced?"

"She was killed. An accident." I was tired of telling this story. So, I didn't. If he asked, I would make something up. I don't know why. I just would.

"I'm sorry."

"Me, too."

"Kids?"

"One."

"How old?"

"Fourteen."

"Boy? Girl?"

"Boy."

"Live with you?"

"No."

"Where is he?"

"With her parents."

"See him much?"

"When I can," I lied. He was getting a little too close to the bone, and I was starting to squirm a little. I don't like to squirm.

"You got a big agency?"

"I don't want you getting the wrong idea, Dubin. I'm no big-time private investigator. I'm a skip tracer. I find people who don't pay their bills, or who skip out on their spouses. I'm the lowest of the low. If I were a book, I would have been on the remainder shelf a long time ago. Now that we've pretty much exhausted me as a topic of conversation, let's get back to why I'm here."

"Sure thing. One more question. You packin'?"

"No."

"Why not?"

"The last time I carried a gun, the only one who got hurt was me. Why don't we get back to how you might be able to help me."

"If we must. I thought of something after you left."

"What's that?"

"The kid."

"Sean."

"Yeah. He never actually took a class with me—though I don't know why, since I'm the best damn professor in the department. But professors talk, and from what I heard, the kid was very much into books."

"I would hope so. He was in grad school for them."

"I mean books as objects, not necessarily as literature."

"What's that supposed to mean?"

"Dana could probably tell you more about it, but I understand over the years he'd collected a number of valuable signed first editions."

"Ever see any of them?"

"No."

"But it's what you heard."

"Yes."

"And this is supposed to help me how?"

"You're the detective, Swann. I'm not about to tell you how to run your business. It's information that might help you. It's up to you to figure out how. They broke Watergate by following the money, maybe you should follow the books." He laughed. "I wish some of my students would do that."

I took a sip of my beer, buying time, trying to figure out why Dubin was telling me all this. It could have been he was honestly trying to help. It also could have been he was trying to throw me off the trail. But if so, why? Maybe it was time to throw a grenade into the crowd and see who got hit by the explosion.

"I think you know a lot more than you're telling me, Dubin. My guess is you asked me to meet you to find out what I knew," I said, staring him down.

"I always know more than I tell, Swann. It's what keeps the balance of power in my favor. But if guys like me didn't try to keep information from guys like you, then guys like you wouldn't have a job. Let's see how good you are at finding out what I know and what I don't know."

"You know what they used to say about Lyndon Johnson when asked how anyone would know if he was lying? When he touched his brow, he was telling the truth. When he touched his neck, he was telling the truth. When he opened his mouth, he was lying. That's kinda the philosophy I've used in life. Everyone lies, it's just to what extent."

"I guess that's what you're going to have to decide when it comes to me."

"Now that we've got some of our cards on the table, got any other information about Sean you'd like to share?"

Mike arrived with our drinks and set them on the table. Dubin nodded thanks. "What I've given you so far should be enough to earn you paying for the drinks, don't you think?"

"I believe I could manage that."

"Don't forget a nice, big tip for Mike. Someone's gotta pay his way through business school."

"Why shouldn't it be me?" I said as I pulled my wallet from

my back pocket, removed two twenties and threw them on the table.

"Change?" Mike asked.

"Keep it," Dubin said. "My friend here's a big tipper."

"Thanks," said Mike.

"So, when all is said and done, you think you're making any progress finding them?" Dubin asked as he pushed back his chair.

"Hard to say."

"Frankly, if you ask me, you look a little lost."

"Like Daniel Boone once said, 'I can't say I was ever lost, but I was bewildered once for three days,' " I said.

12
HIGHER EDUCATION

The evening had to end. I was tired. I had things to do. And although I'm sure Dubin could have gone on all night—and I believe he would have, if I'd let him; the man was filled with fascinating stories about writers he'd met, actresses he'd fucked, and students who'd gone on to bigger and better things—I finally excused myself. But only after promising I'd keep in touch. It was the truth. I had a feeling I'd be seeing him again, whether I liked it or not.

"You're an interesting fellow, Swann," he'd said as he walked me to the elevator bank and shook my hand with a grip that could have squeezed an orange dry, "and there's a paucity of interesting folks in the world. We're a minority, my friend. Let me know how it goes when you speak to Dana. These days the best I can do is live vicariously. I've got the characters in my books, of course, but they just do the same thing over and over again. The words remain the same, only the interpretation changes. Once I've figured a book out, it loses all interest for me. The good ones, of course, are always revealing new secrets, but they're rare. Now you come along, and with you, the possibility of a new chapter being written. I'd like to read that chapter, Swann, so I'm hoping you'll keep me in the loop."

I can shoot the shit as well as the next guy . . . sometimes even better. And I can spot a shit-shooter with an ease that sometimes surprises me. Sometimes I'm wrong. Usually, I'm not. But no matter. I can match anyone shot for shot, which is what I was about to do. "Dubin, my new friend, I will try to do just that. And who knows? Between the both of us, we might actually find this kid. But I'll tell you this right up front. I don't split fees."

He laughed. "Don't worry, Swann, I don't need your money. I'm stealing enough from the university now, and I've got a very nice pension waiting for me when I retire. If my ex-wife dies before me, I'll be sitting even prettier. But repeat that at my trial, and I'll deny every word."

I stepped into the elevator and pushed eight, but it stuttered for a moment before the door closed. Dubin didn't move, standing there, his arms folded across his chest, smiling at me, until the door shut. For all I knew, he was still standing there when I reached my room.

Was he full of shit? Did he know more than he was saying? I didn't know. But keeping that possibility in mind was essential. In my line of work, if you believe what's on the surface, if you fall prey to the predictable, you're sunk. The world is filled with Sandy Koufaxes. Just when you think the ball is coming at you it makes a sharp turn and you wind up swinging through air. Besides, I've never met anyone who didn't know more than they were saying. And if I did, they wouldn't interest me.

Dubin was right about one thing, though. Our jobs weren't that dissimilar. Both of us had to collect information, synthesize it, deconstruct it, put it back together again, then come to a conclusion that answers that ever-elusive question, what does it all mean?

He was a literary detective, I was a literal detective. Not nearly as good as those his students might read—Chandler, Hammett, MacDonald, Parker, Stout and Poe—because I'm flesh and blood, and the world is not nearly as neat as those writers make it out to be. All they have to do is enlighten and entertain. The stakes are a lot higher for me. Dubin works in the fictional world, where readers might get disappointed or students might earn a lower grade. I deal in the real world, where people get hurt, emotionally, physically, sometimes both. But if I allow myself to think about that too long, I'd quit, which, come to think of it, is what I did a couple years ago. But now I was back and though it felt right, I still found myself wondering, what if, in the end, the hokey-pokey really is what it's all about?

Lying in bed, too wound up to sleep, I had yet another meaningless epiphany. What Dubin does and what I was doing wasn't so different from what I was doing only a few days ago for the New York City Community Cable Company. It was all about communication. A lack of it is what probably set Marcy Phillips on the road away from her father. He didn't listen. She didn't listen. They spoke a different language. They were on a different page. Who gives a shit? Communication breaks down, and there's nothing left to hold people together. But look, I'm no shrink. That's not my job. My job is not to understand why Marcy was estranged from her father, why she might even hate him, though that wouldn't be difficult to understand since he was a pompous ass, but to find her and see if the lines of communication could be reopened.

I had more of the pieces of the puzzle than when I'd started, but they didn't add up to much. It's a mistake to try to put the pieces together too quickly. If you do, you often wind up with a fuzzy image, a picture that might seem to make sense, but doesn't. The clearer the picture, the closer you are to the answer; the closer you are to the answer, the clearer the picture. It's like showing a letter box film on a conventional set. You get the general idea, but everything is out of proportion. You're not seeing what you're supposed to see. I've learned to take what I find out, file it away a while and then, when I've got enough of the puzzle pieces, I put them together and see if they make sense.

Unfortunately, sense doesn't always result in truth. And then you just have to throw the pieces back in the box and start all over again.

I was up early the next morning. Made myself a cup of coffee. Packed up my things. Before I checked out, I headed back to the business center, where I went online and booked a flight to Boston, leaving Syracuse at eleven A.M. Then, I Googled everyone involved in the case: Sean, Marcy, Dubin, Dana Simmons and last, but surely not least, Carlton Phillips.

Dubin had led a checkered life as an actor, writer and professor. He'd written a number of well-thought-of critical essays on Hammett, Chandler and MacDonald, comparing them to the more traditional genre writers like Agatha Christie and Erle Stanley Gardner. There was also an interesting essay on the noir writers, like Big Jim Thompson, Cornell Woolrich and James M. Cain. There was an entertaining look at the adaptations of their books and stories into film, focusing on Cain's *The Postman Always Rings Twice*, *Mildred Pierce* and *Butterfly*. Dubin's specialty, though, was twentieth-century American fiction, and he was regarded as one of the foremost experts on the post–World War II Jewish-American writers, like Mailer, Roth, Bellow and Malamud.

There was also plenty about Carlton Phillips—his firm, cases he'd worked, charitable and professional organizations he belonged to. But there was one thing that caught my eye. A dozen years ago he'd been brought up in front of the bar association on charges of misconduct. Unfortunately, there were no details, but it was definitely something to look into. I had a friend, Goldblatt, a shady, disreputable character, a disbarred attorney who still had some connections to the bar association, and I shot him an email to see if he could come up with some details.

Sean was pretty much a blank slate. There were a few photographs of him having to do with his high school graduating class. And there were a couple mentions of him on a site devoted to rare books. He recently listed a book on eBay that he wanted to sell, an autographed copy of a signed, first edition of James Jones's *From Here to Eternity*. The bidding was up to $2,500, but there was a note that the item had been removed.

As for Marcy, there was even less; just a mention of her in a bio of her father and a high school yearbook photo.

There were the usual educational items about Dana Simmons, along with a couple of photos of her, obviously taken from a Syracuse University publication. She was a knockout. Long, dark hair, dark eyes and a killer smile. She, too, had several articles published in literary magazines, as well as a few short stories and poems. Her specialty was twentieth-century European and American fiction.

There were several small threads to pull here, but I wouldn't know which ones until I was farther along. Now, it was time to head to Boston.

★ ★ ★ ★ ★

PART 3
BOSTON, MASSACHUSETTS

★ ★ ★ ★ ★

"If it was so, it might be; and if it were so, it would be:
But as it isn't, it ain't."
—Lewis Carroll, *Through the Looking Glass*

13

THE CURSE OF THE BAMBINO
STRIKES AGAIN

I don't like Boston much. It isn't because of the Red Sox or the Celtics. It isn't because I got dumped by a girl there when I was twenty-two. It isn't because the people talk funny. It isn't because they think they're better than anyone else. It isn't because you can't get a decent slice of pizza or a good bagel there.

It's because I'm a New Yorker, through and through. People in Boston, unlike Chicago, where they own up to being the Second City, have the audacity to think they're better than New Yorkers. It is not my job to disabuse them of that notion, though I would if they asked me to.

Nevertheless, there is something oddly comforting about the city. Maybe it's the history—what other city has something like the Freedom Trail that snakes through the city streets, marking sixteen historical sites? Or maybe it's the scenic Charles River, which separates the city from Cambridge. Or maybe it's because it's the home of Robert B. Parker's fictional hard-nose detective, Spenser.

For the short time I was in Boston, I lived on Marlborough Street, just off Copley Square, a quaint section of the city that housed many students who attended Boston University or one of the many other schools of higher education, as well as the much wealthier old-line Bostoners who preferred the neighborhood to the stuffier Back Bay. By day it was fine, but at night the alleys were overrun with rats that, in the winter, literally threw themselves against the back doorways in a futile attempt to escape the cold. I lived on the bottom floor and my door opened up onto the alley, and in the morning, when I would leave, I would occasionally find a dead rodent, run over by a passing car, in my path. Most of my time was spent either strolling along the Charles, pining for the Hudson, or even the far less scenic and characterless East River, or haunting the newsstand at Copley Square, waiting for the New York newspapers to arrive.

But I wasn't in Boston to reminisce. I was there to talk to Dana Simmons who, I hoped, would provide me a lead to finding Sean Loomis.

As soon as I got off the plane, I gave her a call. She lived in Cambridge, she informed me, not far from Harvard, where she was attending a summer seminar.

"Why don't you meet me at the Harvard Bookstore," she said. "It's got a nice café and we can talk there. The place actually adds a few IQ points," to which I replied, "I can use all the help I can get."

A half hour later I was browsing through the bookshelves when someone tapped me on the shoulder. "Mr. Swann, I presume."

I turned around to find a stunning woman, around five-seven, slim, with dark, shoulder-length hair, flawless skin, slightly tanned with a few freckles sprinkled over her nose, like pepper on an omelet, and high cheekbones that left her face in a perpetual smile. She was wearing faded jeans and a pink tank top. "That would be me."

"I'm Dana Simmons."

"How'd you recognize me?"

"Look around. One of these things doesn't belong."

She was right. I was, by at least twenty years, the oldest one in the room.

"My bad," she said. "It's kind of crowded in here. What say we go across the street to a place that's a little quieter?"

"Fine with me," I said.

"Follow me," she said.

Anywhere, I thought.

She walked quickly. She was either in a hurry, or she was a woman with a purpose. I guessed the latter. When we got to what turned out to be a funky little coffee shop, she opened the door and held it for me. I didn't think twice about going in before her. There was something about her that made me think that not only didn't she mind, but that she would have been offended if I hadn't. I did not want to offend her. Not even a little.

"Hey, Dana, how ya doin'?" called a bearded man behind the counter.

"Just fine, Derek. Okay if we grab a seat in the back?"

"Anywhere you like, baby. The place is yours."

"I wish," she said as she led the way to a small, round table in the back. "It's kind of self-serve here, especially this time of day, what with Derek being the only one around. So what would you like? It's on me. That's not a problem, is it?"

"I have no problem with anyone paying for me. Even you. Coffee. But none of that fancy frappacino crap."

"Something to eat?"

"I'm good."

While she was getting our order, I scanned the café, which held about a dozen small tables. There were line drawing portraits of recognizable writers, poets, artists and philosophers on the walls, and a couple of bookcases overflowing with hardcover and paperback books on the two walls closest to where we were sitting. Most of the books seemed to be the New Agey, self-help kind of junk people think that by reading their lives will change, only to be disappointed when they learn they are still their same, pathetic, unhappy selves.

Dana returned with two iced coffees and a couple of muffins.

"I know you said you didn't want anything else, but these muffins are the best. All organic. If you don't want it, I'll probably eat both of them. Unless you do the honorable thing and stop me."

"I don't eat anything unless it's chock full of preservatives."

"Really?"

"Why do you think we're living longer? It's the damn preservatives. They preserve food, so it makes sense they'd preserve us, too, doesn't it? I eat as many Twinkies as I can get my hands on."

"Interesting concept. Try one anyway. Make believe it's got all that crap in it."

I took a bite.

"Not bad, right?" she said.

"Not bad."

"I wouldn't lead you astray."

"I hope not."

She meticulously sliced her muffin into four equal parts and popped one in her mouth. "So, you're looking for Sean Loomis."

"That's right."

"Because you're really looking for Marcy Phillips."

"Right again."

"What makes you think they're a couple?"

"What makes you think they're not?"

"I didn't say they weren't. I just asked you why you thought they were."

"Are you trying to tell me they're not?"

She smiled.

"You're jerking my chain, aren't you?" I said, taking a bite of my muffin. A couple of crumbs dropped to the table and I swept them into my napkin. No matter how hard I try, my place at the table always seems to be the messiest. I don't know why. But it could be worse. It could be all over me.

"Yes. I am. Pretty good, huh?" she said, gesturing toward my muffin, which was now half its original size.

"So good, I'd swear it's filled with preservatives."

"You're a funny man, Swann. You don't mind my calling you that, do you? It suits you better than Henry."

"Why should I mind?"

"Most people don't like to be called by their last name."

"I'm not most people."

"I think that's probably a good thing. But I don't want to waste your time. You're here to talk to me about Sean Loomis. What would you like to know?"

"I want to know where he is, but to do that, I need to know who he is and what he's like."

"He was only my student . . ." She stopped and sipped her coffee. She was measuring everything she said. That meant she knew something that could help me. But it also meant it was going to be difficult getting it from her.

"And?"

"He's very smart. A genius, maybe."

"So I've been told. Look, I don't know why you're making this so difficult, but if you're protecting him for any reason . . ."

"Why would I be protecting him?"

"Don't know. I'm guessing your vocabulary is a lot larger than mine, but all I'm getting is true–false answers. When someone answers questions like that, it makes me think they're trying to keep something from me. I don't like that. It makes my job more difficult. I like things nice and easy. I'm a very simple man, Dana. I don't do what I do for the challenge. Or the glory, of which, by the way, there is none. I do it for the . . ." I rubbed my fingers together. "I'm not tenured and I don't have a pension to fall back on. I need to produce or I perish. It's as simple as that. In order to find Marcy Phillips, I have to find Sean Loomis. I think you can help me in that endeavor. Let's just cut to the chase, because if we don't it's going to be a long afternoon and you know what? In the end I'm going to find out what I need to know anyway. Do you know where either of them is?"

Her face hardened, her voice took on a different, more annoyed tone. "Why would you possibly think I'd know where they were? I only know them as students. Sean was in my graduate seminar and Marcy was an undergrad."

When someone becomes defensive, I know I've hit a nerve. No time to back off. "I think you have a personal relationship with one or both of them," I said.

"What's that supposed to mean?"

"It means I think you socialized with them."

"I don't socialize with students. That would be unprofessional."

"You'd be surprised how many people do unprofessional things, Dana. Like skipping out on their obligations. Like lying, cheating and stealing. You think the academic world is immune to that kind of behavior?"

She broke into a half-smile. "Maybe worse."

"Yeah, maybe worse. Why don't you tell me what you know about Sean," I said.

"For one thing, he knows as much, if not more, about books than I do. Not only the books themselves, but the authors. I've actually learned a lot from him."

"Like what?"

"The back story of particular books. Anecdotes about the authors."

"How did he know that kind of stuff?" I probed.

"I don't know."

"Sure you do," I challenged.

"I heard he bought and sold some rare books, so I guess it was part of his business."

"He made money that way?"

"You'd have to ask his accountant."

"I'll take that as a yes. Why was he in grad school if he already knew so much?"

"Because he's smart enough to now he didn't know everything, which might be one of the attributes of genius. I wouldn't be surprised if in the back of his head, Sean might be considering teaching at some point. He has that kind of personality. He likes knowing things, and he likes letting people know he knows things."

"Do you think he left school because he learned everything he could learn from you guys?"

"You'd have to ask him that."

"Unfortunately, I can't do that. But I will when I find him. When was the last time you saw him?"

"Some time near the end of last summer."

"Where?"

"Here."

"Excuse me."

"I saw him here. Right where you're sitting, as a matter of fact."

"Why were you here, and what was he doing up here?"

"I graduated from Harvard. It's home to me. I come back every summer either to take a class or teach one. Sean was here because I helped him find a job at the Houghton Library."

"Do you find jobs for all your students?"

"Don't be ridiculous."

"I try not to be, but sometimes I just can't help myself. Why'd you do it for him?"

"I didn't get him the job. I just helped. I heard they were

looking for someone to work in the library and I knew Sean, with his interest in books, would be a perfect person to help out. They're always shorthanded during the summer months."

"How long did he work there?"

"Six weeks or so."

"That's not the whole summer. Why'd he leave early?"

"You'd have to ask him or the head librarian."

"You don't know?"

"No. I don't."

"When you met with him, was that before or after he left his job?"

"I don't remember."

"You would have remembered if he'd spoken to you about leaving, though?"

"I suppose I would."

"What about Marcy? Was she up here, too?"

"Maybe she visited him a couple of times, but I can't say how much time she spent here. I think I'll get a refill. You?"

"I'm fine." While she was gone I tried putting some of what she'd said together, but it wasn't giving me much of a picture. Maybe I'd know more after I visited the library and spoke to the head librarian. I was hoping the reason he left might help me track him down. I could sense that Dana was holding something back. I wasn't sure if she was protecting Sean or herself. It didn't matter. Eventually, I'd get the answers I needed. Like Aeschylus, I've always believed "the facts will appear with the shining of the dawn." And if dawn doesn't come quick enough, I whip out a flashlight.

When she came back, I tossed in another grenade. "You haven't said anything about the plagiarism incident."

"You know about that?"

"Yes."

She shook her head. "Dubin told you?"

"Is it supposed to be some kind of secret?"

"Not now, obviously."

"Tell me about it."

"It was a joke."

"Really?"

"Yes. Really."

"Then why was he suspended?"

"Because Richard didn't find it that funny."

"Why bother to report it if you considered it a joke?"

"I didn't report it. I just mentioned it to Richard, in passing. It was amusing."

"But he didn't find it that funny, did he?"

"I guess not."

"It's kind of odd Sean would do something like that."

"Not if you knew Sean. He loves pushing the envelope."

"You don't mean to suggest he thought there was a chance you wouldn't recognize your own work, do you?"

"I've done a lot of writing over the years, Swann, and it was a pretty obscure passage, but trust me, I know my own words and thoughts when I see them. When they come out of someone else's mouth, I don't have any trouble recognizing them. I think he was just testing me. Sure, I was a little shocked when I saw it, but I knew he wasn't stupid enough to try to actually get away with it. I like to think it was more of an . . . homage."

"How's that?"

"You know, like writers who include little jokes, often self-reverential, in their work. Nabokov did it all the time. *Lolita* is chock full of allusions and little inside jokes, literary and otherwise. You are familiar with Nabokov, aren't you?"

"I'm not as ignorant as I might appear to be."

"I didn't think you were ignorant. In fact, I think you're quite bright, actually. As far as Sean is concerned, I believe he was just playing around."

"Seeing what he could get away with."

"Yes. In the end, his prank was harmless. We gave him a slap on the wrist, simply because we had to. So, is there anything else you need to know from me?"

"Is there anything else you need to tell me?"

"Not that I can think of. I wish you luck finding what's her name, but I don't think anything else you ask me will get you any closer to her."

"If you say so, Dana."

"I do. So, what will you do with the rest of your time in our lovely city?"

"I'll hop over to the library and see if I can talk to the head librarian, or anyone else who might have known Sean. Then, since I'm on the clock, and there's nothing else to check out here, I'll probably head back to the city."

"It might be late by the time you're ready to leave."

"The shuttle runs late."

"It does. But why not wait till tomorrow? If you need a place to stay, I can put you up for the night."

"Are you coming on to me, Ms. Simmons?"

She laughed. "I've got an extra bedroom."

"Tell you what, if I get hung up and it's too late to hop the shuttle back home, I'll give you a call."

"Sounds good. And, just in case, I'll make sure I have some clean sheets ready."

14

THE BOOKWORM TURNS ALL
RIGHT. BUT IN WHAT
DIRECTION?

The Houghton Library, tucked comfortably between the larger Widener Library and the slightly smaller Lamont Library, was in one corner of Harvard Square, off Massachusetts Avenue, facing Quincy and not far from the café. Dana pointed me in the right direction after she filled me in on a little of the library's history.

In the late thirties, the librarian of Harvard College suggested a separate, temperature- and humidity-controlled library building for rare books and manuscripts and a few years later, in 1942, the new library was opened. Till this point, rare books had been housed on the ground floor of Widener, in what was known as the Treasure Room. Now they had a home of their own, and over the years the collection of rare and valuable books and manuscripts had grown, so much so that now parts of it had to be housed in the adjacent Pusey and Lamont Libraries.

Dana told me to ask for Elizabeth Lawson, the head librarian, and as I waited for her at the front desk, all sorts of library memories shot through my mind. As a kid, the library was my refuge. I read voraciously, an escape from a childhood that was less than ideal. A father who had emotional problems that resulted in his being aloof almost to the point of being invisible, until he actually was, when he took off not so unexpectedly, never to be heard from again. A mother who meant well, but who wasn't able to take care of anyone, especially two boys, since she could hardly take care of herself. As Colonel Rupert once remarked about Babe Ruth when he repeatedly asked to manage his beloved Yankees, "How could he manage the team when he can't even manage himself?"

But sad tales of family histories bore the hell out of me. Especially mine. What's done is done. Move on. Looking back only results in tripping over yourself. As the Tom Hanks character said in *A League of Their Own,* "There is no crying in baseball," and that should pretty much go for life, too. If Carlton Phillips and his daughter could manage that, they'd be much better off. Wipe the slate clean and start writing a new history. But the chances were that wasn't going to happen. It rarely does. People hold onto things, especially bad things, much too long. They let the past shape their future. Big mistake. But without those mistakes, I'd be out of a job. Grudges, anger, disappointment, frustration and lack of communication—anything that drives people apart or causes them to act irrationally or totally in self-interest—keeps me working. So you won't hear me complaining. Or crying.

Before I could wander too much farther down Memory Lane, a woman I presumed to be Elizabeth Lawson emerged from a back room and headed in my direction. She had the look of being someone in charge. In her late forties, with short cropped auburn hair, she was wearing a very conservative dark suit. The only deviation from this dress for success outfit were her large, bright red framed eyeglasses, which gave the impression that she either had a secret life or yearned for one.

"May I help you?" she asked sternly as she planted herself directly in front of me, her arms folded tightly across her ample chest.

"You Elizabeth Lawson?"

"I am."

"I was hoping you could give me some information about

Sean Loomis. I believe he used to work here."

"And you are?"

"Henry Swann."

"And you would be interested why?"

"Because I've been hired to do a background check on Mr. Loomis by a potential employer."

I don't know why I lied. I just did. It's not necessarily because lies get to the truth more efficiently, although that's sometimes the case. It's not because lies come easily to me, though they do. I'm not proud of that. It's a loathsome habit and I should be ashamed of myself. As William Golding wrote, "What a man does defiles him, not what is done by others." The way I see it, there are many ways to defile myself, and I've tried most of them at one time or another. Do I feel bad about it? Sometimes. Does it ever stop me? No. Lying is a tool of the trade. Lies can get you to the truth. If you're good at lying, and I am, lies often pay off. The trick is to tell lies that, as Oscar Wilde once said, "Seem to have a stamp of truth upon it." Keep them simple and plausible and consistent, and you can get away with it.

"Most people would contact former employers by phone or email," she said in that officious way librarians have picked up from lives of shushing people to remain quiet.

"I guess I'm not most people. I take my job very seriously."

She looked me up and down and suddenly I felt as if every lie I'd ever told was suddenly going to come back to haunt me.

"Do you have some identification?"

"Identification?"

"Yes. You know what that is, don't you?"

"I believe I do." I reached for my wallet. I should have been ticked off by her attitude, but I wasn't. I liked that she had an edge. I liked that she wasn't buying whatever I was selling. Maybe it was the challenge it offered. No matter. I was up to it. "Would my driver's license do?" I took it out and handed it to her. I could have told her to go fuck herself, but I didn't. I don't care much for authority, and yet when presented with it my first reaction is usually to submit to it. Fortunately, that doesn't last long. A *fuck you* might come later.

She removed her glasses and examined my license closely, as if she were a cop who'd stopped me for speeding. She looked up, then back down at the document.

"You don't take a very good photo."

"I wasn't feeling my best that day. Late night, if you know what I mean."

"Well," she said, handing the license back to me, "you seem to be who you say you are. You wouldn't happen to have a business card, would you? Something that tells me who your employer is."

"I'm self-employed, ma'am."

"You said you were working for a company that was checking up on Sean."

"I'm an independent contractor. Always have been." I leaned forward and half-whispered, "I hate working for the man."

She smiled. I now had a hint of the real Elizabeth Lawson. Beneath those red glasses beat the heart of a former rebel.

"But I'd be glad to give you my personal business card." I took one from my wallet and handed it to her.

"Henry Swann Investigations . . ."

She looked up and handed it back to me.

"Keep it." I handed it back. "I've got plenty. So, have I passed the test? Can I possibly get some help here?"

"I'm still not sure I should be answering your questions. This proves who you are, but it doesn't prove why you're asking questions about Sean."

"Any reason I shouldn't be asking about him?"

"No."

"Then why not answer them? Unless, of course, you . . . and

he . . . have something to hide."

"There's nothing to hide, Mr. Swann. He worked here. Last summer . . ." her voice trailed off.

"Yes?"

"Nothing."

"I know you've got more to say, Ms. Lawson. What was he like? Who were his friends? What did you think of him?"

"I'm very uncomfortable talking about a former employee, especially Sean."

"Why's that?"

"It doesn't seem . . . ethical."

"Ms. Lawson, I've got a job to do. I'm just a working stiff who's been hired to check out someone's references. There's nothing unethical about that. In fact, it's all about due diligence. You're just part of the process. So, why don't you just give me a break here. I'm not asking for his Social Security number— we've already got that. All I want to know is what you thought of him."

"All right. He was very smart and a good worker. I have no idea who his friends were. He was here to work, you understand, not socialize."

"I understand. It is a library, after all. Shhh." I put my finger up to my lips.

"Yes. It is."

"How long did he work here?"

"I believe it was about six weeks."

"That's not the whole summer."

"He left early."

"Why was that?"

"You'd have to ask him."

"Was there a problem at work?"

"Not necessarily."

"You know, Ms. Lawson, all this is confidential. What you tell me will go no farther than Sean's potential employer. But if you're holding something back that would reflect on his ability to do the job, then I think you owe it to everyone to let me know what it is."

"What kind of job are you talking about?"

"I'm not at liberty to divulge the exact nature of the work, but I can tell you that Sean would be entrusted with some valuable works of art."

"Is that so?"

"Yes, and so if there was any kind of situation he was involved in here that I should be apprised of, it would be much appreciated."

When she hesitated a moment, I knew I'd struck a nerve. I looked around, lowered my voice and said, "There's no one here but you and me, Ms. Lawson, and I can promise you that I'm not going to divulge who gave me this information. But it's important I know everything about Sean Loomis that might impact on his, shall we say, character."

"Well, something did happen, but there's no proof that Sean was involved . . . and frankly, I don't think he was."

"I'm not a cop, Ms. Lawson, and you're not going to have to testify to anything."

"There are a lot of valuable articles kept here."

"I know."

"Books, manuscripts . . ."

"Yes."

"While Sean was working here, something was found to be missing."

She hesitated. I could tell she liked Sean. She didn't want to get him in trouble or, in this case, lose him the possibility of a good job. She wanted me to be responsible for extracting the information. That way, later, she could absolve herself of any guilt. I had no problem helping her out.

"What was it?"

"A signed, first edition of F. Scott Fitzgerald's *Tender Is the Night.*"

"You suspected Sean took it?"

She shook her head. She looked down at the floor. I knew exactly what she was thinking. "I guess it was possible, though I really didn't think so. But a funny thing happened."

"What was that?"

"A few days after the book was found missing, it showed up in the stacks of another one of our libraries. I don't know how it could possibly have gotten there. But there it was. It was only found by accident."

"As Huck Finn said, 'Dey ain' no sense in it.' What do you make of the matter?"

"Perhaps it was someone's idea of a prank."

"But you thought Sean might have been behind it?"

"I liked Sean and I doubted he would be so foolish as to risk being involved in something like the theft of a rare book, especially since he might be a likely suspect, but I suppose it was possible."

"So you fired him."

"No! We wouldn't do that simply because we had suspicions. We'd have required proof. Sean knew he was under suspicion, since we questioned everyone who worked here. He denied knowing anything about the theft, of course, and when the book turned up, he came to me and said he couldn't work here anymore because he didn't think we trusted him. I tried to explain that we had to question everyone, but he was adamant about leaving. I was very sorry to lose him, because he did an incredible job here. He went through practically everything we had and updated our catalogue, adding important notes about many of our rare editions. He really is brilliant. And very dedicated."

"What kinds of notes?"

"There's often more than the mere text involved in rare books and manuscripts. Many of them have a history."

"Like what?"

"For instance, Jack Kerouac wrote *On the Road* on a roll of teletype paper, and so that manuscript would be extremely valuable, more valuable than the galley generated by the publishing company, for instance. Sean uncovered a story about Kerouac going into Robert Giroux's office with the manuscript under his arm, which Giroux said looked like a roll of paper towels. When he asked what it was, Kerouac yelled, 'Whee!' and unfurled the roll of pasted-together teletype paper across the office floor. Giroux asked how he'd done it, and Kerouac answered that he'd never taken it out of the typewriter. He asked how he'd make corrections and Kerouac got angry and said, 'There aren't going to be any corrections. This was dictated by the Holy Ghost.' He proceeded to roll up the paper, walked out of the office, and took it to another publisher.

"He also found that Norman Mailer had the copy editor of *Why Are We In Vietnam* remove the *n* he placed on the word *dam* in the last sentence of the book because he not only wanted the allusion, but the word turned around spelled mad. Sean was very good collecting these kinds of anecdotes and adding them to the catalogue."

"So now, a year later, do you think he had anything to do with the theft?"

"I wouldn't exactly call it a theft . . . and I can't imagine he would have been involved in a silly, potentially serious prank like that. For what possible reason?"

"Maybe the book was switched for another edition?"

"You mean counterfeited?"

I nodded.

"We had experts check it out. It was the real thing. We're not stupid, Mr. Swann. We know how to do our jobs."

"I'm sure you do, Ms. Lawson. It's part of my job to be cynical. This kind of thing, well, he's applied for a job that requires the utmost security. We can't have him working around valuable items if he's been guilty of a theft like the one you've described. Have you had any contact with Sean since he left?"

"No."

"So you don't know what he's been doing for the past year?"

"I assume he went back to Syracuse, to finish up his degree."

"Is there anyone else you know who might be able to talk to me about Sean's reliability?"

"He had references. You could check those."

I shook my head. "Worthless. The ones he chose, the ones anyone would choose, are those he's sure would say good things about him. I'm hired to find out the truth, not someone's made-up version of it."

"Why would you think Sean's references wouldn't provide you with the truth?"

"As incredible as it might be to believe, most references are either a figment of the imagination or faked. Faking references is not difficult. People get away with it because they're rarely checked thoroughly. That's why they hire people like me. Are you the one who hired Sean?"

"Yes."

"How'd he get to you?"

She hesitated a moment. I knew she was either going to lie, avoid answering or, if she did tell the truth, that it was significant.

"Dana Simmons. I assume she's the one who sent you in my direction," she said with an edge to her voice that led me to believe she had a problem with Dana. My first thought was that maybe their relationship wasn't entirely professional? I glanced at Lawson's left hand. No wedding ring. Of course, it was possible that their problem lay somewhere else, but usually people are adept enough at covering their feelings about insignificant things. This was something more serious.

"I'm sensing Dana is not one of your favorite people," I said, trying to dig a little deeper.

"I hardly know her," she snapped.

She was lying.

"It's pretty obvious you don't like her."

Her eyes shrank and she stared at me as if I still hadn't returned a long overdue book. "There are a lot of people I don't like, Mr. Swann, but that's my business and I don't see what it has to do with your mission here. Now, I've got other things to do, and I've told you all I can about Sean Loomis, so I'm afraid we'll have to end this interview."

15
WILL YOU STILL LOVE ME TOMORROW?

It was late. I was tired. I didn't want the hassle of taking a flight back to New York that night. But that's not why I called Dana Simmons. I called her because I thought she had more to tell me about Sean Loomis and Marcy Phillips. I was also intrigued about her connection to Elizabeth Lawson. Lawson was lying when she said she hardly knew Dana. She wouldn't have given Sean such a plum summer job on a recommendation from a stranger. But why deny it? It was something I needed to find out.

It only took one ring for Dana to answer.

"Hey," I said. "It's Swann. Just wondering if the offer to crash at your place tonight is still on the table."

"It is."

"I'd like to take you up on it."

"Good. But don't eat."

"Why not?"

"Because I've made dinner."

"How'd you know I'd show up?"

"Who said I prepared it for you?"

Her place wasn't far, so I decided to walk. Not because I wanted to save Carlton Phillips's money, but because I think best when I'm on the move.

This case was getting complicated, which meant it was getting interesting. I don't particularly like complicated. But I do like interesting. I've had more than my share of cases that put me to sleep, those run-of-the-mill repos and bill-skippers. Standing on corners, waiting for the right moment to break into a car, hotwire it and take off. Pulling sorry-ass drunks out of bars and returning them to their spouses, who then stiff me on my fee. I prefer challenges. Sometimes I rise to them, sometimes I don't. But when I do it makes me feel good about myself. Those times are few and far between, so I relish them.

The key to finding Marcy was finding Sean. The key to finding Sean was to first uncover who he was and what he was up to. No one is who we think they are or, for that matter, who they think they are. That's what makes the job tough. It's not enough that I know what time it is. I have to take the watch apart and find out what makes it tick. Whatever Sean was up to, whoever he really was, it wasn't good, and I was beginning to believe that Carlton Phillips was right to be worried about the welfare of his daughter. There were red flags waving in my face. The plagiarism. The missing, then found book. What I perceived about a conspiratorial silence about Sean among those who knew him. Why were they protecting him? What did he need protecting from?

The mere fact I was having such a tough time finding Sean told me something funny was going on. Most people aren't hard to find. They leave a trail your grandmother could follow. You look them up in the phone book. You find them at their job. You get in touch with a family member or a friend. The Internet makes it even easier. Think about it. Unless you're the Unabomber, or on the run, most of us have someone who knows where we are or how to contact us. That's because, although everyone has something to hide, they aren't actually in hiding. They live their lives out in the open. Most of us are, by nature, creatures of habit. We take the same seat in the theater. We eat at the same restaurants. We frequent the same bars. But people like Sean are different. They live in darkness, a darkness they create and then embrace. They keep secrets. They shun routines, because they know that if you have a routine, you're easy to find. These people are never where you'd expect to find them. But in a way, that unpredictability, that urge to remain hidden, makes it possible for someone like me to find them. They break connections, because if you're connected, you're easy to find. Even though they forge relationships with people, they're not real. It's as if they're written in disappearing ink. They're there and then they're not. To find them, I have to begin to think like them, act like them, be them. I am an impersonator of lost souls. I know them well, because in many ways I am one of them.

My job is to read what's written in disappearing ink before it completely fades from the page. Then I take what I read and make sense out of it. I make connections. Not just any connections, but the right ones.

This is what went through my mind as I headed toward Dana Simmons's place, hoping she would provide more information about Sean before he totally disappeared into the page.

"Nice place," I said as Dana, dressed in tight, faded jeans, torn at both knees, and a crimson Harvard T-shirt, let me in the place, which was on the ground floor of what looked to be a very nice, very expensive townhouse. She smelled good. Lemony. And though she hadn't dressed up, I could see she'd applied makeup. It was as if part of her wanted me to think she couldn't care less if I were there, while another part wanted to impress me. Either one was fine with me.

"Don't get the wrong idea," she said as she took my hand to lead me farther into the house. "It's not mine. Just on loan for the summer while my friend's in London. She's an English professor, doing some research over there."

"Lucky you. If I'd known English professors could afford

something like this, it's possible I would have taken a completely different career path."

"Most of them don't, unless they divorce wealthy lawyers."

"Guess I'll just have to aim lower."

"Is that all you've got," she said, gesturing toward the knapsack I had slung over my shoulder.

"I travel light."

"Hungry?"

"A little."

"Good. I'm starved. I thought since it's such a nice night, we could eat out back, on the deck."

"Fine by me."

"I'd show you around, but the upstairs is off-limits."

This is a word I do not like hearing. Tell me not to touch something because the paint hasn't dried, and that's just what I'm going to do. Just to make sure you're not lying. And so, I couldn't help but wonder what was upstairs.

"Why's that?"

"Jen keeps her stuff up there, and she doesn't like anyone messing with it. Would you like to wash up first?"

"Sure."

"Bathroom's on the way. Follow me."

We walked through the living room, then passed through what I assumed were two bedrooms on either side of the hall.

"Here it is," she said, gesturing to her right. "When you're finished, just walk straight through the dining room, past the kitchen, then through the back door. You shouldn't have any trouble finding me."

"Don't worry, that's what I do," I said as I ducked into the john.

I'm a born sneak. I go into someone's bathroom and I can't help opening the medicine cabinet. What's in there tells you a lot about the person—sometimes allowing, if you will, for a

Sherlock Holmesian moment. I ran the water, then opened the cabinet, where I found the usual items—hand cream, lotions, toothpaste, Tylenol, Band-Aids, a razor, shaving cream, a couple of prescription bottles, one for Prozac, the other for a generic antibiotic. I closed the cabinet door, looked down and spotted two toothbrushes in the cup. One was new, the other had the bristles worn down. The simple explanation for things is often the best. But my job is to go beyond simple. I assumed Dana had her own bathroom connected to the bedroom, so this was a spare. It could have been that the owner of the place had left some of her stuff there. Surely that would be a logical answer, but it was also possible that Dana'd had another recent guest. Maybe two. Male or female? Or both? There was no way of knowing. There was also no way of telling how recently the other person or persons had been there, or whether they were still there. Up the forbidden stairs, maybe? The only thing I could do was keep my eyes peeled for any other sign that someone else was in the house.

Dana was outside lighting candles as she stood beside a table filled with several platters of food, none of which looked the least bit familiar.

"Sit," she said. "I didn't know if you were a wine or beer kind of guy, so I've got both."

"Wine gives me a wicked headache," I said.

"Beer it is. Corona okay?"

"Perfect."

She disappeared into the kitchen and when she returned she handed me a frosted bottle. "You don't look like the kind of guy who needs a glass." She said down opposite me. "Dig in."

I hesitated a moment.

She smiled. "You look a little confused, Swann. Need some help?"

"Possibly, though despite what you might have heard, I have

149

mastered the art of the knife, fork and spoon."

"You can't possibly know how happy that makes me."

"So, what've we got here?" I said. "I don't recognize a damned thing."

"I'm vegan. No meat, no poultry, no fish, no dairy. But I promise, I'm a pretty good cook," she said as she moved to my side of the table and started spooning stuff onto my plate. "I think you'll like it, and even if you don't, it'll be good for you. A very nice change of pace for your body, I'm sure."

"I'm not used to doing anything that's good for me," I said, staring at my plate. "My body doesn't take well to change."

"Then it'll be a new experience. You like new experiences, don't you, Swann?"

"It's tough enough for me to get used to the old ones."

"Then it's time to shake up your world a little." She sat back down, scooped some food onto her plate, and started eating. I watched her as I sat in a near paralytic state, my fork poised over the plate.

"Mmmm. Excellent, even if I do say so myself," she said.

I put my fork down and took a swig of beer.

"Jesus, Swann, you look like a deer caught in the headlights. You don't have to be loaded to eat this meal. You don't want me to come over and feed you, do you? Because I will, if it comes to that."

"I think I can handle this on my own."

"I would hope so."

I took a bite. It wasn't bad. I took another. I knew I could make it through, as I pictured a nice, big, fat cheeseburger at the end of the rainbow.

"I knew if you took a chance you wouldn't be disappointed. Trying something new can actually be rewarding. You ought to add that concept to your repertoire."

"It's not bad," I said, moving food around the plate with my fork, "but don't think you've converted me."

"That's the last thing I'd want to do. Now that the experimental period is over, you're on your own. I think what we need is some music," she said, rising from her chair. "Any requests?"

"Whatever you're in the mood for."

She went back into the apartment and a few seconds later the backyard was filled with the kind of Latin music I recognized well from my days in *El Barrio*.

"Interesting choice," I said as she slid back into her seat.

" 'Buena Vista Social Club.' Thought you might like it."

"Why's that?" I asked suspiciously.

"No particular reason."

"You know my office used to be in Spanish Harlem."

"Really?"

"Done some homework on me, have you?"

"Why would I do that?"

"It's something I would have done."

She smiled enigmatically. "But I'm not a detective, am I?"

She was having fun. So was I. Now it was time to get down to business, and maybe take back a little of my mojo. "I spoke with Elizabeth Lawson, the librarian who hired Sean."

"Find out anything interesting?"

"Possibly."

"What might that be?" Dana asked, taking a sip of wine.

"That he left the job early."

"Early meaning he cut out before closing time every day?"

"Early meaning he didn't make it through the summer."

"I told you he was only here six weeks. Did you find out why?"

"When someone leaves a job early, it either means they've found something better, that working conditions sucked, or they didn't get along with their boss."

"Which one was it?"

"I'm betting you know. You got him the job. You were pretty close to Sean. I'm assuming he confided in you."

"I wouldn't say we were 'close,' at least the way I think you mean it."

"How do you think I mean it?"

"Do I have to draw you a picture?"

"Pictures are worth a thousand words."

"I teach literature, Swann. I'm partial to words."

"You're not trying to tell me you didn't have any contact with him the entire summer, are you?"

"I would never tell you anything that wasn't true. We spoke a couple of times—and we probably ran into each other on campus. But I wasn't here the whole summer. I was back and forth between here and Syracuse, and I even took a couple of weeks off to go to London on holiday. I'm sure you have some idea why he left, so why don't you enlighten me?"

"There was that situation with a missing book."

"Do tell."

"You don't know what I'm talking about?"

"Nope," she said, grabbing a slice of bread, seven-grain, she made sure to inform me earlier, and using it to move some food onto her fork.

"While Sean was working in the library a signed, first edition copy of *Tender Is the Night* went missing."

"I'm surprised I didn't hear about that," she said coolly. "And Sean was suspected of the theft?"

"Far as I can tell, there were no actual suspects. The book turned up a few days later in the regular stacks at another library on campus. No harm, no foul. That's probably why word didn't get out. But Sean left the library soon after the book was found."

"And to you that means he had something to do with it?"

"Can you think of any reason why someone might steal a rare book, then return it within a matter of days?"

"To read it?"

"Funny."

"Honestly, I can't imagine why. Maybe whoever stole it got cold feet. Or was afraid they'd get caught when they realized it wouldn't be so easy to dispose of."

"I was thinking it might have been done by the same kind of person who'd plagiarize his own professor's work."

"Gosh, I never thought of that," she said with a cute half-smile.

"You think this is some kind of joke?"

"Not if I thought it was as serious as you obviously do. But please, Swann, let's get a grip here. Even if the thief was Sean, and neither of us can be sure of that, what would he be guilty of? Harmless pranks? In either case, no one was hurt. Maybe whoever did it, and let's even say it was Sean, was trying to make a point about how easy it was to steal a book from the library in order to point out the lack of security."

"It's possible he's just out to prove how far he can push the envelope, to show how much he can get away with. But maybe it's more than that."

"What would that be?"

"I have no idea. I was hoping you might be able to help me come up with something that made more sense."

"I'm afraid not. I'm not saying Sean isn't capable of doing everything you're talking about, because he might well be, but I can only extrapolate from my experiences with him. He is a bit of a jokester, a provocateur, which is why he did that plagiarism bit. I guess he might be capable of playing a game with that book, because if he was responsible, that's obviously all it was. A game."

"And you really have no idea where he is now?"

"No. But there is something . . ."

"Don't make me beat it out of you."

"I doubt it'll come to that."

"Let's have it," I said, knowing full well that whatever she was going to tell me was fully orchestrated. She knew she was going to wind up telling me; it was just a matter of when and how.

"I saw him not long ago."

"When?"

"About a month ago."

"Why didn't you tell me this earlier?"

"I didn't speak to him. I just saw him walking across the street from me. And to be completely honest, I'm not even positive it was him."

She took another sip of wine and pushed her plate away. "It was in the square. Late afternoon. I was on my way home from a class. I was in a hurry. I was waiting for the light to change. Just before it did, I saw him crossing the street in the other direction, across from me. At first I didn't recognize him, because he was wearing a suit and carrying an attaché case. I'd never seen him in a suit before. It was so out of character that for a moment I honestly wasn't sure it was him."

"But now you think it was. Why?"

"It was his walk. It was distinctive because he had a very slight limp."

"A limp?" No one had ever mentioned Sean having a limp before.

"He told me it was the result of an injury he got a few years ago in a car accident. Evidently, he broke his ankle and it never healed quite right. It wasn't noticeable unless he was walking quickly. Or when he was tired. At least that's what he told me."

"So, he was walking rapidly?"

"Yes."

"Like he was trying to get away from someone?"

"More like he was in a hurry to get somewhere."

"Why do you say that?"

"He wasn't looking behind him, and I'd think if he was trying to get away from someone he would be."

"Or maybe he was trying to get away from somewhere he'd been."

"We'll never know for sure, will we?"

"Not unless I find him and ask him."

"Which is exactly what you're going to do, right?"

"That's the plan. That's the only time you saw him in the past six months?"

"The one and only. Scout's honor," she crossed her heart with her index finger. It's a gesture that's been used on me before. Sometimes it means what it signifies. Usually, it's just the opposite.

"Why didn't you mention this earlier?"

"It slipped my mind."

"I don't believe that."

"Believe what you want."

"I usually do. So, what's with you and Elizabeth Lawson?"

"What do you mean?"

"She doesn't like you. What's the deal with you two?"

"I have no idea what you're talking about."

"You're lying to me, Dana."

She sat up straight and looked me right in the eye. "I resent that accusation. I don't lie."

"Everyone lies, honey. Not just occasionally. All the time. Sometimes the lies are inconsequential . . . the social kind. Sometimes they're used to manipulate. Most of the time they're to hide something."

"I'm not hiding anything."

"Maybe. Maybe not. But if you are, eventually I'll find out."

"You're pretty sure of yourself, aren't you?"

"I am. But it's not because I'm smarter than you or anyone

else. It's because I know human nature. Lying is in our genes. It's a form of self-preservation. It's what makes us a so-called higher life form. I understand that."

"You're cynical."

"I prefer to call it practical. Right now, it doesn't matter what went down between you and Elizabeth Lawson. It's enough for me to know it's something. If it's important, I'll find out what it is."

"Not if there's nothing to find out."

I smiled. She got up and started to clear the dishes. "How about some dessert?"

"I don't think so."

"I've got some great soy ice cream. You'd never know it wasn't the real thing," she said, as she headed back toward the kitchen.

"Then why not just have the real thing?"

"Because this would be better for you."

"If I did what was better for me, I wouldn't be in this business."

She stopped at the door and turned to face me. "I think you know what's best for you, Swann. I think you just don't care. I could use some help here," she said as she stood in front of the door, her hands filled with dishes. I got up, took some of them, then opened the door for her. I went inside with her. She put the dishes in the sink. So did I.

"I'll wash," I said.

"You don't have to do that."

"I know. I want to. I like taking something dirty and making it clean."

"Suit yourself," she said. "When you're finished, you can vacuum the floors."

While I washed the dishes, she prepared dessert. When we were both finished, we went back outside.

It seemed to have grown warmer, but now there was a slight

breeze blowing. We sat across from each other; the only light, cast by two flickering candles, softened the chiseled features of her face. The sound of crickets filled the night air. Neither of us said anything for a moment or two.

"Noisy," I said.

"You call that noise?"

"I'm a city kid. City noise doesn't bother me. Country noise does."

"This ain't the country, Swann."

"It is to me."

"You really have to get out more."

"They're communicating with each other."

"I guess they are."

"What do you think they're saying?"

"I don't know. What do you think?"

"I think it's meaningless noise. Just a way to let the other crickets know they're around."

"I think it's probably more than that," she said.

I shrugged. "We'll never know."

"Eat your ice cream. It's melting."

"It's not ice cream."

"Whatever it is, eat it before it's soup."

I took my spoon and dipped it into the gelatinous ball in my bowl. "It looks like ice cream," I said.

"Isn't that amazing."

I brought some to my mouth. It was coffee flavored. It wasn't bad. And maybe, just maybe, by eating it, I'd add an extra few days to my life. Question was, what would I do with them?

Dana smiled as I dipped my spoon in again. She followed suit. "You know, Swann, you're a very attractive man. Especially when you get contemplative. I suspect you're a lot more complicated than you let on."

"Are you flirting with me, Dana? Because if you are, under

the circumstances, I'd have to ask myself why."

"The circumstances being that I'm a dyke?"

"You are?"

"It's what you've heard, isn't it?"

"How do you know what I've heard?"

"Word gets around."

The only way she could have known is that she'd spoken to Dubin. That meant there was a whole lot of conversation going on about me and what I was doing. The more conversation, the better, because that meant people were interested, which meant they had a vested interest in what I was doing. Sean + Dubin + Simmons + ? = Marcy Phillips. At least that's the way it was supposed to work.

"Well, are you?"

"A dyke?"

"Yeah. Is that something that would matter to you?"

"Should it?"

"Not unless you were interested in me."

"I'm here, so I guess I'm interested."

I felt her foot rub up against the calf of my leg. She was smiling. I knew what that smile meant. It wasn't about sex. She was playing with me. And the funny thing was, I didn't care. Not a bit. She was doing what every red-blooded female would do in that situation: she was using the possibility of sex to get what she wanted. The question was, what did she want? I could let it go as far as she wanted to take it and find out, or I could change the rules of the game. I decided to do the latter. It wasn't because I wouldn't have enjoyed the game, or even taking her to bed. She was a beautiful, sexy woman and I'm a man presented with the opportunity for sex, which is very difficult, if not impossible, to resist. It wasn't because I was beat, because no man is ever too tired to have sex when it's presented to him on a platter. It was because I'm the one who likes to do the manipulating, and in this case I could do that by playing against the grain, by turning down anything Dana was offering. It would make her work harder. And the harder she worked, the more possibility there was of her slipping up.

"You know," I said, "what you're doing with your foot isn't necessarily going to get you what you want."

"Really," she said, moving her foot higher up on my leg. "What do you think that might be?"

"I wouldn't presume to guess. The truth is, Dana, you're probably a lot smarter than I am. I'm sure you're a lot more complicated. Most everybody is. I suspect you know a lot more than you're telling me, and I have no idea why you're not telling me what it is. I'll find out, though, with or without your help. You can bank on that because, although I might not be as smart as you are, I'm tenacious. Tenacity sometimes makes up for a lot of other things."

She withdrew her foot and smiled at me. "Can't blame a girl for trying, can you?"

"Nope. The truth is, I probably would have enjoyed screwing you, whether you're straight or not. It probably would have been very exciting. And I like being excited."

"Then why not?"

"I'll keep you guessing about that. Maybe another time, another place."

"Oh, I'm not so sure about that. This could very possibly be it for you, Swann."

"My loss, I'm sure."

"Yes, it is. It's been a long day and I'm pretty tired," she said. "I'll show you where you'll sleep, and then I think I'll turn in."

"Okay," I said as we both rose and I followed her out of the kitchen. She pointed to a bedroom on the left, across from what I assumed was hers.

"The sheets are clean, and you can use the towel over there

on the chair, in case you want to shower. If you need anything else, let me know."

"Thanks. I will. By the way, you're here alone, right?"

She looked around. "You see anyone else?"

"Sometimes, it's all about what you don't see."

She turned on her heels. "Then I'll keep you guessing about that."

"You're not pissed, I hope," I said as she opened the door to her bedroom.

"What if I am?"

"That'd be a shame. But you'll get over it."

"I'm sure I will. I have an early class in the morning, so I'll probably be gone when you get up. Just close the door behind you when you leave."

"What about locking it?"

"You don't have to worry about that. This is a very safe neighborhood."

"Really?" I said, arching my eyebrows. "You could've fooled me."

★ ★ ★ ★ ★

PART 4
NEW YORK CITY, AGAIN

★ ★ ★ ★ ★

"I have yet to see any problem, however complicated, which, when looked at in the right way, did not become still more complicated."

—Poul William Anderson

16
WHO SAYS YOU CAN'T TELL
A BOOK BY ITS COVER?

Books. Books. Books.

They seemed to be the key to finding Sean and Marcy. I couldn't quite put together how books played into this, but I knew they did. I figured I had to learn more about them, not what was inside them, but what was beyond and behind the pages. The best place to do that was back in New York City.

By the time I awoke from what turned out to be a very deep sleep, Dana was gone. She must have left, like the fog, on cat's feet, because I hadn't heard a sound. She left a note for me on the kitchen counter.

Swann,

   Sorry I didn't get a chance to say goodbye. Help yourself to anything in the fridge. Believe it or not, last night was fun. I hate losing and I hate being thwarted, but I suspect we're alike in that regard. Hope you find Sean, and if you do, say hello for me.

   And no matter what happens, don't you feel a lot healthier this morning?

                                          Dana
            P.S. I brewed some coffee for you. Help yourself.

I zapped the coffee in the microwave, poured myself a cup, and sat at the kitchen table, giving myself a moment to plan my next move. Alone in the house, or at least I thought I was alone,

I now had the opportunity to check the upstairs. I don't know what I expected to find, but uncovering secrets is what I do. There was no way I was going to leave without checking out the upstairs.

There was a door at the top of the second landing. It was locked. I pressed my head to the door to see if I could hear anything. Nothing. I knocked gently. No response. I tried a credit card, wedging it between the doorjamb and the edge of the door, but the lock was too sophisticated to be beaten by such a rudimentary trick. It made me wonder why someone would use that kind of lock inside a house. Was it because there was something to hide? Or was it to protect something valuable? There was no way I was going to get in there short of taking the door off its hinges, so I had to accept that this was one secret that was going to remain hidden.

Back downstairs, I spent the next ten minutes roaming through the house, looking for anything that might give me a hint as to where Marcy and Sean might be and maybe even help me figure out who Dana was and what part she'd played in their disappearance. In Dana's room, I went through a couple of drawers and found nothing but clothing. There were a few books left around, including one on the nightstand, a copy of Thomas Pynchon's *The Crying of Lot 49,* which she was obviously in the middle of reading. I picked it up and thumbed through it. She'd made some notes in the margin. I guessed she was planning to teach it in the fall. I put it back exactly where I'd found it, a skill I'd picked up when I used to go through my father's porn magazines I found in the back of the closet when I was a kid. The other books, stacked in a pile near the window, were American classics—Faulkner, Hemingway, Fitzgerald, Dos Passos, Cather. I was tempted to thumb through them, too, to see if I could find any clues, but it was getting late and I needed to make it back to New York before noon.

An hour later, I was on the shuttle back to LaGuardia.

When I stepped off the plane and checked my cell, I found a message from Goldblatt, telling me he had some information for me. I found an isolated seat in the terminal and gave him a call.

"You've got something for me, Goldblatt," I said, stretching my legs far out into the aisle.

"You got something for me, Swann?"

"Ah, *plus ca change, plus c'est meme chose.*"

"Huh?"

"That's French, Goldblatt."

"Fuck the French. I got what you asked for, now what's in it for me?"

"Helping out a friend?"

"Stop playing with me, Swann. I got better things to do."

"Like what? You're a disbarred lawyer who spends his time looking for some disreputable way to make a buck."

"I resent that."

"But you can't deny it."

"No. But I can still resent it."

"How much?"

"Five hundred bucks. And that's non-negotiable."

"I'll give you two-fifty, and that's non-negotiable."

"So when can we meet?"

"Can't we just do this over the phone and I'll send you a check?"

"You gotta be kidding. I'm supposed to trust you?"

"We've known each other a long time."

"I know my mother, but I still cut the cards."

"I'll be back in the city in half an hour. Meet me at Veselka's."

I arrived before Goldblatt. I wasn't surprised. Goldblatt's always late. He never has a reason, he just is. I knew that and so

I should have stopped at my apartment first. But hope springs eternal . . .

Ten minutes later, Goldblatt, looking like he'd slept in his clothes—a rumpled polo shirt, a filthy seersucker jacket, and shiny pants that had one time belonged to a suit—arrived. He sat down, holding a beat-up leather attaché case to his ample stomach.

"Nice outfit," I said.

"My suit's at the cleaner," he said, smoothing out what little hair he had with his hands.

"When's the last time you shaved?"

"April. What's it to you? I'm starved," he said, cradling the attaché case in his lap.

"You got state secrets in there?"

"Huh?" he said, grabbing a menu.

"What the hell have you got in there?"

"Stuff."

"What stuff?"

"Important stuff, okay? Stuff that's none of your damned business."

"Okay. Okay. Don't be so touchy. What have you got for me?"

"First we order, then we talk. You're paying, right?" He buried his head in the menu.

The waitress came over. "What're ya havin', gents?"

"You go," said Goldblatt, "I'm still considering."

"I'll have a western omelet, toast on the side. White."

Goldblatt shivered. "Eggs? I hate the sight of 'em. Even hate the word."

"Too bad. That's what I'm having. Close your eyes."

"And you," said the waitress.

"I'll have a turkey on rye with tomato and Swiss cheese. No mayo. Russian dressing or Thousand Island, or whatever the hell you call it here, on the side. And I'll have the kielbasa and sauerkraut and give me some of those cheese blini, plenty of apple sauce. And you might as well add some sour cream, on the side."

"Do you want me to bring all that together?"

"As a matter of fact, just bring the kielbasa, and I'll take the sandwich to go. And honey, why don't I just hold onto this menu, in case I want something else."

"You stocking up for winter?"

"Fuck you."

"The information you have better be good, Goldblatt."

"You get what you pay for. Which reminds me," he said, holding out his hand.

I went into my wallet and counted out five fifties. He reached for them.

"Not so fast. One at a time, Goldie."

"I hate when you call me that. It makes me sound cheap."

"God knows, I wouldn't want you to feel that. Now, what have you got on Phillips?"

He brought the attaché case from his lap, put it on the table, and snapped it open. He pulled out a sandwich covered in plastic wrap, and placed it on the table. Then he pulled out a couple of yellow legal pads and bunch of papers, which he started riffling through.

"What the hell is all that?"

"You think you're the only client I got, Swann?"

"I'd hardly call the people you deal with clients."

"I know it's here somewhere. Ah, here it is." He triumphantly pulled out a rumpled piece of yellow paper torn from a legal pad. "Carlton Phillips, right?"

"How the hell did you ever make it out of law school?"

"Hard work, my friend. Hard work. So, you want this or not?"

"Shoot."

"Okay, nineteen ninety-four, one of his clients filed a complaint against him. Said Phillips sold assets that weren't his and then kept the proceeds."

"What assets?"

"That took some digging."

I handed him another fifty.

"A rare manuscript."

"What happened to the complaint?"

"It was dropped."

"Why?"

He held out his hand. I fed him another fifty.

"Phillips came up with proof that the manuscript had been given to him in lieu of payment for a job he did for the client. Seems the client didn't know how valuable the manuscript was and Phillips did. No crime in that, though."

"Anything else?"

He smiled. A third fifty passed hands.

"When his wife filed for divorce, she claimed, among other things, that he was physically abusive. And that he hid assets. But that's old hat. Every woman says that about her husband, and every husband does it. I can't tell you how many cases I was involved . . ."

"This isn't about you, Goldblatt. We can roam down Memory Lane another time, when I'm not paying. What happened in the divorce?"

"He paid her a nice settlement and, presto, the problem was gone."

"Anything else?" I slid a fifty across the table, just as the waitress brought our order.

"I did some poking around, just because I like you, Swann, and I found that although he's never gotten into any real trouble, he's certainly skirted the edge. But he's also got a reputation as a damn good lawyer. You want I should keep on it?"

"Sure, why not? It'll keep you busy. And since I'm obviously taking care of the next three meals you're having, you might as well stay on the payroll."

He held out one hand, his other holding half a blintz on a fork. I placed the last fifty in his palm, then dug out another twenty and handed it to him.

"Much obliged," he said, not bothering to empty his mouth, as little pieces of applesauce dribbled down his chin.

"Wipe your face," I commanded as I dropped two twenties on the table and left.

What Goldblatt told me might solidify my sense that Phillips was a scumbag, but it didn't really help me find his daughter, or make sense out of what was happening. But maybe he'd come up with something else.

As soon as I dropped my bag off at my apartment, took a quick shower and changed my clothes, I walked over to the Strand, on Broadway, the largest bookstore in New York, proudly boasting "18 miles of new, used and rare books." It was one of the last of the used bookstores in the area, most of them having succumbed to the twin plagues of higher rents and super-bookstores, like Barnes & Noble and Borders. When I was a kid, I used to haunt these second-hand book emporiums, scarfing up cheap, hardcover remainders, most of which were now stored in the basement of my building.

I asked to talk to someone about the book business and was sent up to the third floor to speak to a fellow named Jon Kravetz, who, they said, might be able to help me.

If possible, Jon, who looked to be in his early forties, was even worse dressed than me. He was tall, over six feet, lanky, and his hair was long, his beard thick. He wore a red Strand T-shirt, a pair of worn, faded blue jeans that looked this close to disintegration, and a pair of brown work boots that were practically falling off his feet. Obviously, neither he nor I subscribed to George Bernard Shaw's estimation of a man's position in life, "He's a gentleman: look at his boots."

"So, dude, how can I help you? If it's about selling books, you're on the wrong floor. That's downstairs—and if you are selling them, don't expect to get rich. At least not here."

"I'm not selling and I'm not buying. I just need some information."

"Look around you, dude, that's what we're all about. You want information, we've got the books to give it to you. Or, if you're just looking to entertain yourself, we've got that, too. But hey, you'd better get it while you can, because reading, at least reading books, is a dying art. Ten years from now, we're out of business. Guaranteed. You want a book, you go to the library, or you borrow it from someone who's still got one. They'll be putting books in a time capsule, and fifty years from now someone'll open it up, find a book and say, 'What the hell is this?' It's all about the computer now. Everything's going to be online. You push a button and it's delivered to you like that." He snapped his fingers. "Take it from me, dude. I know of what I'm speaking."

"I'm sure you do"—and you do a lot of it, I thought—"but that's not the kind of information I need. Ever hear of Sean Loomis?"

"I know Sean. Righteous dude. He's in and out of here all the time. Since he was a kid."

"When was the last time you saw him?"

"Few weeks ago, maybe. He was in here with this chick he hangs out with."

"Know her name?"

"He didn't introduce us."

"What's she look like?"

"Pretty chick. Dark hair. Slim. Young. Early twenties, maybe."

"You've just described about half the female NYU college students." I took out Marcy's photograph. "How about this?"

He looked at it. "I guess that could be her."

"Could be?"

He looked closer. "The hair's longer in this picture, but yeah, like I said, I guess it could be her."

"Why's Sean here so often?"

"He's a book dealer, dude. That's what we do here. We buy and sell books. Sean's a whiz. He's always coming in here with something interesting. Besides, he likes hanging here talking books. He's always interested in the new stuff that comes in. But we're not the only place he deals with."

"Like where else?"

"Private dealers."

"Anyone in particular?"

"He used to do business with a dude named Ross Klavan. He's one of the biggest. And the best. Cool dude. He brokers all kinds of important collections. From what I hear, Sean was once kind of like a protégé of his."

"Know how I'd get in touch with Sean?"

"Not exactly."

"What's that mean?"

"I mean, I've got a P.O. box for him, and an email address, but that's it. Dude moves around a lot."

"Let me have what you've got."

"Don't know if I can give out that kind of information, dude. That might fall under the category of privileged communication. I'd have to check with my boss. Or maybe contact Sean and see if it's cool."

"Why don't you do that."

"My boss isn't here today. I can email Sean and see if he gets back to me. But I gotta tell ya, he don't always answer right away. Why don't you give me a call or stop by tomorrow, and I'll see what I can do for you. Or leave your phone number or email."

"This might help." I pulled out my wallet, took out a business card, and wrapped a twenty around it.

He laughed. "Dude, you think this is like the movies or something? I like my job, so you're just going to have to wait till I get the okay from my boss or from Sean."

"Worth a try," I said, tucking the twenty back into my wallet. "In the meantime, how would I find this Ross Klavan?"

"He works out of his apartment. That's something I can hook you up with."

"I'd appreciate it."

He went into his back pocket and took out a stack of business cards, thumbed through them, then handed me one. "He gave me a shit load of 'em. I refer someone to him and he makes a buy or a sale, he throws me a couple of bucks. It's all on the up and up. A finder's fee."

"Good to see you're not allergic to money." I took the card, glanced at it—it was an address on Second Avenue, in the low-twenties—and tucked it in my wallet. "You come up with any information on Sean and I wind up connecting with him, I'm not averse to coming up with a finder's fee, too."

"Sounds like a plan, dude. And hey, while you're here, take a look around. Maybe there's something you'd like. I can give you a righteous ten percent off. Just show my card at the cash register and you'll get the discount." He took one out, initialed it, and handed it to me.

"Thanks, dude," I said, taking his card and stuffing it in my wallet.

I never can make it through a bookstore without dropping some cash, so I did just what Kravetz suggested. By the time I roamed through the bins of review copies, I'd picked up several novels, including the latest Philip Roth, a used hardcover copy of Saul Bellow's *Herzog,* and a pretty worked-over copy of Ellison's *The Invisible Man.*

17
BOOK SMART

I gave Ross Klavan a call and asked if I could stop by. I didn't tell him the truth. Not that any of us knows what that is, anyway. We all know that if you tell a lie often enough, it can become the truth. What if a lie leads you to the truth? Does the lie then become part of the truth?

I told Klavan I was a journalist researching an article on rare books and rare book dealers. This could have been the truth. I'd get information I needed, and he'd get to talk about himself and what he does for a living. That's what people want. To talk about themselves and have someone listen to what they have to say. I provide a public service, listening to people when no one else will.

At first, Klavan, who had a deep, resonant radio announcer's voice, was hesitant. "I don't need and I don't want the publicity." But when I told him it was just for background, he capitulated and invited me up to his place, which he called his home/office. "I've got a lunch at one," he said, "but I should be back by three. Be on time. I can only give you an hour or so. There's an auction at Sotheby's I've got to attend."

"No problem," I told him, and this time I wasn't lying, because if I can't get what I need in an hour, then I'm not doing my job very well.

I had a few hours to kill before our meeting, so I shot up to the public library on 40th Street and Fifth Avenue to do a little research on Klavan and the rarified world he inhabited. I found a profile of him in a three-year-old airline magazine and learned that Klavan, like many rare book dealers, grew up wanting to be a writer. In his case, it was poetry. No surprise why he gave that up. When I was at Columbia, I interned for a few months at a small literary magazine. That was back when I thought I wanted to write the Great American Novel, before I realized it had already been written. Numerous times. And even if it hadn't been, I wasn't going to be the one to do it. The magazine was run by a poet, and many of the people who came in and out of the office were poets, too. They were all pretty crazy, not beyond envy, backstabbing and out-and-out destruction of their competitors. It didn't surprise me. After all, what the hell were they fighting for? None of them made a living writing poetry. Even if they did get to the top, wherever that was, the heights weren't all that high. Usually the plum they were battling over was a university position teaching poetry. I was alone in the office one afternoon when a fellow, wearing tight leather pants, leather vest and a black silk scarf wrapped around his neck, walked in and asked to see Daniel, the editor, who lived upstairs, in the penthouse, no less, of a rundown building in the west 30s. I told him he wasn't in the office.

"Where is he?" he asked.

"Upstairs."

"Give him a call and tell him Peter Salonga is here to see him."

I gave Daniel a call.

"There's a guy down here named Peter Salonga who wants to see you."

"You're kidding."

"Nope. He's here, all right."

"Hold him there. Don't let him leave. I'll be right down."

"He'll be right down," I said to Salonga, who took a seat in the office.

A few minutes later, Daniel came bursting through the door wielding a baseball bat. I started to get up to get between them because I was afraid he was going to kill the guy. He took one look at Salonga, stopped, laughed, and said, "You sonuvabitch!" He dropped the bat and pulled the visitor into a bear hug.

It turned out the guy was an old friend of his, another poet, named Norman Church. I had no idea who that was until later, when I found that Salonga had given Daniel's most recent book of poetry a savage review.

With guys like that to deal with, it was no wonder Klavan saw the light and decided he could still make his living on words, but in a far more profitable way.

While he was still trying to make his mark in the world of verse, he took a job at the Strand, where he became interested in rare books. After a couple years, he opened his own business, working out of his tiny East Village studio apartment, not far from where I lived now. In those days the East Village, especially Alphabet City, as it was known—Avenues A, B and C—was a thriving drug market, a dangerous place to live or visit. I figured Klavan must have been a tough cookie if he was running his business from there, because the chance of being ripped off by junkies who prowled the 'hood were extraordinarily high. Klavan stirred up some controversy when the owner of the Strand accused him of poaching customers. Klavan refused to back down, arguing that anyone interested in buying or selling rare books was fair game. His first big score came when he sweet-talked a Wall Street lawyer into letting him handle the sale of his valuable collection of early twentieth-century American first edition novels. From there, Klavan branched out into buying, then reselling, at what appeared to be enormous profit, rare manuscripts and letters. The profile mentioned his primary competitor, Teddy Rabinowitz, who also began his career working at the Strand. From the photos of both of them, it was clear that Rabinowitz, clothed in a custom-made, cream-colored suit, was the yin to Klavan's yang.

Frankly, I didn't understand the whole business. The same words appeared in a first edition that sold for thousands of dollars as in the paperback edition you could pick up secondhand for a couple of bucks. There was no intrinsic value to a first edition. You can't wear a book. You can't look at it like a painting, admiring the brushstrokes or the composition. You can't form it into jewelry. You can't eat it. It's just a damned book. A collection of words on paper. And yet it seemed that some of these signed, rare first edition books could often go for thousands of dollars. That was the real mystery, one I wasn't about to solve.

Klavan's building—by this time he'd moved uptown a bit—faced the very exclusive Gramercy Park, which was locked to all except those residents who had a key. It would have been easier getting into that park, though, than getting through Klavan's building security. First there was the doorman, who not only demanded to know who I was seeing but also for some kind of identification. Then there was the concierge, who called Klavan to verify that I was, indeed, an invited guest. The elevator was programmed by the concierge only to go to the appointed floor. Once the elevator opened onto the ninth floor, I stepped directly into Klavan's apartment.

I took a few steps into the cavernous room and called out, "Anyone here?"

"With you in a second," came a booming voice from somewhere in the back of the apartment. "Just find a seat, any seat, so long as it's not behind my desk."

I entered into what could have passed as one of the most extensive private libraries in the world. The hum of the air-conditioning, cranked up high, filled the high-ceilinged room. The walls were lined with various-sized bookcases, some shoulder height, others floor to ceiling, all crammed with books.

In the middle of the room there was a huge desk, covered with papers and books. Against one wall, sandwiched between two large windows, there was a computer station, and interspersed throughout the room there were a number of other small tables, several of them covered with glass exhibition cases, the kinds you'd find in a museum. They protected either manuscripts or books with brightly colored dust jackets. In one was a vintage copy of *Catcher in the Rye*. In another, a copy of *A Farewell to Arms*. They appeared to be in remarkably good condition, and seeing them sent chills up my arms. It was almost like being in the same room with the authors, and suddenly I could see the appeal of collecting these rare, first edition books. I even imagined Salinger and Hemingway fondling their books for the first time, as if they were newborns.

While I waited, I checked out some of the books on the shelves. They were in remarkably good shape, a noteworthy representation of every well-known writer throughout the last couple of centuries. I was about to pull one from its perch when a man I presumed to be Klavan walked into the room. He was about five-nine, and he had the build of a linebacker: stocky and well-muscled. He was clean-shaven, including the top of his head. He was wearing baggy blue jeans and a black Grateful Dead T-shirt, and was wearing a pair of Birkenstock sandals. He looked familiar, and then I realized it was because he looked very much like a slightly younger version of Richard Dubin.

"Sorry to keep you waiting, man. Had to take a crap. My assistant would have let you in only she called in sick today. She does that a lot. You don't think it's me, do you?" He smelled his armpits. "Not bad. Guess that shower last week's still good. And before you complain about the temperature, it's for the books. They like it cold. And so do I."

He shook my hand heartily, pumping it up and down. "Nice to meet ya, man. Hope you're not allergic to books. Or dust.

No matter how often we dust 'em off, the dust just seems to come back. It's the city. Fuckin' books are a dust magnet. You know how Quentin Crisp dealt with dust, don't ya?"

"Can't say as I do."

"He figured dust only got so high—you don't see dust a couple inches high, right? So, when it got bad enough to see, he'd open the door and the windows and the dust would blow to either side of the room."

"Very clever."

"I met him a few times, down in the Village. Strange, foppish, little man. Loved the hair. I think it was his, but who can be sure. Most good writers I know are very good at reinventing themselves. Especially when they're trying to avoid writing. He was very entertaining. His stuff doesn't go for much now, but you never know what the future will bring, when a writer is going to be discovered by a new generation. Happened with Henry Roth. *Call it Sleep* died a quick death when it was first published, but when Kazin rediscovered it, it became a classic and now a first edition is worth a small fortune. My business is up and down, like the stock market. One minute you're ridin' high, the next minute it's, 'so and so who?' So your name's Swann, huh?"

"That's right."

"Any relation to Swann Galleries?"

"Not that I know of."

"Just a coincidence, huh?"

I nodded.

"I do some business over there."

"Never been there myself."

"You ought to. Especially if you're doing an article on rare books. Now what magazine did you say you write for?"

"I'm freelance."

"But you have an assignment, right?"

"Not exactly. I'm putting together some information so I can pitch a piece to the *New Yorker.*"

"Really? Now that would be very nice, wouldn't it? Si New-house has mucho bucks to throw around, from what I under-stand." He rubbed his fingers together. "Met him once at an auction. Strange, little man. Not very friendly. Kinda looks like one of those lawn gnomes. Have you written for them before?"

"It'd be the first time."

"And some of your other credits would include?"

"Mostly trade stuff you've probably never heard of. I'm try-ing to move into the more commercial markets."

"Don't think I would have heard of them either," he said as he plopped himself in his desk chair, which squeaked as his ass hit leather. "That wasn't a fart."

"I didn't think so."

"Actually, Swann, and I call you that not out of a lack of respect, but because I call everyone by their last name and yours kind of trips off the tongue, I would be remiss if I didn't check you out before I invited you here. There's some very valu-able material in this room and, as you can see, once you enter my little den there's very little security. Other than those snipers across the street who've got their weapons trained on us at all times, of course."

He laughed.

So did I.

"So, let's cut the crap. I know you're a private investiga-tor . . ."

Okay, so he knew who I was. But that was okay. I had him sized up as someone who'd respond better to the direct ap-proach anyway. "Since we're laying our cards, or rather my cards, on the table, just so there's no misunderstanding, calling me a private investigator is like calling Dan Brown a writer."

"Ouch!"

"I'm a skip tracer. I find people and things that are lost.

Sometimes I bring them back, sometimes I don't."

"And what, pray tell, is the lost object or person that you're looking for now and, more importantly, how the hell do you think I can help you?"

"I'm hoping you can lead me to Sean Loomis."

"Loomis, huh? What'd he do, cold-cock an old lady for her book collection?"

"Is that something he'd be capable of?"

He laughed. "Just kidding. Truth is, Sean's not a bad kid. He's actually steered some pretty good deals my way. It's just the way this business can be sometimes. You know . . ." He passed a finger across his neck and made a gurgling sound.

"I thought I should learn about your business if I'm going to have a better shot at finding Sean. Assuming, of course, you can't make life easy for me by telling me how I can find him."

He shook his head. "No fucking idea. Why is it so important you find him?"

"I'm not really all that interested in finding him. It's his girlfriend, Marcy Phillips, I'm after. She's missing, and I'm assuming she's with him, or at the very least he can point me in her direction."

"And you're looking for her because . . . ?"

"Her father hired me."

"Her father wouldn't happen to be Carlton Phillips, would he?"

"You know him?"

"He's been a customer, though I haven't seen him in a while."

"What's your impression of him?"

"Sonuvabitch. But don't take that the wrong way."

"There's a right way?"

"Toughness is sometimes an admirable trait, though not when it's used against me or you. Know what I mean?"

"I'm not sure."

"What I mean is that in his business—the law—and my business—books—pansies don't last long. You gotta man up. If you don't, you're eaten alive. You gotta respect someone who's made it to where he is, even if you don't want to go to the movies with him."

"What kind of stuff has he bought . . . or sold?"

"He's mostly into original manuscripts and letters, though he's certainly bought some books in his time. He has, or had, as far as I know, quite a collection of Joyce and Beckett. I sold him some of it and he got a bunch of things from that sonuvabitch Rabinowitz."

"That would be Teddy Rabinowitz."

"You've done your homework, baby, haven't you?"

"It comes with the territory. You obviously don't much care for him."

"You can tell, huh? Well, it's no secret. Let's just call him my arch nemesis and leave it at that. It seems he's always there just when I'm about to close a big deal and somehow, he's the one who winds up in the catbird seat. Truth is, I had a bit of a falling-out with Sean because he started selling stuff to Teddy instead of me. This isn't for publication—of course, that's not your game"—he smiled mischievously—"but I wouldn't be surprised if Sean wasn't feeding him a little information about deals I was close to making." He rubbed his fingers together. "Otherwise, it would be quite a coincidence that he seemed to catch the fish just as I was about to reel him in. And for Chrissakes, I was one of Sean's mentors. He sought me out early on and he was so talented, so knowledgeable, that I took him under my wing." He laughed. "Son of a bitch turned out to be so good at it, he went off on his own."

"Just like you did."

He smiled. His teeth were amazingly white, so white they almost glistened. I couldn't help wondering if they were real, or if they'd been artificially enhanced.

"Yeah. Just like me. Maybe that's why I liked the little bastard. Saw a lot of me in Sean. He's a hustler, just like me, just like Rabinowitz, only Rabinowitz dresses nicer, talks better and is a lot smoother than Sean and me. To his credit, though, Teddy knows who the fuck he is. He refers to himself as a combination scholar and grifter. But let's face it, you've got to be in this fuckin' business, or you'd swim with the fishes. Teddy's pretty much sewn up the business with the Ransom Humanities Center at UT. Not that I wouldn't have done the same thing if I could have. I think it's that I don't make a good first impression, if you can possibly imagine that."

"You're doing fine with me. What's Ransom?"

"It's part of the University of Texas. They have an incredible collection of books and manuscripts and papers of renowned writers. They're the elephant in the room. But they ain't pink. They're real. Very real. And they've got a shitload of money to throw around. And way too much of it is thrown Teddy's way, because he's managed to sew up the estates of a lot of prominent writers. Can you detect a hint of envy in my voice?"

"I do. But then, that is my job."

"Yeah, I forgot. Big-shot detective. I've got to give him credit. He really put this business on the map. That was some sweet archive deal he made for John Ashberry almost twenty years ago, when a hundred and eighty-five grand was worth a lot more than it is now."

"It's amazing how much money there is in this business."

"I wouldn't be in it if there weren't, pal. Here, let me show you something." He led me to another room, unlocked a door, we walked inside and he flicked the light switch. The room was twice the size of the room we'd come from and filled with glass cases similar to the ones in the main room. "The vault," he said. "Here, take a look at this." He pointed to a case that held an original hardcover copy of *The Sun Also Rises.* The cover art was of a woman, seated, wearing a flowing dress and sandals, her head tilted down and to the side. "Very rare. Nine twenty-six. Inscribed. First edition, second printing, which was just seven weeks after the first printing. Original dust jacket. Guess how much I can get for this?"

"No idea."

"Seventy-five, eighty grand. Maybe more, if the bidders are jazzed up enough."

I whistled.

"And this," he led me to another case that held a copy of *The Great Gatsby,* also with the original dust jacket. "First edition, first issue, fine condition, unrestored dust jacket. Unsigned. How much?"

"A hundred grand?"

"Try a hundred and fifty."

"You're kidding."

He shook his head.

"Yours?"

"I wish. Consignment. But I'm not complaining. I'll make a pretty penny when I sell them."

"Here I always thought it was the words that mattered."

"Grow up, Swann. Everything's about business. Money makes the world go round." He spun his finger in the air. "And sometimes, as rare as it might be, some of that money actually filters down to some of the writers, the poor saps. At least it does to the ones who manage to hang on long enough so their work's actually worth something."

"That's measured how?"

"Not necessarily by talent, though that can't hurt. But only if it's recognized talent. The bottom line is, like any other collectible, it's rarity that matters most, as well as the public's perception of the writer. The more famous or the more notorious you are, the more your book's worth. Plus condition. You take a book like Hemingway's *For Whom the Bell Tolls*. A signed first edition, in excellent shape, with the original dust jacket is worth thousands. You take that same book, same edition, in fair shape, unsigned and without the dust jacket, it's worth bubkis. Why? Not because the words are any different, but because of the rarity of it. It's like virgins, Swann. They're highly valued because they're very rare."

"Does Sean still do business with Rabinowitz?"

"Nope. At least that's the word on the street. Seems they had a falling-out. From what I heard it had to do with the latest book Sean was peddling."

"And that would be?"

"I'm not sure I'm at liberty to say because I'd still like to get my hands on it."

"How about a hint?"

"I admire a man who doesn't take no for an answer, but I really can't say anything other than it's a 'two-for-one' deal. And that's all I can say right now. What do you know about the literary world?"

"I read."

"Most of us do. The question is, what do you read and how much do you know about what you read?"

"English major."

"Yeah, you and every other shmuck who didn't know what they wanted to be when they grew up. But do you still read, or did you read your last book the day before you graduated?"

"I still read."

"What's the last book you picked up and read to the last page?"

"I thought when I came here I'd be the one asking the questions."

"It looks like you were wrong. What we're having here is a

conversation. Give and take. I gave and you took, now it's the other way around. Play the game, Swann, or take a hike."

"Fine, so long as you aren't finished giving."

"Be patient, my friend. Your time will come."

"I was on a Nabokov jag, so it was *Lolita*. And it wasn't for the first time. You're not going to hold that against me. Or jump to any prurient conclusions about me, are you?"

"Oh, I'll jump all right, but the conclusion is one you might like, which is that you're probably smarter than you look."

"That's a compliment?"

"Take it any way you like. I don't give a shit. As it happens, the sale that really put Rabinowitz on the map was peddling the Nabokov literary estate to the New York Public Library for over a million dollars. It took two fuckin' years to get the deal done, but Teddy stuck with it, and for that you've gotta give him credit. But he raised the bar for all of us, and the truth is, no matter how much I dislike the fuckin' guy, he's put money in my pocket and for that one time a year I go to shul, I thank him. Of course, the other three hundred and sixty-four days, I curse the day his mother and father had sex and hope that it was only that one time."

"Kind of harsh, isn't it?"

"My friend, this is all about business. When you're dealing with rare commodities, in this case books and anything literary, like original manuscripts, the field of play is very limited. Duane Reades you see all over the place. Starbucks you see on every fuckin' corner. There's a McDonald's in every town in the country. There's a reason. Because there are enough people who need drugs and toiletries and cheap burgers and fries and drink designer coffee. Take a look around, man. You see bookstores on every corner? No. What you do see, and what you're going to see, is Barnes & Noble and superstores like that taking over. And if I see into the future even farther, which I do, because I'm a fuckin' genius, websites like Amazon.com are going to make bookstores even more superfluous. Eventually, even those superstores will be a nostalgia question on *Jeopardy*. There will be fewer books because people will read on screens, but they will still read, and writers will still be held in high esteem by at least a small part of the population. Books will become artifacts. Artifacts have value. Those of us who deal in rare books and manuscripts will benefit from that. But there's only so much to go around. The best and the smartest and the most cunning will survive. My hating Rabinowitz is just another way of saying that I admire the fuckin' hell out of him. But you won't hear me say that straight out, of course. The sonuvabitch's ego is big enough as it is."

"So explain the business to me. And then explain what Sean Loomis's place in that business is."

"You want a primer?"

"Yes."

He looked at his watch.

"I've only got about an hour before I have to be over to the Swann, but what the hell. I'll give you the Evelyn Woods version. Want some coffee or something to drink?"

"I'm fine. Don't want to waste a minute of that sixty."

"Okay, sit back, relax, and Uncle Ross will give you the scoop on something it took him years to learn."

Klavan kicked off his sandals, leaned back, put his feet on his desk and his hands behind his head and began.

"First off, a lot of people believe Thomas Jefferson was the most famous of all American book collectors. Some people have called his library, which was meticulously organized, 'a blueprint of his own mind,' and I think there's probably a lot of truth to that. By eighteen-fifteen, he'd built a library of sixty-seven thousand books, which was undoubtedly the most important library ever formed by an American at that point in time. And why shouldn't it have been? In a letter to a friend, he wrote that he 'spared no pains, opportunity, or expense' on his collection.

"After the original Library of Congress was destroyed during the War of eighteen-twelve, Jefferson sold his entire library to Congress to make sure the American government had access to the best and most important books published at that time."

"What about value?" I asked.

"Relax, I'm getting there. To begin with, just because a book is old or hard to find doesn't mean it qualifies as being 'rare.' A rare book has to be desirable *and* scarce, plus *important,* which means it had a profound effect when it was printed and still has that effect.

"There are a whole bunch of factors that affect the scarcity of a book, including its printing history, the number of copies printed or sold, the quality of the paper and binding, its popularity, the genre, and if there was any controversy surrounding the publication of the book. Like the first edition of *Lolita,* or some of Henry Miller's books, *Tropic of Cancer, Ulysses* or even Twain's *Huckleberry Finn.* Banned books can translate into bucks.

"One important factor in determining the value of the book is the dust jacket. The first use of dust jackets goes back to the mid-nineteenth century, but since they were created to protect the book in transit, they were generally tossed out, so very few of those early jackets survive. But by the early twentieth century, dust jackets became an art form and they became an important part of the book, especially for collectors. Among the scarcest of dust jackets are those of *The Great Gatsby and The Sun Also Rises.* And with dust jackets condition is also very important, the worse the condition, the less value."

Klavan talked for sixty minutes straight, hardly ever coming up for air, and then, as a bonus, added another ten. After he'd finished his little primer, which was a fascinating tour through the history of rare book collecting, I had a much better sense of what I was dealing with. I had a few questions, but there wasn't time unless I wanted to accompany him to Sotheby's.

"You can ask your questions on the way," he offered, and I accepted.

Outside, he announced, "We'll walk a while." He patted his belly, "I could use the exercise."

As we headed north, walking briskly—"to get my heartbeat up," he said, I tried using the information I'd already gotten from Klavan to get a fix on what might be going on with Loomis. I had this nagging feeling in my gut that everything wasn't on the up-and-up with the kid. If that was true, my job just got more difficult.

"Are there many forgeries in the business?" I asked.

He looked at me and smiled. "You're always going to have that problem when money's involved. But it's not an easy task fooling the experts, and when there's the potential for big bucks, experts like me are going to be consulted."

"But it happens?"

"Sure. It ain't a perfect world. Where there's a will, there's a way. Check out a guy named Thomas James Wise."

"Who's he?"

"An early twentieth-century English book collector and owner of one of the world's finest private collections of English literature. He was also a forger. In the mid-thirties, two young book experts, John Carter and Graham Pollard, published something called *An Enquiry into the Nature of Certain Nineteenth Century Pamphlets,* in which they proved that Wise had invented pedigrees for worthless books and pamphlets, including a book of sonnets by Elizabeth Barrett, and passed off forgeries as the real thing. He's not the only one. There are a lot of suckers in the world, Swann, and I'm guessing you've come across your share of them. You know what Amarillo Slim said: 'Look around the table. If you don't see a sucker, get up, because you're the sucker.' I'm not too proud to admit that I've gotten up from my fair share of tables, my friend."

"So someone could forge a signed copy of a rare book?"

"Yeah. But it's not as easy as it sounds."

"Why's that?"

"First of all, they'd have to get their hands on a first edition. Not impossible, but costly, unless they stumble across a copy in some yard sale, which has happened, but it's getting more and more unlikely. The book would have to be in near pristine condition, with the dust jacket virtually untorn and unblemished. The real bucks are if it's autographed, and that's not easy to forge because everyone's signature changes over the years, so the forger would have to get a sample of the writer's signature at the time it was supposed to have been signed. For instance, when you were twenty, let's say, your signature was very different from the way it is now. My guess is that it's sloppier now, more rushed, and probably shorter, because you don't take the time to form all the letters. I remember years ago, before I really got into the business, I got my hands on what I thought was a John Wayne letter. I got all excited. He'd just died and I figured it would be worth a bundle. And it might have been, except that it was a fuckin' forgery. I found that out when I took it to Hamilton's, they took one look at the date of the letter, then at his signature, and pronounced it bogus. It was probably signed by his press agent or secretary. Happens all the time. I have a friend who does that for Barbra Streisand. All her signatures on those photos people asked for are his, not hers."

"But if you had a sample of someone's signature it would be easy?"

"Easier. Not easy. But even with a sample, you and I couldn't pull it off well enough to fool an expert."

"Even with practice?"

"It would take more than practice. It would take an artist

who could look at the signature, then practice it till it came naturally. Believe me, if we tried it, it would look stilted and obviously faked."

The wheels in my head went round and round. "But an artist might be able to pull it off? Like maybe a trained calligrapher?"

"I guess."

We stopped for a red light.

"What are you thinking, Swann?" Klavan asked.

"I'm thinking about a book that went missing from the Houghton library."

"What book?"

"Fitzgerald's *Tender Is the Night.*"

"How come I don't know anything about that? Something like that, word would get around."

"It was just missing a couple of days, then they found it."

"So?"

"Maybe someone took it just to examine the signature. Took a picture of it. Copied it. Then maybe gave it to someone, an expert calligrapher, who might have been able to forge it."

"Possible, I guess. But there are other ways to get one over on even the best expert. Safer ways. Ways that are much more difficult to detect."

"That would be how?"

"Books become even more valuable in terms of what we call their association."

"What's that mean?"

"Okay. Let me give you a hypothetical. Let's say Joe Shmo was an ambulance driver in the Spanish Civil War, and he meets a young guy named Ernie Hemingway. They hit it off. They become friends. They drink together. They whore together. The war ends, they go their separate ways, but keep in touch. After Hemingway writes a little novel called *The Sun Also Rises,* he gives a signed copy to his good pal Joe. Shmo, who's not much of a reader and couldn't care less who his pal, Ernie, turns out to be, just sticks it in the attic with some other mementoes and forgets about it. Joe croaks. His family gets rid of his possessions, which include that signed book. A dealer buys the whole lot, finds the book, sees that it might be worth something, then learns that Joe actually had a connection to Ernie. Bingo! That book suddenly becomes even more valuable than it would if it was just another signed copy. That's called an association, which is just another way of saying there's a good story connected to the particular copy of the book.

"If you want an actual case, take the inscription Hemingway made in *The Sun Also Rises:* 'To Sylvia with great affection— Ernest Hemingway, Paris, November 1926.' Hemingway hung out regularly at Sylvia Beach's bookshop, Shakespeare and Company, along with a lot of other 'Lost Generation' writers like Gertrude Stein, Morley Callaghan, Fitzgerald, and Miller. In this case, the association is extraordinary, which creates an enormous increase in value of what's already a very desirable rare book."

"So, just because someone owned or handled a particular book, that makes it more valuable?"

"You got it. And sometimes it creates havoc, and in one case, at least, resulted in a literary feud."

"What was that?"

"V.S. Naipaul was a friend and mentor to Paul Theroux. Theroux inscribed several of his books to Naipaul, 'with love.' One day, Theroux was browsing through a rare book catalogue and saw that Naipaul had put those books up for sale. That pretty much ended their friendship, but it made the books even more valuable."

"Could someone create an association where there wasn't one?"

"Swann, my friend, you've got the devious mind of a criminal.

Sure, it happens. But you've got to be pretty smart, and you've got to know an awful lot about the writer's life to get away with it. And you've got to have guts."

"Sean's that smart."

"Yeah. He's that smart."

"And he's got guts?"

"Yeah, he's got guts."

"And he's well versed in the lives of literary people?"

"Yeah."

"That might explain why he went for his master's, to learn even more."

"It might. Or it might be that he just loves literature."

"Yeah, and I like casing cars for a living. So let me get this straight. I go out and find a legitimate signed copy of, let's say, a relatively rare Henry Miller novel, or maybe something more contemporary like Salinger's *Catcher in the Rye,* and I pay X dollars for it. Then I create an association for it, preferably one no one can check—like Salinger's going to come out of hiding to refute it, even if he hears about it, right? And the sexier the association, the more it's worth. Then suddenly, that book becomes worth Triple-X. Am I right?"

"I hope you put that mind of yours to good rather than evil."

"So it could happen?"

"It could, and I'm sure it has."

"My faith in mankind is renewed."

"Pretty cynical, aren't you?"

"I come by it honestly. You deal with the kind of people I've dealt with for ten years, you know it's all about self-interest. What's in it for me? It's all about want, Klavan. People want what they can't have. They want what they can't afford. They want what someone else wants. They want what will make them feel special, important. You want. I want. They want. It's what makes the world go round and without it, I'm back working for the cable company."

"Huh?"

"Long, boring story. Anyway, I'm guessing if someone like Sean was dealing these association books, someone would know about it?"

"If someone's smart enough to figure that out and how to make it work, then they're smart enough to be careful about controlling the number of books they sell that way. And if they aren't, if they're greedy, then sure, I guess it would become known fairly soon."

"But you don't know anything about this going on?"

"I don't. But put yourself in Sean's position. If, in fact, he was doing this, would he deal with someone who knew him? Someone who might question how he was getting his hands on these books?"

"I guess not."

"Which is why if he were doing it, and I have no reason to believe he is, I'd be totally in the dark."

"And in the clear in terms of aiding and abetting him."

Klavan stopped, turned and faced me, his tone turning serious. "I'd have way too much to lose, Swann. I've got a good business here. I've got standing in the community. People trust me because I don't rip them off. Why would I risk all that just to make a few more bucks? You've seen my place. I've probably got millions of dollars' worth of books there. If I needed money, I'd just auction off parts of my collection. But I don't. And I wouldn't. And you know the reason I wouldn't?"

"Because you love books."

"That's right. Because I love books. I love having them around me. I love smelling them. I love touching them. I hold them up to my face and rub them against my cheek. I sleep with them. I eat with them. I even fuck with them, if I'm lucky enough to get someone to cooperate. On occasion, I even love reading them. Besides, I make more than enough dough selling other people's collections to afford me the luxury of having my own."

"Has Sean sold you any books lately?"

"What's your idea of recent?"

"Within the last year."

"Yeah."

"How many?"

"One."

"When?"

"Maybe six months ago."

"Did you check it out?"

He hesitated a moment. "I didn't have any reason to."

"Maybe you should."

He shook his head. "No need. He'd know he could never put anything over on me."

Suddenly, it seemed like a good idea to put some doubt in Klavan's head, to shake things up a little bit. "Sean is Sean, and I happen to know he's capable of doing some unexpected things."

"Yeah? Like what?"

"Like plagiarizing, even when he knew he'd get caught."

Klavan stopped dead in his tracks. His head dropped. He ran his hand down his face, squeezing his cheeks.

"You're thinking about it, aren't you?" I said.

"You've rocked my world, Swann. What's this plagiarizing thing you're talking about?"

"He handed in a paper that he plagiarized to the professor he stole it from."

"That's pretty much the definition of stupid, don't you think?"

"You know as well as I do that Sean isn't stupid. He did it for a reason. I just don't know what the reason is. Yet. What was the book?"

"Fitzgerald. *Tender Is the Night.* It was an association copy. He said it was owned by Sara and Gerald Murphy, who were the models for the main characters. I paid a lot of money for that book, Swann."

"If I were you, I'd check it out."

"I might just do that," he said, his deep voice dropping off, reflecting a bit of doubt that hadn't been there before. I didn't feel very good at that moment. He'd believed in this kid, he'd liked him, and I'd shaken that belief and now maybe he didn't like him quite as much.

"Is there any way of checking to see if Sean has been actively selling any books lately?"

"There is."

"Would you do it for me?"

"You've got me hooked, Swann. I'll see what postings I can come up with, and I'll make a few calls. If he has been out there hawking books lately, I'll know it."

"Thanks. And if you do come across any Loomis sightings, you'll let me know?"

"At this point, I don't see why not."

18
Jonesing for Trouble

I left Klavan at 57th and Madison and headed back downtown. I had some thinking to do, so I figured the walk would do me good. The weather had changed. It was a little cooler now, the air clearer, the humidity much lower. Even though it was mid-July, there was a hint of fall in the air, as if Mother Nature was giving us a warning that there was something a lot more ominous around the corner. "Winter is icumen in . . ." I muttered over and over again as I picked up the pace.

By the time I hit Gramercy Park, it was almost six. Workers were spilling out of their offices, heading home. But foot traffic on Irving Place is never heavy, which sometimes gives it the feel of a small town. To the discerning eye New York is, despite what outsiders think, really just a series of small neighborhoods, each one with a distinctive feel. Less than a half a mile away from my apartment in the East Village, I could be a continent away from home.

I stopped for a light at 19th Street and glanced diagonally across the street. The sidewalk was pretty much empty except for a guy wearing a tan trench coat and a fedora, also waiting for the light to change. Odd get-up, I thought. There wasn't a hint of rain in the air or in the forecast. And although it was appreciably cooler than it had been, the temperature was still hovering in the mid-seventies. But then, nothing in New York surprises me. That's why I like it. You never know what to expect. The misfits, oddballs, jerk-offs and loners eventually wind up here. I didn't have to. I was born here.

I looked away and crossed the street. When I looked back over to my left, I saw that Trench Coat Man had crossed, too, and was now matching me step for step. Was he following me? Was I imagining it?

When I reached the corner of 17th, I had the light to cross, but instead I stopped for a moment and looked back, as if I'd forgotten something, or wasn't sure where I was headed. Three beats. One. Two. Three. I bent to tie a shoe that was not untied. I sneaked a look over to the other side of the street. Trench Coat Man was there. Like me. Stopped. He caught me looking at him but instead of looking away, avoiding eye contact with me, he smiled broadly and tipped his hat. He was following me, and he didn't mind if I knew it. I made a left, east, toward Third Avenue. I took a few steps. I stopped. I looked back. I didn't see him.

I meandered home, crossing where the lights allowed. It was a game I played. Trying to make it to my destination without stopping. If I timed things just right, I could do it. If not, I'd find myself waiting at every corner. Every so often, I'd look around for Trench Coat Man, but he wasn't there.

I crossed 14th Street and headed down Second Avenue, past the movie theater at 12th, past St. Mark's Church on 11th, where I'd attended way too many poetry readings when I was younger. At St. Mark's Place, I crossed over to the east side of the avenue, and continued downtown. When I got to the corner of 7th, as I prepared to make the turn east, toward First Avenue, I glanced to my left and there, sitting at an outside table at a Mediter-ranean restaurant called Virage, was Trench Coat Man. He was reading a newspaper and a glass of wine sat on the table in front of him. I stopped. I stared at him. He looked up. We made eye contact. He didn't pull his eyes away. Neither did I. He smiled. I did not. He put down his newspaper and raised his glass, holding it out in front of him, as if he were toasting me. I considered just walking away, then thought better of it. I approached his table and stood over him. He had picked up the newspaper again and seemed to be reading it.

"Do I know you?" I said, deliberately leaning way too far into his space.

He cocked his head to one side. The hat threw an ominous shadow across his face, but still I could see he was about forty, clean-shaven, longish dark sideburns, with a nose too large for his face. He had a small scar running down his left temple to just below the eye. "I don't think we've been formally introduced, if that's what you mean."

"But you know who I am."

"Indeed, I do," he said with the hint of a strange accent I couldn't quite place. English? Southern? Australian? German?

"Why are you following me?"

He laughed. "Mr. Swann, I'm sitting here enjoying a glass of wine, reading my newspaper, minding my own business. I would have to be ambulatory if I were to be following you. And obviously, I'm not. It appears more likely that you're following me."

He unnerved me. *How did he know my name?* But I didn't want to let him know it. "Why would I do that?"

"You tell me. But you're here, so why don't you sit down and join me? Perhaps you'd like a glass of wine. Please. It's a beautiful evening and I could use the company."

"I appreciate the offer, but I'm a little busy at the moment."

He shook his head back and forth. "We're all much too busy these days. We need to take more time for ourselves. You know what they say about all work . . ."

It was driving me crazy, trying to place his accent, which seemed to change with every word he spoke. It was probably faked, and badly. Why?

"Speaking of which, why don't we save some of that precious

199

time by you telling me who you're working for?"

"I don't work, Mr. Swann. I just have fun."

"Lucky man."

"It's true. I am a lucky man. How about you?"

"Not really."

"That's too bad. Well, luck is like the weather, it can always change."

"Yeah. Hope springs eternal. What's with the trench coat and hat in the middle of summer?"

"Stylish, don't you think?" he said, running his hands down the lapels of the coat.

"I think you look like a joke."

"Oh, I'm anything but a joke, Mr. Swann. In fact, you ought to take me quite seriously. Nevertheless, if it bothers you . . ." He stood up, removed his trench coat, folded it carefully and put it on the chair next to him. He was wearing a light green summer sport jacket. He looked like a lime popsicle. When he leaned over, I thought I spotted a bulge at his side.

"Is that a gun in your pocket, or are you just glad to see me?" I cracked.

"Maybe both," he said, smiling.

"Should I be frightened?"

"We should all be frightened, Mr. Swann. It's a frightening world out there," he said as he waved his arms. "A prudent man is aware of the risks of just getting out of bed each morning, and so he minimizes those risks as best he can."

"I've made a career out of minimizing. By the way, I never did catch your name."

"You're absolutely correct. We haven't been formally introduced, have we?" He extended his hand. "John Paul Jones here."

I took his hand, which had a large, silver ring with a jagged design on it. I could only imagine what he used that for.

"Whether I'm pleased to meet you or not will have to be determined later, I suppose."

"Very prudent of you." He held my hand firmly, a little longer than was necessary. Message received.

He removed his hat, placed it carefully on top of the coat, and ran his hands slowly through his slick, black hair. "One should always avoid hat hair. I'm afraid it's one of the consequences of style. Ah, I see the waitress peeking out from inside. Are you sure you wouldn't like something to eat or drink? My treat."

"I'm good."

He took a sip of wine. "Not bad. I've had better, of course, but for an establishment such as this, in a neighborhood such as this, I'm rather pleasantly surprised. Have you, by chance, ever eaten here before, it being a neighborhood place and all?"

So he knew where I lived, and he wanted me to know that he knew. He probably knew a lot more about me and he wanted me to know that, too.

"Can't say as I have. But since we're probably both busy men with better things to do, why don't we skip all this melodramatic bullshit, and you tell me what you want from me?"

"What makes you think I have anything better to do? This is precisely what I want to do. In fact, I'm enjoying myself quite a bit."

"Wish I could say the same."

"I don't mind saying that I'm a bit disappointed. I'd hoped you, too, would enjoy our conversation."

"But we're not really having a conversation, are we?"

He extended his hands, palms up. "Of course, we are. Two men of the world, here on a lovely summer evening, beautiful women in all kinds of provocative attire passing by. What more could one ask for?"

"I suppose you've got something there."

"Are you sure you wouldn't like something to eat? Or drink?"

"Like I said before, I'll pass. I'm not a fan of breaking bread, or anything else, with someone I don't know."

"Oh, Mr. Swann, don't be silly. We do know each other. Or at least I know you."

"Jesus, this is getting old. Can't we just cut to the chase and you tell me what you have to tell me?"

"I see I'm making you cranky, and that's the last thing I wanted to do. Here's the chase. I'd like you to do me a personal favor. I'd like you to stop your search for Sean Loomis."

"Why would I want to do you a personal favor? I don't even know you."

"Because you do me a favor and perhaps one day, when you need one, you'll have a new friend who will be glad to do a personal favor for you."

"I don't need any new friends. Fact is, I don't have much use for the old ones . . . or they for me. Besides," I leaned forward, "I'll let you in on a little secret, I'm not looking for Sean."

"Of course you are."

"I'm looking for Marcy Phillips."

"Please, Mr. Swann, don't take me for a fool. If you do, you'll wind up regretting it." He paused a moment. I thought I saw him make a small move for the bulge on his side. "And you wouldn't want that, would you?"

"Is that a threat? Because if it is, it's kind of clichéd, don't you think?"

"A threat? Why on earth would I threaten you?"

"I can't imagine. Why do you want me to stop looking for Sean?"

"I'm not at liberty to discuss that."

"Well, like I said, it's not a problem, because I couldn't care less about Sean Loomis. It's his girlfriend I'm concerned with.

And frankly, Mr. Jones, I'm starting to worry about her well-being."

"You have nothing to worry about."

"Can't help it. It's my nature. I think we're finished here, so I'm going to let you enjoy your wine and the beautiful evening. I can't say it was a pleasure, Mr. Jones . . ."

He rose. "Oh, I was so hoping that one day you'd look back on our meeting as a fond memory. But if you don't stop looking for Sean, I can assure you that you haven't seen the last of me."

I shrugged, took a few steps, then turned back, leaned back into him and whispered, "By the way, I hope you've got a permit for that thing under your jacket."

I crossed the street and ducked into the doorway of a building, whipped out my cell phone and dialed 911.

When the operator answered, I said, "There's a very scary-looking guy sitting outside Virage restaurant, on Second Avenue and 7th Street, and he's got a pistol that he's waving around. He's wearing a light green jacket and has dark hair. He's put the gun back under his jacket, but I'm afraid he's going to pull it out and use it."

The operator said they'd send a squad car right over. I waited long enough to see it arrive and two burly cops, their hands on their sidearms, approach Mr. Jones, who looked pretty startled.

"Don't fuck with me, my friend," I muttered under my breath as I headed in the direction of home.

19
SOMEWHERE, OVER THE RAINBOW

I was hungry. I stopped at the local pasta joint on First Avenue and 5th Street, Three of Cups, a restaurant best known by people in the 'hood as the place where Quentin Tarantino accidentally punched out a waitress. I sat outside, over a plate of pasta, keeping half an eye out for the guy in the trench coat.

As I was getting ready to pay the check, my cell phone vibrated. It was Klavan.

"Swann," he said excitedly, "you son of a bitch, you set the seeds of doubt growing in my mind, so I made some calls and went on the Internet. I've got some info for you, pal."

"Shoot."

"I hate to be played for a sucker, Swann, so I needed to find out as soon as possible. You were right. The book he sold me, which, fortunately, I haven't resold yet, is definitely suspect. I'll know for sure when I give it a closer look and then bring it to a few other experts. As for other activity, right again. I checked my sources, and there have been a bunch of books being offered for sale with associations that raise my antenna. Including that big one I mentioned. Guess where they're coming from?"

"Rabinowitz."

"Bingo! In the past three months Teddy's been hawking copies of association books by Malamud, Miller, Hemingway, Fitzgerald and Faulkner. He might have been fooled the same way I might have been . . ."

"Or he might be in on it."

"My gut tells me no. Like me, he's got too much to lose, and he's much too successful to get involved in something so sleazy and so potentially ruinous. More likely, he's getting them from someone he trusts . . ."

"Like Sean Loomis."

"Like Sean Loomis."

"Where are the books showing up?"

"A dealer in London."

"How recently?"

"Couple of weeks ago. I know the dealer. I can give you his contact info."

"If I'm going to get good information, I have to do it face to face."

"You'd go over there?"

"Yeah."

"Name's Robert Prescott. His shop's The Book Shelf, on Charing Cross Road. He caters to a very hoity-toity crowd. I'll alert him you're showing up."

"Don't."

"Why not?"

"The element of surprise works wonders. Someone's been following me, which means there's a leak somewhere. The fewer people who know what I'm doing and when I'm doing it, the better."

"Who's following you?"

"Some guy in a trench coat. Very nineteen-fifties. We had a little tête à tête."

"You're kidding. Did you find out who he's working for?"

"No. But I'll find out. Eventually. One thing I do know is that there's money involved, probably big money. When there's money, there's always an element of danger. If Marcy Phillips is still involved with Sean, if she's traveling with him, I don't want to risk her getting hurt. Unless, of course, she's in on it with him."

"I assume you know what the hell you're doing. But if you're going there soon, booking a flight is going to be expensive."

"I don't have to worry about that. It's not coming out of my pocket."

"There's one other thing I should tell you."

"What's that?"

"The book I mentioned. It's one I never even knew existed. It's a pristine copy of Hemingway's *The Sun Also Rises,* with an inscription to F. Scott Fitzgerald. From word on the street, the inscription is very personal."

"What's that supposed to mean?"

"I don't know details, but from what I hear it may set the literary world on end. Maybe it's hype. Maybe not."

"How much would something like that be worth?"

"If it's really that earth-shattering, I'm guessing to the right private collector, we're talking well into the high six figures. When word hits the street, there'll be plenty of people interested. I wouldn't go so far as to call it the Holy Grail of American book collecting, but it's damn close."

"Think it's for real?"

"No fuckin' idea. But I'll tell you this, if I were bidding on it, and I'm not, I'd be extremely careful with my due diligence. If it is real, it could break someone's bank."

I wrote down the information, promised Klavan I'd keep him in the loop, then called the airline and booked a flight for the next evening.

It pained me, but I figured I ought to check in with Phillips before I left, so I gave him a call.

"Have you found Marcy yet?" he asked gruffly.

"No."

"That's not what I wanted to hear."

"I know what you wanted to hear, but you didn't hire me to blow smoke up your ass. I'm sure you've got plenty of people who work for you who'll gladly take care of that job."

"I don't like your attitude, Swann."

"I don't give a shit what you do or don't like about me. This is professional, not personal. If you don't like the way I'm doing my job, then fire my ass. I'll keep what you've paid me so far, and we'll both walk away happy."

"You don't like me, do you?"

"I don't. But that's okay. I hate everybody because that way I don't have to waste time and energy hating myself."

"I paid for service and I expect to get it. Why are you calling me?"

"To tell you I've booked a flight to London for tomorrow. I have a feeling Marcy and Sean might be there."

"What makes you think that?"

"I don't discuss process with clients."

"What the hell is that supposed to mean?"

"You hire me, I do what I do."

"In case you've forgotten, you're my employee."

"I pride myself on my memory. By the way, I understand you're a book collector."

"What does that have to do with anything?"

"You sound a bit defensive. Got something to hide?"

"What I do with my spare time, Swann, is my business and my business alone."

"Sean deals in rare books. You never told me that. It makes me think it's something you didn't want me to know. And for the life of me, I can't figure out why that is. But it leads me to believe there are other things you're keeping from me."

"You know everything you have to know."

"You've dealt with Sean?"

"That's irrelevant."

"I guess I have my answer. What I can't figure out is why you're holding back."

"I told you, you have all the relevant information. My business is my business, and it has nothing to do with Marcy's disappearance." There was a moment of silence. "All right. If you have to go to London, then go. But this isn't a paid vacation. I trust you'll be back in the States by Wednesday."

"I'll be back when I'm back." I wanted to ask him about his transgression with the Bar, but I decided I'd had enough conflict for one day. I'd hold that back for another time, a time when I needed to shake things up again.

★ ★ ★ ★ ★

PART 5
LONDON, ENGLAND

★ ★ ★ ★ ★

"The most difficult way is in the long run, the easiest."
—Henry Miller

20
LONDON BRIDGE IS FALLING DOWN

I'd been to London once before, in the early eighties, well after the British Rock invasion hit our shores, a full fifteen years after the breakup of the Beatles. The country was in the midst of the "troubles" between Britain and the IRA. I arrived only a few months after the bombing at Harrods. The economy sucked, and the mood was serious, far from the swinging London Petula Clark sang about, and yet I was there to have some fun and to walk in the steps of some of the great writers I admired. I was in my late twenties, still drifting, looking for something a little more meaningful to do with my life than attending rock concerts and chasing women who were much faster on their feet than I was. It was the trip I should have taken after leaving college. Rather than head to Paris, where most of the American expatriate writers went to find themselves after World War I, I chose what I thought of as the easier path: a country where we spoke pretty much the same language.

The fact that England was a country in turmoil suited me fine. So was I. It was a place with a solid history it wasn't afraid to flaunt. Unlike New York, physical change came more slowly. I didn't have the sense that if I went to sleep and woke up the next day, things would be out of place. They would be right where I left them. This was the way I liked it—neat, sensible, rational. I needed a sense of permanence, a sense that there were answers to questions, not questions leading to other questions. At the time, I believed in God, a god, some god, any god, because I believed the world was a rational place and that there was some kind of divine plan. It's what probably propelled me into detective work, because as someone once pointed out, a detective has to believe in a divine being if he's going to believe in solutions. At the time, that made sense. It was only later that I found that coherence is a construct we lay on top of the incoherent things that occur in order to make life tolerable.

I roamed the streets of London, soaking up the atmosphere. I frequented pubs, where I listened to folks talk about football—soccer to me—and politics, listening to people badmouth Margaret Thatcher, whose approval rating had just shot up to a whopping thirty-two percent.

But the world had changed in the two decades since I'd been in London. It was a change I recognized the moment I arrived at Heathrow, stumbled out of the terminal, making my way through customs with little trouble since I was traveling light, and hopped a cab to London. It was a change brought on by the explosion in communications. Isolation was now impossible. We lived in a world community, connected by the barely visible chips and wireless gadgets. Instead of maintaining our differences, we were becoming the same. Communication was bringing us together, erasing some of our differences. But it was also tearing us apart. Maybe the less we know about others, the better off we are.

The sky was slate gray, much the way I'd left it twenty years earlier, and it appeared as if it had rained less than an hour earlier, as the streets were still slightly damp. My first stop was what they liked to refer to as a boutique hotel not far from The Book Shelf, recommended to me by Klavan. "It ain't the Plaza," he explained, "but they change the sheets, the towels are clean and it's quiet enough to get a good night's sleep."

I checked in, dropped my bag in the room, which though immaculate was only a little larger than a prison cell, then headed over to Charing Cross Road, which many Americans knew as the result of correspondence between the American author, Helene Hanff, and the staff of Marks & Co., subsequently written as a book and then made into a movie with Anne Bancroft and Anthony Hopkins.

I found the small shop not far from Foyles, Borders and Blackwell's, the much larger, more established bookstores in the area. Outside, there was a table filled with used books. Inside, the shop was cramped and poorly lit, books everywhere, on shelves and on tables. A dank, mildewy scent permeated the store, which was empty, except for a small, thin, silver-haired fellow who was putting books on a shelf. He had on wire-rimmed glasses and was wearing a striped shirt, bowtie, and suspenders holding up a pair of gray slacks that seemed at least two sizes too large for him. When he saw me enter, he gave me a half smile but continued what he was doing. Not wanting to come on too strong, I moved through the shop slowly, picking up the occasional book, hoping he'd approach me before I had to approach him. When he finished what he was doing, he retreated behind the counter, where he picked up a newspaper and began reading.

I was in no hurry. I was enjoying myself, thumbing through worn editions of Dickens, Dafoe, Austen and T. S. Eliot. Several minutes passed before he finally looked up, lowered the paper, pushed his eyeglasses down the bridge of his nose, and said, "May I help you?"

"Just browsing," I said. "You've got a very interesting shop here."

"American," he replied, not in an accusing tone, but rather victoriously as if he'd just picked up some deep, dark secret I was trying to hide.

"That's right," I said. "You've got a sharp ear."

"It's more the way you're dressed," he said, probably refer-

ring to the Gap jeans, T-shirt and dark blue Banana Republic
V-neck sweater I was wearing. Of course, they were all made
elsewhere, China, Vietnam, the Philippines, but that probably
made them even more American.

"Compliments of the Gap and Banana Republic," I said,
"though I believe you have those stores here, as well."

He came out from behind the counter. "Are you here on
holiday or for business, sir, if you don't mind my asking?"

"A little of both," I said as I moved closer to him. I've always
enjoyed the British reticence, a nice contrast to the American
brashness, a trait that I humbly acknowledge in myself. And yet,
when necessary, I can behave as reticently as the next guy. "But
wherever I go, I can't help stopping in at local bookstores. I'm a
bit of a bibliophile."

"You don't look like the usual customer I have in here, if you
don't mind my saying."

"I'd like to take that as a compliment, though I'm not sure
that's the way it's meant."

"Didn't mean to offend you. Not at all. I just meant that my
usual customer is a bit older, a bit more, well, established."

"Better dressed?" I said with a smile.

"Oh, no, I didn't mean that a'tall."

"I'm used to it. I'm kind of an amateur collector, if there is
such a thing, and I was wondering if you had any American
signed first editions. Hemingway, Fitzgerald or maybe a bit
more contemporary, like Malamud or Salinger. I'm especially
interested in signed copies."

"A collector, are you?" he said, eyeing me suspiciously.

"Yes. My name's Henry Swann," I said, extending my hand,
"and you wouldn't happen to be Robert Prescott, would you?"

"Indeed, I would," he said, extending his hand to meet mine.
"And how would you happen to know who I am?"

"I believe we have a friend in common, or perhaps even two."

"And who would they be, may I ask?"

"Ross Klavan, for one."

"Yes. I have had the pleasure to make Mr. Klavan's acquaintance."

"Sean Loomis would be the other."

His eyes dropped. He knew him. But he wasn't going to admit it.

"You're acquainted with him, too, aren't you?"

"A lot of people come in and out of my shop," he said, moving back behind the counter and busying himself with some paperwork that had lain dormant before I'd mentioned Loomis. "I suppose he might have been one of them. I might know him by sight."

"It's not important, really. I just thought you might know him. What about those books? Would you happen to have any to show me?"

"I did have both a Dos Passos and a Salinger pass through here recently, but I'm afraid you're a bit too late. I sold both of them a few days ago."

"That's too bad, though it doesn't surprise me. My timing's been pretty bad lately. They wouldn't have happened to have been association copies, would they? I'm especially interested in those."

He looked up and stared at me over his glasses, obviously deciding just how much he should tell me. "They would."

"You seem to be playing your cards very close to your vest, Mr. Prescott. Any particular reason?"

"I don't know what in the world you mean by that."

"I think you do. In fact, I think you know exactly who Sean Loomis is, and I think Sean's the one who provided you with those books."

The sweet, kindly bookseller suddenly turned stern. "My customers demand discretion, Mr. Swann. I'm sure you can understand that."

"I can. Especially if some of those books might not be all they're cracked up to be."

His head dropped. "I don't know what in the world you're talking about."

"Not that you're to blame. Sean is very good at what he does. I'm sure he sold you a cock-and-bull story before he laid those books on you. Of course, you'll be the one holding the bag when the books turn out to be frauds. I might even be able to help you if you'd just tell me everything you know."

"Who are you?"

"I'm just who I said I was. Henry Swann."

"But who are you really and why are you here?"

"I'm here to find Sean Loomis, not to get you or anyone else in trouble. Truth is, I'm not even here to get Sean in trouble. I just want to find the young woman I believe is traveling with him."

"Well, Mr. Swann," he said, fiddling with a pencil, "I wasn't lying when I said I didn't know Sean Loomis, because, in fact, I don't. All our business was accomplished over the phone. He sent the books over with a young woman, and it was she to whom I gave the money."

"Did she give you a name?"

"I believe it was Michelle."

Michelle. I rolled the name over in my mind. Something clicked. Sandy Brennan told me Sean's girlfriend was named Shelly, short for Michelle. I pulled Marcy's photo from my pocket.

"Is this her?"

He took it from me, pulled his eyeglasses up, and stared at it closely. "She was dressed far more conservatively, but I believe there is a strong resemblance."

"Her name's Marcy Phillips. Mean anything to you?"

"No."

"Maybe you know her father, Carlton Phillips."

His eyes opened wide, his forehead wrinkled. "Why should I?"

"Because her father is a book collector. It's a small community, and I suspect over the years you've probably done business with him."

"I've done business with a lot of people, Mr. Swann, and not all of them use their real names, and some of them use agents to do their buying."

"But not Carlton Phillips. He's a hands-on kind of guy. The way I see it, it's very possible you were really buying the books from him."

"I suppose anything is possible."

"How long ago was the sale made?"

"Earlier this week."

"I need to find this woman, Mr. Prescott. Anything you can do to help me would be much appreciated. I believe her father would be even more appreciative, and I think he might be able to show it in ways I couldn't possibly imagine."

"I really don't know anything," he said as he pulled over a stool and sat.

"I think you do, Mr. Prescott. Tell me how Sean Loomis contacted you and what you know about him."

He hesitated a moment, which meant he was editing his story. That's okay. I can read between the lines as well as anyone. "A month or two ago, I received a call from Teddy Rabinowitz. He's a rare book dealer . . ."

"I know who he is."

"Of course you do. Well, Teddy, whom I've dealt with countless times over the years, said that a young man, a protégé of his, would be in London, and he had some very interesting books of noted American authors he'd like to deal. You would think the market for these authors would be larger in America, but that's not necessarily the case. Many European collectors value those books quite highly, especially those of the American expatriates. Often, if sold privately, those books can garner higher amounts over here. So it wasn't odd that he was coming over here to deal with someone like me. Teddy knew I had several important contacts who might pay top dollar for the right books."

"But you never met him?"

"We only spoke on the phone. He said he was in London, but that he'd sustained an injury. I believe he said he'd slipped and twisted his knee or his ankle and wasn't able to leave his hotel. He said his assistant would be glad to bring the books over for me to examine, along with their provenance. He told me a little about the books, and he even gave me a short description of their associations, but he said that he would write them out and that his assistant would deliver that along with the books."

"And she did?"

"Yes. They were lovely, actually. Both the books and the association descriptions. They were precise and very well written and, as a result, very convincing. I had no doubt they were true. The books themselves were excellent editions, with the dust jackets virtually intact."

"Any chance they were forgeries?"

"I've been in this business a long time, Mr. Swann. I'm adept at separating the wheat from the chaff. I don't mind saying that I can spot a forgery a mile off. There are too many things that must align. I've seen my share of fakes in my lifetime, some of them clumsy and some of them quite artful, which is precisely why I know these were the real thing."

"But there's no way you could possibly know if the associations were real."

"Well, that is certainly a little more difficult, but as they say, if it looks like a mallard and it quacks like a mallard, then in all likelihood it is, indeed, a mallard. The associations Mr. Loomis provided were impeccable. And if they aren't true, then my hat is off to him, because he is perhaps as much of a creative, imaginative artist as the writers who wrote the books he was selling."

"Do you remember anything he might have said that would lead me to where they were staying?"

"Let me think." He ran his hand through his hair. He was buying time, wondering if he should help me, wondering what was in it for him. I needed to get him on my side.

"It would be in your best interest to help me, Mr. Prescott. That's the only way you're going to know if you sold the real things. If they're fake, then it's your reputation that's going down the tubes. If you help me and I find out the truth, you'll come out smelling like a rose, if you're the one who blows the whistle on the whole operation."

His eyes popped open. He'd seen the light. I'd converted him. "Well, he did say that he also hoped to do some sightseeing while he was here, and I believe he mentioned that the Bloomsbury writers were some of his favorites. In fact, as I recall, he did say that's why he was staying in the Bloomsbury Square area."

"That covers a lot of territory."

"I'm afraid it does. But hold on a minute, I recall he asked me how his representative would get from Russell Square to this address, so I presume he was staying in that neighborhood, which would be adjacent to Bloomsbury Square."

"That pins it down a little. You wouldn't happen to have a London guidebook here that includes a list of hotels?"

"I would," he said, gesturing toward the end of the counter. He reached over and plucked a small book from its stand. "This should provide the sort of information you're looking for."

"Thanks," I said, pulling out my wallet. "I'm afraid I haven't had time to convert my money, but I think this should take care of it." I peeled off a twenty and handed it to him.

"Indeed. If you give me a moment, I'll figure out your proper change."

"No need," I said. "Before I leave, let me ask you: what kind of impression did the girl make on you?"

He made a face. "I'm afraid we didn't converse very much. She gave me the package, I opened it, gave it a look, said I'd get back to her boss as soon as I had time to examine the merchandise more closely, then she left."

"How were you supposed to get back to Loomis?"

"He was going to call me the next day."

"Did he?"

"Of course."

"And . . . ?"

"I told him I was very pleased with the books and their provenance, and that I would be glad to sell them on consignment. He said no, he wasn't going to be in London long enough, and that if I wanted them I'd have to buy them from him, for cash, and then resell them. I knew I couldn't manage that, and so I told him I was afraid that I would have to decline. He then lowered his price for one of the volumes, John Steinbeck's *The Grapes of Wrath*, and we came to an understanding on that one."

"I hope it's legit."

"I fervently believe it is. And so does the gentleman I sold it to."

"I guess so long as that's what he thinks, there is, as we say in America, 'no harm, no foul.' "

Frankly, I wasn't much worried about some wealthy collector getting ripped off. After all, if he thought he had the real thing, what difference did it make if he didn't? And without getting all existential, if the association was faked, and if it was accepted as truth, then it would be true, wouldn't it? And so, ultimately, what harm was there? Who was hurt? Sure, there was a crime, fraud, but if someone believes a lie to be true and no one is injured, what's the real harm of that lie? The words in the book remain the same. The meaning of those words remain the same. The ideas communicated by the book remain the same. The only problem I foresaw was that in my experience, when there's money involved, there's also a chance of violence. So I knew I had to step carefully, because if Loomis was pulling off a scam and he knew someone was on to him, that might result in trouble. Now, I was right in the middle of it.

I took the guidebook and shook Prescott's hand. "Thank you, Mr. Prescott, and perhaps the next time we meet I'll be able to spend a little more time enjoying the wonderful books you've got here in your shop."

"I hope so, Mr. Swann, and I wish you good fortune in finding Ms. Phillips. And please give my regards to her father and tell him I hope to be doing business again with him at some time in the future, because I do have some lovely works by Kingsley Amis."

"I will," I said, as for the first time it dawned on me that Carlton Phillips's name was cropping up a little too often in this investigation. It made me begin to wonder just what role he played in all this, other than hiring me to find his daughter.

21
EVIDENTLY, THE SUN DOES SET ON THE BRITISH EMPIRE

I found a nearby pub, ordered some food, and pored over the guidebook I'd purchased from Prescott. I jotted down a few hotels in the Bloomsbury area, then called each of them to see if Loomis had checked in. None of them had a guest by that name, but when I described Sean and Marcy, I finally hit pay dirt at the Hotel Russell. They'd registered as Mr. and Mrs. Cliff Irving. Very funny. They hadn't checked out yet. I rang their room. No answer.

I wanted to get right over there, but jet lag got the best of me, so I headed back to my hotel to take a nap. I hadn't slept in more than twenty-four hours, and not only did I have a pounding headache, but my mind was too foggy to concentrate.

Before I got to the elevator, the desk clerk called me over. "Excuse me, Mr. Swann. Someone has left this envelope for you."

I took the envelope, went upstairs, kicked my shoes off, threw myself down on the bed and opened the envelope. Inside, there was a piece of paper folded over three times. Printed in large, block letters across the front of the hotel stationery was the message, *If you don't want trouble, stop looking for Sean Loomis.*

Threats piss me off. They get in the way of what I'm trying to do. They also accomplish what they're meant to: they frighten me. My first response is always flight rather than fight. But threats also tell me that I'm on the right track. And what usually supersedes flight is anger, the problem I have with authority, with people telling me what to do.

The only one who knew where I was staying was Klavan, but why would he send the note? He was the one who'd led me in this direction. Preston? I hadn't told him where I was staying. Phillips? The only way he could know was because he was paying the bills and could check on where I was using the company credit card. But why would he want to keep me from finding his daughter? The obvious person was Loomis himself, but my gut told me no. Why would he take the chance of appearing at my hotel to deliver the note? And how did he know I was looking for him? How did he even know I was in London?

But if it wasn't any of them, who could it be? Possibly the mysterious Mr. Jones? Where did he fit in the case? Who'd hired him? Or was he working on his own? Why was I being warned off the case? Because I might blow the lid off a possible book scam? Because finding Marcy might lead to some other secrets being uncovered?

I tried to sleep, but couldn't, despite the fact that my body felt so heavy I could hardly lift myself from the bed. My mind was racing, trying to put together the pieces of this puzzle. My job was to find Marcy Phillips. Marcy was connected to Sean Loomis. Loomis was connected to some kind of rare book scam. I didn't care about that. I only needed to find Loomis, which would, in turn, lead me to Marcy. But Loomis wasn't easy to find, because he might be deeply involved in some kind of illegal operation. Was he working alone? I doubted it.

I made a mental list of the major cast of characters: Carlton Phillips, Marcy Phillips, Sean Loomis, Richard Dubin, Dana Simmons, Ross Klavan, Teddy Rabinowitz, Robert Prescott, Mr. Jones. How did they fit together? What or who did they have in common? What did any or all of them have to hide?

I gave up on the idea of sleep. I hopped in the shower, then headed down to the hotel restaurant, where I downed two cups of coffee that weren't strong enough. Before I headed back out to the Hotel Russell, I approached the desk clerk.

"I was wondering if you could tell me who left that note you gave me a little earlier."

"I'm sorry, sir, but I don't know. It was in your mail slot when I arrived on duty."

"Is the person who was on duty when it was delivered around?"

"I'm afraid not, sir. She's gone home for the day."

"Could you tell me how I could get in touch with her?"

He shook his head. "I'm sorry, I can't do that, sir. Perhaps if you'd like to speak to the manager. I believe he's at lunch now, but he should return within the hour."

"Maybe later," I said, hoping I wouldn't need to know after my trip to the Hotel Russell.

"Is there anything else I might do for you, sir?"

"Not that I can think of," I said.

"Well then, have a good day, sir."

"I hope so," I said, "but somehow I don't think that's going to happen."

The Hotel Russell dominated the east side of Russell Square, across from the Russell Square Gardens, not far from the Russell Square Tube Station on the Piccadilly line. It was an enormous structure, large enough to hold, according to my guidebook, 373 rooms, which had been "furnished to a high standard with your comfort a priority." The hotel included the Tempus Bar and the Fitzroy Doll's restaurant and was, again according to the guidebook, "the perfect location for your conference, meeting or event."

I approached the front desk and, with a straight face, asked for Cliff Irving's room number.

"I'm afraid we can't give out that information, sir," the desk clerk replied. "But if you'd like, I would be happy to ring up his room and see if he's in."

"That would be very kind of you," I said. I watched as he punched up four keys: 4913. After several seconds, he said, "I'm afraid there's no answer."

"That's strange. I was supposed to meet him here. Perhaps he's waiting for me at the bar or in the restaurant."

The desk clerk shrugged and went back to what he was doing. I figured the extension number was correlated to the room. I headed toward the bank of elevators. There was a middle-aged, well-dressed couple waiting to go up.

"Excuse me, but I wonder if you might be able to help me."

The man turned to me and smiled. "American."

"You, too?"

"You betcha."

"Minnesota?"

"Close enough, my friend. Fargo, North Dakota. Where do you hail from?"

New York sometimes puts people off, so I opted for the Midwest. "Chicago, that somber city . . ."

"Geez, I thought it was the Windy City."

"That, too. I was just quoting what someone else called it."

"I see." He didn't, of course, but that was okay. "The wife, Sarah, and I have been there several times. So, what can we do you for?"

"Well, I'm staying here too and, I'm embarrassed to say, I've forgotten the phone extension to my room and I've got a buddy over there." I pointed to some stranger seated in one of the plush chairs. "We're just running out, and I wanted to give him my number, so he doesn't have to bother with the operator. I'm a little embarrassed to ask the desk clerk. You know how it is. They think all us Americans are idiots anyway. I know the extension is a form of our room number, but I just wanted to make sure."

"It's the room number with a four in front of it," said Sarah, who, tugging on her husband's sleeve, seemed to be in a hurry.

"Just what I thought. Thanks . . . and I hope you enjoy your stay in London."

"So far, so good," he said as his wife pulled him into the arriving elevator.

I knocked on Room 913. No answer. I knocked again. Still nothing. I looked around. Down the hall, there was a house-cleaning cart. I walked toward it. The room door was open and inside a dark-skinned, elderly woman was making the bed. I rapped on the door a couple times. She looked up. I walked in.

"I'm sorry to bother you, but my wife's waiting downstairs. She forgot her sweater, and she's got the room card key. I'd hate to go all the way down there, do you think you could open the door for me, so I can just pop in and grab it? It'd just take a second and I'd be awfully grateful," I said, pulling out my wallet. "It would be a real pain going all the way downstairs."

"All right," she said as she put her hand in her pocket, pulling out a card. "What room is it?"

"Nine thirteen. And here's something for your trouble." I pulled out a twenty and handed it to her. That made me feel good. I figured she could use it. Maybe it would make Phillips feel good, too, since it was his twenty, though I doubted it.

The room was immaculate. There were absolutely no outward signs that anyone was staying there. I checked the closet. Nothing. Not a single item of clothing. The dresser. Nothing. The beds were made. There didn't seem to be anything in the bathroom that the hotel hadn't put there. On top of the desk was a writing pad and a copy of *TimeOut London*, probably provided by the hotel. I was about to give up when I noticed there was something under *TimeOut*. It was a copy of the current *Esquire* magazine, something I was sure the hotel didn't provide. It was a subscription issue, which would have given me an address where Loomis was getting his mail, except that he'd torn off the address label, leaving only bits of adhesive. I sat down on the edge of the bed and thumbed through it. Page 140 had been torn out.

I tucked the magazine in my back pocket, went back downstairs and approached the desk clerk.

"Excuse me, I was supposed to meet my friends, the Irvings, but there doesn't seem to be any answer when I knocked on their door, and I was wondering if perhaps they'd checked out."

"I'll see if that's the case, sir," he said as he punched some keys on his computer. "No, they haven't."

"That's strange. Maybe they took a walk. I'll come back in a bit and see if they've returned."

"Would you like to leave a message, sir?"

"That won't be necessary."

I went to the gift shop and picked up a copy of *Esquire* and turned to page 140, where I found the missing page.

How to Vanish . . . Forever
Need to completely erase yourself? Here's how. We're not asking why.

The one-page article offered three stages of disappearing, which included misinformation, disinformation and reformation. There was nothing in there that I didn't know—after all, it was my business to find people who were trying to disappear—but it certainly would be a big help to anyone who wasn't familiar with the strategy. It appeared as if Sean, and with him, Marcy, was getting ready to go underground. Sean had probably checked in on a credit card in the name of Cliff Irving, so skipping out on his bill wouldn't be very difficult. I guessed he'd booked the room for a week, and this was probably midway through his stay. If I was going to find Marcy, I didn't have much time. If I were lucky, I could follow the Cliff Irving money trail unless, of course, he also had a credit card with another name.

First, I'd try the various airlines, to see if Cliff Irving had booked any flights. If that didn't work, I was going to try the rent-a-car places and railroads. I didn't have to. Mr. and Mrs. Cliff Irving had booked a flight for New York City the day before. That meant they were already back in New York. There was no reason to remain in London, so I could keep my flight home for later that day.

I headed back to my hotel where there was another note waiting for me, this one written in large, bold, red letters.

Swann, this is your final warning. Forget about Sean Loo-mis. And if you don't, you'll have to pay the consequences.

A Friend

I folded it up and tucked it in my pocket. I asked the desk clerk who'd left it for me. He said it was given him by a "poorly dressed, middle-aged gentleman" who said he'd been asked by someone named Vrain Lucas to leave the note for me. Had the desk clerk ever seen him before? No. Could he describe him a little better? Afraid not.

Vrain Lucas? Who the hell was he? I wasn't about to waste time trying to find out who it was. Frankly, I didn't give a shit. I thought it was an idle threat, simply meant to throw me off my game. I didn't think I was involved with a violent group. What were they going to do, throw a book at me?

When I got back to my room, I found it had been tossed, and not very gently. The few possessions that were in my backpack were scattered on the floor. My bed was pulled apart. All the drawers were open. There was nothing to find, so I knew the mess was nothing more than an exclamation point on the note left for me.

At the airport, check-in went smoothly and, since I was almost two hours early, I found a comfortable chair in an almost empty section of the airport waiting area, well away from my boarding gate. I pulled out a copy of a Robert Parker Spenser novel I'd picked up at the airport gift shop, and started to read.

I was well into my book when I sensed someone hovering over me. I looked up to see a man in a dark green trench coat standing maybe five feet in front of me, his hands in his pockets, staring at me. He was in his mid-forties, had dark, close-cropped hair and a mustache.

"Can I help you?" I asked.

He didn't say anything, but continued staring at me.

"Do I know you?" I asked.

No answer.

"Hey, pal, something I can do for you?" I pressed, raising my voice slightly to show I meant business.

He said nothing, but moved toward me. My eyes followed him as he sat down beside me, leaving only inches between his arm and mine, close enough so I could smell his cheap, lemon-scented after-shave. He looked straight ahead. He removed his hands from his pockets. They were enormous. On his left hand, which was closest to me, he wore two large silver rings, one on the middle finger and the other on his second finger.

"Look, pal, it's a big airport. There are plenty of seats around," I said, waving my arm. "You wanna give me some space here."

He turned his head, looked at me, and a half smile appeared on his face. He was freaking me out, but I didn't want to give him the advantage by showing fear.

"Do I know you?" I repeated.

He shook his head slightly, from side to side. "I don't believe so, Mr. Swann," he pronounced in a clipped, British accent.

"But you obviously know who I am."

"Yes." He paused a moment. "I do."

"How do you know that?"

"I don't think that's particularly relevant."

"It's sure as hell relevant to me. You're in my space, pal, and I don't appreciate that," I said, straightening my back, tensing my body, to show him I meant business, which, of course, was the last thing on my mind. But to show weakness would be a mistake. I have always adhered to Will Rogers's admonition that "Being a hero is about the shortest-lived profession on earth." There's no physical confrontation I won't run away from. But sometimes, by showing you're not averse to violence if you're pushed far enough, you manage to avoid it. Of course, it's only a theory and I can't say that it always works. But it's always worth a try.

I made a half turn in his direction and jutted my chin forward. "So, either you move or I move."

"Suit yourself. But frankly, Mr. Swann, I don't give a damn what you think," he said in a voice so gentle you would think he was whispering sweet nothings in my ear, which made the whole situation a little more freaky, not to mention scary. Still, I wasn't quite ready to back down.

"You got a name?" I asked.

"I do."

"Mind telling me what it is?"

"Mr. Smith."

"Yeah. Sure. Well, Mr. Smith, obviously you think you have some business with me, so we might as well get it out in the open, because I've got a plane to catch."

"If"—he paused again—"you're lucky."

"I don't have to be lucky to catch that flight, my friend. As a matter of fact, I think I'll just take a little walk over to the gate right now and maybe, on the way, I'll bump into airport security and suggest they check out the annoying fellow in the green trench coat."

"Well, you could do that, I suppose, but I don't really think that would do you much good."

"Really?"

"Yes. Really."

"Why's that?"

"Well, for one thing, I believe you want to make your flight, and that would slow things down considerably since inevitably you would be held to explain just why you've asked them to detain me for no other reason than I sat down next to you and I was, in your word, 'annoying.' And for another, I don't believe it would be in your best interests."

"What do you know about my best interests?"

He turned and looked straight ahead. He put his hands back into his coat pocket. I tensed up.

"Take a deep breath and relax," he said. "This is not the movies, nor is it one of your dime store detective novels, Mr. Swann. We don't need to use violence anymore. It's ultimately ineffective unless we're willing to go all the way." He smiled. "At this point, we're not. In fact, there are far more effective ways to get one's point across."

"What ways might that be?"

"You're a very inquisitive man, Mr. Swann. Perhaps you're writing a book?" He emphasized the word book. I got his point. I knew why he was sitting next to me. I just didn't know who sent him.

"What do you want from me?"

He chuckled. "Personally, Mr. Swann, I could not care less about you, but I have friends who feel that you've, shall we say, overstepped certain boundaries."

"I never did learn how to color within the lines."

" 'Tis a pity."

"It's a trait that's paid off for me on occasion."

"Perhaps this is one of those times. Perhaps not. Which brings me to my point. I've been authorized to engage your services."

"I'm all ears."

"It would necessitate dropping what you're working on now."

"I've been a multi-tasker all my life, so I could actually work on two things at once. And once I've started something, I'm not the type to give up on it. Besides, I think I'm almost finished with the case I'm working on now."

"My mistake. I thought you were finished."

"That is your mistake."

"Then you don't wish to hear how much remuneration is involved?"

I shook my head. "Truth is, it might tempt me to the point where I'd go against everything that's dear to me. As Oscar Wilde said, 'I can resist everything except temptation.' "

"Wilde got himself in a lot of trouble, Mr. Swann, and that could happen to you, too. If you're not careful."

"Oh, I'm careful. Very careful. Now, if there's nothing else, I have a plane to catch. But before I leave, perhaps you'd like to tell me who hired you to make what I assume is a very generous offer?"

"I'm afraid I'm not at liberty to divulge that."

"Oh, come on. It's obviously someone who has something to lose, a lot to lose, from my investigation. It wouldn't be Sean Loomis, would it?"

He looked away from me.

"I suppose I'd get the same reaction no matter what names I threw at you, so I'm just going to save us both a lot of time and get on my plane back to New York. And you might pass along a message to whoever hired you, and that is, as much of a money-grubbing low-life as people might think I am, or I think I am, there is a level at which I'm uncomfortable about sinking any lower. Which, I have to admit, sometimes surprises me."

"You might consider that you're making a grave mistake, Mr. Swann. There will, I assure you, be consequences." He threw his head back and to the left. I looked over and saw a man dressed in a black leather jacket and jeans, his hands folded across his chest, leaning against the wall. He wore a silver earring in one ear, his dark hair was slicked back and he was wearing aviator sunglasses. He was looking straight at us. He smiled at me. There was something vaguely familiar about him, but I couldn't quite figure out what it was.

"I'd be interested in knowing what those consequences are, but not right now," I said. "And by the way, you see that guy over there in the black leather jacket? He wouldn't happen to be with you, would he?"

Mr. Smith didn't bother to look up. "What would make you think that, Mr. Swann?"

"Because he keeps staring at us, and we can't possibly be that interesting."

"You seem a little paranoid to me, Mr. Swann. Do I really look as though I can't handle this myself?"

"We could all use a little help, Mr. Smith. But if you say you don't know him, who am I to argue?" I got up. "I'd like to say it was a pleasure making your acquaintance, but we'd both know I was lying through my teeth." I picked up my knapsack, stuffed my book into it and started to walk away.

After a few steps, I stopped and looked back. Mr. Smith was gone. I looked to the side, and there was the man in the leather jacket. He removed his sunglasses. It was none other than Mr. Jones. He folded the glasses and stuck them in his jacket pocket as he moved toward me.

"We have to stop meeting like this, Mr. Jones. People will begin to talk."

"You're a very funny man, Mr. Swann."

"On occasion. Love the earring. Nice touch."

"You almost got me in a lot of trouble."

"I can't imagine how."

"That little stunt you pulled at the cafe."

"I don't know what you're talking about."

"I'm sure you don't. Well, no matter. One does what one has to do."

"Are you following me, Mr. Jones?"

"Why would I do that?"

"You tell me."

"Obviously, we have similar interests, which cause our lives to intersect."

"Maybe we're soul mates."

"Maybe we are."

"Are you with Mr. Smith?"

"I have no idea to whom you are referring."

"The dude I was talking to. You were watching us pretty closely."

"If I'd known him, I certainly would have come over and chatted with both of you."

"Funny, because I got the sense you knew each other. My bad." I looked at my watch. "My plane leaves in half an hour. I think I'd better get over to the gate. Unless, of course, you have something to tell me."

"No. Nothing."

I turned to leave. I took a few steps.

"Oh, there is one thing, Mr. Swann."

I turned.

"What's that?"

"It wasn't a very pleasant experience for me, dealing with the police. I think I owe you one."

"I'm sure you'll figure out a way to repay me, Mr. Jones. But I wouldn't count on it working out the way you'd like it to."

★ ★ ★ ★ ★

PART 6
NEW YORK CITY

★ ★ ★ ★ ★

"He who secretly meditates a crime is as guilty as if he committed the offense."

—Juvenal

22
The Chicken Comes Home to Roost

Traffic was surprisingly light, and it was only thirty minutes before we emerged from the Midtown Tunnel and hung a left, headed downtown for the East Village. It was early Saturday evening, and the city, in the throes of mid-summer, had that empty holiday feel, as many New Yorkers abandoned their apartments for a weekend at the beach or in the country. But within an hour or so, the East Village would be teeming with visitors, most of them young and from the boroughs, looking for a good time. I stopped looking for that a long time ago. If a good time is out there, I wouldn't know how to find it.

All I wanted to do was hit the sack. It seemed like I hadn't slept in days, and I was pretty much running on fumes. I hiked up the three flights to my apartment and was about to slip the key into the lock when I noticed that the door was slightly ajar. No one else had a key, including our nonexistent super, who pretty much existed only on paper. He had a voice, but not much else, since I'd never actually seen him, especially when there was work to be done.

I listened for a moment to see if I could hear any sounds from inside. Nothing. Gently I pushed the door open, stopping halfway again to see if I could hear anything. Nothing. I stepped inside. I flicked on the hall light. Nothing. Only the dim light from the hallway illuminated the small foyer that led to the the living room, which was not much bigger. I dropped my knapsack to the ground, making sure it hit loud enough to make a noise, alerting whoever might be in the apartment that they were not alone.

I pulled out my cell. "If anyone's here, I might as well tell you I'm calling nine-one-one," I lied.

Still nothing.

I relaxed a little, though I was still ready for someone to jump out of the darkness and lay into me.

I moved slowly into the living room and fumbled for the light switch on the wall, found it and clicked it on. Light flooded the room.

"Jesus Christ," I hissed as I surveyed the place, which looked as if it had been turned upside down and tossed around, as if in a blender.

My first thought wasn't that something had been taken—hell, what did I have that was of any value?—but that it was going to take hours and hours to put the place back together again. I headed into the bedroom.

I heard something that stopped me in my tracks. I listened carefully. It was a series of beeping noises. I looked around, trying to figure out where the sound was coming from. I spotted my cordless phone on the floor, half hidden under a pile of clothing. I picked it up, hit the OFF button, then checked the battery indicator. It was two-thirds charged, which meant that it was within the last hour or two that someone had been there. I put the phone back in the cradle and wandered through the apartment to see if anything was missing.

I could see it wasn't a robbery. The TV was still there. The VCR. The stereo. The camera I kept in the closet was still there, too, although it was now on the floor mixed in with the rest of my things. My laptop was lying in a corner. I saw a mark on the wall, about waist high, and figured it had been thrown there, then dropped to the ground. I found the cord and plugged it in, to see if it still worked. It did.

Either someone was looking for something, or it was just another way of warning me off the Loomis case. Or maybe it was to let me know how vulnerable I was—as if I didn't know that—and also to disrupt my life as much as possible. It wasn't going to work.

I was in the midst of straightening things up when the phone rang. It was Sandy Brennan. Her voice was clipped, almost panicky. "I've got some information about Sean," she said. "Meet me at the diner."

"I'm pretty beat, Sandy. Just flew in from London. Is it something we can talk about on the phone?"

"No."

"Okay." I said, staring at the mess I still had to clean up. "Give me an hour."

"You won't be sorry." She hung up the phone before I could say anything else.

Sandy Brennan, wearing a short, tight black skirt and a tight pink tank top, was waiting outside the diner, leaning against the wall, furiously puffing on a cigarette when I arrived. As soon as she saw me, she tossed the butt on the ground and stubbed it out with the toe of her high-heeled sandals.

"What's so important you couldn't tell me on the phone?"

"It's not what, it's who."

She stuck her hand in the purse that hung on her shoulder, pulled out an open pack of cigarettes, removed one and popped it in her mouth, then fumbled around for something to light it with.

"Those things'll kill you," I said.

"No such luck," she said as she finally fished a pack of matches out of her bag. She tried to light one, but her hand was shaking so much that she couldn't manage it.

"Here," I said, reaching for the matches. I struck one and lit her cigarette.

"Now you're an accomplice," she muttered, sucking in smoke.

"It's not the first time and it won't be the last. What's wrong?"

"There's someone inside wants to talk to you."

"Who's that?"

"You'll see. Last booth in the back."

She took a drag on her cigarette, held the smoke for what seemed like forever, then exhaled it slowly.

"You'll be here when I'm done?" I asked.

She shrugged, turned and blew smoke into the air.

I pushed open the door and walked inside. There were a couple of people at the counter and a threesome at one of the front booths. In the back, I could see a guy in the last booth, his back to me. He had dark hair and he was bent over. It was only when I walked up to the booth and past the figure that I figured out who it was.

The long, lost Sean Loomis.

23
THE VEIL IS LIFTED. KIND OF.

I slid, uninvited, into the seat opposite Sean Loomis, who was reading a paperback copy of Thomas Pynchon's *Gravity's Rainbow*. He didn't bother to look up. I didn't bother to say anything. His hair was long, almost shoulder-length, much longer than in the photo I had of him. He had three or four days' worth of stubble and was wearing a plaid, button-down shirt, buttoned up to his neck.

We sat for several moments in silence until finally, still without lifting his eyes from the page, he muttered in a raspy voice, "I understand you've been looking for me."

"Half true."

Finally, he looked up. "What's that supposed to mean?"

"It means I've been looking for Marcy, but in order to find her I had to find you. The truth is, Sean, I don't give a flying fuck about you."

"That's too bad, because I feel oh so deeply about you."

"Yeah, I'll bet. Let's cut to the chase. Where's Marcy?"

He put down the book, tore off a piece of the paper placemat, stuck it in as a place holder, closed the book, then knitted his fingers together, holding them up so they half covered his mouth. I knew whatever was going to come from his lips would be lies or, at the very least, half-truths.

"What makes you think I know where she is?"

"If you're trying to tell me you don't know where she is, then you're lying through your teeth."

"I don't like you in my business."

"I'm only in your business because I'm looking for Marcy. You tell me where she is, I move right on out of your business. Besides, between you and me," I looked down at his book, then back up, "I think your business is just about over."

"I don't know what you're talking about."

"Your shady little book business."

"I buy and sell rare books. There's nothing shady in that."

"Nothing, so long as you're selling the real thing."

"You don't know what the fuck you're talking about. I'm just a middle man. I find the goods. I deliver the goods. End of story."

"If that's what you want me to think, fine with me. We can make this short and sweet. Just tell me where Marcy is and I'm out of here, and what you do from then on is your business."

"It's not as simple as that."

"What's that supposed to mean?"

He bowed his head. His voice lowered. "I don't know where Marcy is. Really. I don't."

"I find that hard to believe, Sean. You just got back from London, and you were traveling with her, Mr. Irving."

"You know about that?"

"It's my job to know things like that, Sean. I know where you were staying, and I know about your little scheme to disappear."

"I don't know what you're talking about."

The expression on his face had changed, and this time I knew he might actually be telling the truth, or at least what he believed to be the truth.

"I found the magazine."

"Man, it's like you're talking a different language. I don't know what magazine you're talking about."

"*Esquire.* I found it in your hotel room. There was a page torn out. On the page was an article about disappearing."

His face was blank, but I could see the wheels turning. He honestly didn't know about the magazine and was trying to figure out what was going on. And then it hit me. Maybe it wasn't Sean who wanted to disappear. Maybe it was Marcy.

I took a shot. "Sean, let's talk about Marcy. About how she's used you."

His eyes opened wide. "She didn't use me."

"I think she has."

His head sank. "I love her."

"I know you do," I said in my most sincere insincere voice. "And you've done a lot for her. You'll feel better if you tell me about it. That's why you had your mother get in touch with me, isn't it? You really don't know where Marcy is, and you're hoping I can help you find her."

He nodded.

"She took advantage of you, Sean. You don't owe her anything. You need to tell me all about it, so I can find her and put an end to this. The truth is, I've pretty much figured everything out."

He stirred his coffee, then dumped two more teaspoons of sugar in it. I could see he was close to tears. I almost felt sorry for him. But I didn't. Emotions can be faked too easily. I should know. I do it all the time.

"I know this is tough for you, man. So here's what I think. You met Marcy at Syracuse. You fell for her. Hard. She fell for you, too. Because you were smart. You loved books. So did she. She knew you dealt rare books, she told you how interested she was in them. You taught her the business, including the stuff about associations. She was the one who came up with the idea of forging autographs—that's why you stole the Fitzgerald book from the Houghton Library—so you could find someone who could copy it. I suspect you did it with others. But then Marcy raised the ante. She knew, with all your knowledge, that you'd be able to come up with some very imaginative associations, and that was the next step. Am I right so far?"

His eyes locked into mine. He didn't say anything. He didn't have to.

"There are pieces missing, Sean. My gut tells me there are other people involved in this. I need your help, before Marcy takes off and disappears forever. Let's start with the why."

"I don't know why," he said in almost a whisper.

"It's not about the money, is it?"

"No.

"It's about her father, isn't it?"

He was silent. I knew he was trying to figure out the puzzle. He was almost on my side now, so I loosened the line, letting him have all the time he needed. He had to believe we were allies, that I was going to help him get what he wanted. Marcy. The same thing I wanted. But we weren't allies. We weren't friends. I was using him the same way Marcy was. I wasn't sorry about it. Maybe I should have been. But I wasn't. It's what I do.

Finally, he put the truth out there. "She hated him."

"Why?"

"I don't know."

"Sure you do. She told you about it. That's what women do. They share. There's no way she didn't talk to you about her father, Sean."

"I don't want to talk about it."

"That's fine with me. But if you don't, we'll never find her."

"She'd kill me if I told anyone."

"It's your choice, my friend," I said, throwing up my hands in a gesture calculated to make him think I was going to walk.

"She said he . . . she said . . . he molested her."

"When?"

"Lots . . . lots of times."

"That sucks, Sean," I said in my most faux sympathetic voice.

"That's why she hated him. That's why she ran from him. That's why she didn't want to have anything to do with him."

"Makes sense," I said, but what I was thinking was, why the hell would Phillips hire me to find her? Why not just let her go? What did he have to gain by having me bring her back? If she was going to blow the whistle on him, she'd have done it a long time ago. Something just didn't make sense.

"Maybe that's why she's running from you, Sean."

His head jolted up. His face tightened. His body straightened, as if a pole had been rammed through it. "I never touched her like that!"

"I know. But she probably has a hard time trusting men. Trusting anyone, for that matter. You can understand that, can't you?"

His body went limp, like the pole had suddenly been removed. "You think?"

"Makes sense, doesn't it?"

"I guess." He paused a moment. "Maybe she's trying to get back at him."

"What do you mean, 'get back at him'?"

The words stopped. He bowed his head and cupped it in his hands.

"Sean . . ."

"Nothing. I meant nothing."

"She's planning something, isn't she?"

"No."

"I don't believe you."

"I don't know anything."

The pieces were beginning to fall into place. I knew what she was planning. She was going to scam her own father by selling him forged books. But it wasn't about the money. At least it wasn't only about the money. She wanted revenge. She wanted to take something away from him that was more important than money. She wanted to embarrass him. But she couldn't do it alone. She'd been using Sean and maybe others, like Dubin and Simmons, maybe even Klavan and Rabinowitz.

"Sean, listen to me. There are others in on this, besides her."

He shook his head, as if disgusted.

"You created the stories for the associations, Sean, but Marcy needed more than just you involved in this scheme."

He shook his head.

"I know you don't want to believe it, but it's true. You know it's true."

His head hung so low, I thought it would disappear into his coffee cup.

"No," he said emphatically. He stopped. "I guess. Maybe . . ."

"She was close with Dana Simmons, wasn't she?"

"Uh-huh."

"Did she know Dubin?"

He looked up at me, as if surprised that I knew who Dubin was. "Yeah."

"How about Ross Klavan?"

"I don't know. I might have mentioned him."

"Teddy Rabinowitz?"

"She met him once. With me," he said as he picked up a spoon and absently stirred his coffee, without realizing there wasn't any in the cup.

"Who's got the book, Sean?"

"What book?"

"The Hemingway."

"How do you know about that?"

"It doesn't matter. Where is it?"

"Marcy's got it."

"How'd she get it, Sean?"

"She stole it."

"From who?"

"Me."

"How did that happen?"

"I thought I had it when we left London . . . we were show-ing it around. But when I got off the plane, got home and unpacked, it wasn't there. Neither was Marcy."

"What do you mean, 'neither was Marcy'?"

"She said she had to stop at her father's to pick up some stuff, but she never came back. That was two days ago. I haven't heard from her since."

"All right, Sean. I need you to focus. She's got the book. Her next step is to sell it. The logical person for her to contact would be either Klavan or Rabinowitz. Which one?"

"I don't know. Rabinowitz, I guess."

"I want you to set up a meeting for me with him."

"How'm I gonna do that? If Marcy has gone to him with the book, she's probably made up some story about me. Why would he see someone I'm setting him up with?"

"Because he wants to get top dollar for the damned book, that's why. If we play this right, if we follow the book, I'll find Marcy."

"What do I get out of it?"

I hate when people ask me questions. I just want them to do what I say. "I'll see to it that you're kept out of it. Your name and reputation will be clear. The story will stay hidden, and you can go back to academia, get your damn master's or Ph.D., or whatever the hell it is you want. Then you can actually do something constructive with that giant intellect of yours, which, by the way, isn't so damned giant when it comes to women."

"I know. I know." He paused for a moment. "Okay. I'll call Teddy and see what's up. But I don't want to be embarrassed, so I'm going to have to give you a crash course, so you don't look like a fuckin' fraud."

"Fine with me. But we'll do it tomorrow. In the morning. Coordinate with Klavan. I want him along with us. Between the two of you, I should be fine."

On the way out, I passed Sandy, who was still nervously smoking, pacing up and down in front of the diner. When she saw me, she tossed away her butt and moved toward me. "Is everything okay?" she asked plaintively, amid a puddle of half-smoked cigarettes.

"Yeah. You did the right thing in calling me, Sandy."

"I hope so," she said as she pulled the pack out of her pocket. It was empty. She crumpled it up and threw it in a trash can beside the door of the diner.

"You know," I said, "those things are going to kill you someday."

"If my kid don't do it first," she said. And she wasn't smiling.

24
GOING, GOING, GONE

We met in Klavan's office. Sean, who looked liked he'd had a professional makeover, was dressed in neatly pressed chinos and a lime green designer polo shirt with a horse and rider stitched onto the pocket. He'd cut his hair short and was clean-shaven. Klavan, on the other hand, looked even grungier than usual, as he was dressed in baggy jeans a couple of sizes too large for him, and a giant, red tongue Rolling Stone T-shirt. Over croissants and coffee provided by our host, we went over my cover. I was to be representing a Midwestern collector of rare books who wished to remain anonymous. Klavan explained there were plenty of people who could fit that description, so Rabinowitz, or anyone else at the private auction, was unlikely to be suspicious.

Throughout our cram session, I kept my eye on Klavan to see if I could pick up anything that might tip me off to his involvement in the scheme. He could just as well be working with Marcy as Rabinowitz, and so long as I kept that possibility in mind, I protected myself from being blindsided.

"You're gonna have to know something about rare books," said Sean.

"No worries," said Klavan, leaping to my defense. "He's a lot smarter than he looks. He knows his literature, and he knows something about the business from me. I think all we gotta do now is get into a few specifics."

He walked over to one of his numerous bookshelves and

removed a copy of Joseph Heller's *Catch-22*. "Beyond the rarity of the book, you've got to be aware of condition. You've got mint or exceptional condition, which is very rare, you've got fine condition, then you've got very good condition. For rare books, a very good copy might be the best you can hope for, so it's still valuable. This one's dust jacket is pretty much intact, so it could bring as much as four or five grand. And if you want to impress people, there's always the story about the title."

"Like what?" I asked.

"Originally, Heller called it *Catch-18*," Loomis piped up, "but at the same time Leon Uris, who was a big best-selling author, had his book, *Mila-18*, about the uprising in the Warsaw Ghetto, coming out and they didn't want to use the same number. He changed it to *Catch-22*, and we all know what happened with that. Who knows if *Catch-18* would have had the same cachet?"

Klavan returned the book to the shelf, then removed another, Fitzgerald's *Tender Is the Night*. "Here's a real beauty, first edition, inscribed presentation copy, and it's got the rare, original dust jacket, though the condition isn't as good as it could be." He read, " 'You've been so appreciative of my books in the past that I thought this might amuse you.' I could probably get upwards of sixty or seventy grand for this one, if I were willing to part with it, which I'm not."

He picked up another book. "Here's a copy of Puzo's *The Godfather*, which he inscribed to his friend, Joe Heller—'When's the next horse racing game . . . ?' I'd say I could get close to ten grand for that one, maybe more."

"Great story about that one, too," added a suddenly excited Loomis, who seemed to come alive when books entered the conversation. "A lot of these young writers who came to New York had to make a living, and so they got jobs at the men's magazines. Bruce Jay Friedman, you know, the guy who wrote

Stern and then went to Hollywood and became a pretty successful screenwriter, edited one of them. Puzo worked for him, as did a writer named John Bowers. One day, the story goes, Puzo came to Friedman and said, 'I just finished this book and I want to call it The *Godfather*. What do you think?' Friedman considered it a minute or two and then said, 'It sucks. Too domestic.' "

Klavan laughed and threw his arm around Loomis. "This is why I love this guy, Swann. Look at him, will ya? He just loves books and everything about them. He loves 'em so much, he's even willing to dress the part."

"I can see that," I said. And I could. Both of them did. Their enjoyment came not only from reading books, but from knowing about them and about the writers who wrote them. I was almost jealous, wishing I could get so excited about something, anything. But that kind of wonder had long been wrung out of me. Now, I was just out to get through the next day without getting myself beaten up, figuratively or literally.

Over the next fifteen minutes or so, Klavan, his eyes wide, his deep, passionate voice rising several decibels, ran through a number of other titles, including Harper Lee's *To Kill a Mockingbird,* inscribed, "Shoot all the blue jays you want, if you can hit 'em, but remember it's a sin to kill a mockingbird." "Thirty-five grand, at least."

When we finished, they added a few other touches, then pronounced me ready or, as Klavan said, "as ready as you'll ever be. But don't worry. You'll have both of us with you, just in case you fall apart."

Finally, we were finished, with a couple hours to spare.

"How about some lunch, boys? On me," said Klavan.

"The magic words," I said, "but I'll take a rain check. I've got an errand to run before the auction. I'll meet you guys there."

"What's so important you'd turn down a free meal, Swann?"

"Gotta see a man about a horse," I said as I headed toward the elevator.

25
MANO A MANO

"I'll wait," I said to the pretty young receptionist who'd just informed me that Mr. Phillips couldn't see me because he was in an important meeting.

"He might be a while," she said, obviously protecting her boss from some pitiful-looking jerk who couldn't possibly have any real business worth his time. Like everyone in New York, she was something else. From the look of her, probably a would-be actress or artist. At least working in a law firm was better than waiting tables.

"Tell you what, why don't you get on the phone and tell him that Swann is here to see him and that I've got some important information for him. I think that might do the trick."

A moment later I was ushered into Phillips's office, after almost being run over by three fleeing suits carrying armfuls of papers.

"You should have called and made an appointment," Phillips said as he rose from behind his oversized desk.

Once an asshole always an asshole.

"I don't make appointments."

"Maybe you ought to start. Frankly, you don't look all that successful to me."

"I doubt the failure to make appointments is at the heart of my lack of success."

Air escaped from his mouth and made a derisive sound. Obviously, he had almost as much contempt for me as I had for him.

"You've got information for me?"

"Yes."

"Are you going to make me drag it out of you?"

"I enjoy watching you sweat."

"I don't sweat. I was in an important meeting that I've got to get back to, so let's get this over with. You've located Marcy, I assume."

"Not quite."

"What's that supposed to mean?"

"I'm kinda thirsty. You have anything around here for a man to drink?"

"Look, Swann, this isn't a cocktail party. I'm a busy man."

"I'm a thirsty man."

"What do you want?"

"Perrier would be nice."

"You're kidding me."

"What's the matter? Don't I look the type?"

He made a face, picked up the phone and begrudgingly ordered a Perrier for me. Tap water would have been fine. I just wanted to pull his chain. The more pissed off he was, the more off-balance he was, the more likely he'd be to spill the truth.

"Okay, now let's get down to business."

His secretary entered and handed me the Perrier, along with a glass filled with ice. I opened the bottle and poured the contents slowly into the glass, while Phillips tapped his fingers on his desk.

"Can we please move on with this?"

"Fine," I said as I brought the glass to my mouth and took a sip. "Did you molest your daughter?"

His face turned red. His eyes popped open. "What?"

"I asked you if you abused your daughter. The answer's either yes or no."

He turned even redder. His body started to shake. "Why the hell would you think something like that?"

"Because that's what your daughter's saying."

"You're kidding me."

"God's honest," I said, raising my hand. Man, was I enjoying this. I took another sip.

"Who's she telling this cock-and-bull story to?"

"Sean, for one. Maybe others."

"You found the sonuvabitch?"

"Yes."

"Where is he?"

"That's not something you need to know."

"I'm paying you, Swann," he sputtered.

"You're paying me to find your daughter. Sean Loomis is incidental."

"Fuck you, Swann."

"Touchy, aren't we?"

"You just accused me of molesting my daughter. How do you think I feel?"

"Pissed off."

"That's right," he pounded his fist on his desk. "Pissed off."

I looked at him closely, his face, his body language. He wasn't faking it. He *was* pissed off. I believed he was telling the truth.

"Why would she accuse you of something like that?" I said, modulating my tone so he'd start to think he was winning me over to his side.

He took a couple of deep breaths, a technique I guessed he'd learned at some New Age yoga center. All the air seemed to come out of him. He looked smaller as he slumped back into his chair. "I don't know. But if you didn't hear it from her mouth, how do you know Sean isn't lying? Do you really think he isn't capable of it?"

"He's not lying. At least about that. She told him you molested her. Whether she's telling the truth or not, well, that's another thing. Maybe it's one of those false recovered memory things. From what I've read, it happens more than any of us would like to think. It's a lot easier to think the worst of someone, especially since it's usually true. If she is lying, why do you think she'd do it?"

"I don't know," he said, the air making a hissing sound as it escaped from his chest up through his mouth, as if from a punctured tire. Suddenly, he seemed smaller, far less imposing. I almost began to feel sorry for him—well, as sorry as you can feel for someone who was as much of a dick as Phillips was.

"I think you do."

"I told you, we don't get along. That's why she ran. Maybe she's just trying to get back at me."

"This is beyond not getting along. This is serious. And let's say she is 'getting back' at you, for what?"

"I'm not going to say any more. At this point, it's a private affair. I'll deal with it when the time comes. But first, I need you to find her."

"She's going around saying all these terrible things about you. She refuses to have any contact with you. What I'm wondering is why it's so important that you find her. And don't tell me it's for her own protection. From what I gather, this chick can take care of herself."

He hesitated a moment, the way someone does when you know they're either going to lie or edit the good stuff out of what they're going to tell you.

"She has something of mine I'd like to get back." He hesitated a moment. "I need to get back."

"What's that?"

"I'd rather not say."

"Is it valuable?"

"To me, it is."

"To anyone else?"

"That depends."

"You're not going to tell me what it is, are you?"

"I'm not. Are you going to find her or aren't you?"

"Oh, I'll find her. But I'm not sure what I'll do when that happens."

"What's that supposed to mean?"

"It means what it means," I said as I got up. "I think you can call your boys back in here and finish your meeting. I got what I came for."

26
THE STANISLAVSKI METHOD

Another mystery to try to solve: what was it Marcy Phillips stole from her father? And why wouldn't he tell me what it was? I had a good guess what it was. A book. Maybe the book that was going to be the centerpiece of the auction. But how did Phillips get it in the first place, and why would Marcy steal it from him? I could understand not calling the cops on his own daughter if she did steal it, and maybe that would explain why he hired me to find her. It wasn't that he cared about her; it was the book. But what if the book was a fake, or at least a partial fake? Did Phillips know that? Did Marcy? And if it were a fake, who'd rigged it? The smart money was on Sean. Maybe she comes up with the idea. He fakes it. They sell it to her father. He pays for it. She steals the book. He wants it back. She runs off with the book and the money, leaving Sean with nothing. Phillips hires me to find her, but really what he wants me to find is the book.

Other questions remained. For instance, how did Mr. Smith and Mr. Jones fit into all this? Who hired them and why? Or were they working on their own?

The more I tried to connect the dots, the more confused I became. Everything seemed so simple and yet so complicated. There were so many possible connections, all of which could make sense, but I couldn't figure out which ones made the right sense.

One thing I did know was that everything centered around

Marcy and that book. I hoped the auction would bring everything and everyone, especially Marcy, out into the open.

Rabinowitz's place was on 61st and Central Park West. I had about an hour before the auction was to begin. Though the sky was an ominous gray and it looked as if it might rain any minute, I decided to walk across the park. I entered at 59th Street, walked up the east drive, past the entrance to the zoo, then hung a left just below Wollman Rink, which for the summer had been turned into a small amusement park.

I was nearing the underpass that opened up onto the Hecksher softball diamonds when the wind picked up and the sky suddenly turned black. Leaves and papers blew by me as I folded my body over and walked faster. There were a couple of claps of thunder, flashes of bright light, then the sky opened up and sheets of rain, carried horizontally through the muggy air, came down with such ferocity that I knew the storm couldn't possibly last long. The lines, "And God gave Noah the rainbow sign. No more water, the fire next time," kept running through my mind. I made a run for the tunnel. It was only a few yards away, yet by the time I got there I was soaking wet. Leaning against the wall at the edge of the tunnel, I pulled my shirt away from my skin and shook it, hoping that would help it dry out.

I could hear the faint sound of calliope music coming from the carousel slightly north of where I stood. I remembered bringing Noah there when he was four or five. He loved riding the horses. He'd wear a cowboy hat and carry a set of pistols strapped to his side. We had to punch an extra hole in his belt so the holster wouldn't fall off. It was a flashing memory, like the lightning that filled the sky, that I shut down quickly. I heard noise, looked behind me and saw a young couple who'd also sought shelter in the tunnel. Watching them, as they giggled and hugged each other, I felt a momentary sense of longing, a need for a connection, but quickly dismissed it by refocusing on the falling rain. A few minutes passed, the rain let up, and they dashed out, leaving me alone again. The western sky brightened, the clouds parting to reveal a few patches of blue. The air began to smell fresher and feel lighter. A few more minutes, I thought, and I'd be good to go.

I heard muffled footsteps behind me. I turned and saw two figures in the shadows, only a few feet from me. I looked away for a moment and just as I was about to look back, I felt a hand grip my shoulder. I was spun around and found myself face to face with none other than Mr. Jones, who smelled of sweat and rain. I looked to his right and there was Mr. Smith, who grabbed my other shoulder. They pushed me up against the wall.

"Hey, fellas," I said, "no need for the rough stuff. Let's talk."

"The time for talking has passed," growled Mr. Smith as he drew back his arm. I knew what was coming and moved to the side. His blow was deflected by the side of my cheek, and the momentum resulted in his fist smashing into the wall of the tunnel. He groaned and grabbed his hand. "Son of a bitch," he screamed. Mr. Jones, a look of surprise on his face, loosened his grip and, as I pulled away, I smashed him as hard as I could in the stomach, which was soft, like a pillow. I could hear the air gush from his lungs as he keeled over and grunted. I looked around for Mr. Smith, my fists in front of me in a boxer's stance—not that I knew anything about boxing—but he was gone. I looked to my right and caught a glimpse of him running out of the tunnel, in the direction of the rink.

I turned my attention to Mr. Jones, who was bent over, gasping for air. I grabbed him, pulled him upright and was ready to plunge my fist into his gut again when he groaned, "Please. Not again."

I held back, surprised he was giving up so easily.

"The time for talking has passed," I taunted, pushing him

against the wall, my forearm planted firmly on his upper chest, just below his neck. I had no intention of inflicting any more damage, but I didn't want him to think that.

Gasping for breath, he managed, "It wasn't supposed to get this far."

"What's that supposed to mean?" I asked, pressing harder on his upper chest. "You were ready to kick the shit out of me."

"No. Really," he gasped, his voice empty of any menace it held earlier. "I was going to hold you up. I swear. Just . . . just let me go and I'll explain everything."

"Not so fast," I said as I patted him down and pulled the pistol he'd been packing back at Virage out of his side pocket. But something didn't feel right. It was too light. Some new plastic model? I looked at it closely. It was a damned toy. "What the fuck is going on?" I said, reaching for his back pocket where I found his wallet and pulled it loose.

"Let me go and I'll explain everything."

I backed away, and he slumped against the wall.

"Thank you," he said, taking deep breaths, trying hard to catch his breath.

I opened his wallet and pulled out his driver's license. "Johnny Garfield?"

He cupped his head in his hands, still breathing hard. "Asth . . . ma . . ." he gasped. He looked up at me, pleadingly. "Inhaler. Pocket . . ."

"Go for it."

"Th . . . anks . . ." He pulled it out and sucked on it.

"You two are the sorriest excuse for tough guys I've ever met."

He took a deep breath. "We're not . . ." wheeze, wheeze, "tough guys." He breathed in deep again. "We're . . . we're . . ." He took another hit on his inhaler. "We're actors."

"Actors? What the hell are you talking about?"

"We were hired to follow you, to make like we were tough guys, but we weren't supposed to actually do anything to you."

"Yeah, well that fist you cocked and launched toward me looked pretty actual to me."

"Improv," he said.

"What?"

"We're method actors. We just got caught up in it."

"Fuck the method," I said, trying not to laugh at the ridiculousness of it. "Who hired you?"

"I don't know." I raised my arm, closing my hand into a fist—improv. "Honest," he said, flinching.

"Come on . . ."

"No. Really. We were hired through an agency. Our agent sent us up for this. He figured we could use the money."

"Someone had to give you instructions."

"Everything came through email. There was one conversation, but it wasn't with the person who hired us. Some woman who said she was also hired by the guy paying us."

"Did she give you her name?"

He bowed his head. "I don't remember. Man, I'm sorry about this. It was either this or catering, and this seemed, well, this seemed like an interesting gig."

"And you don't know anything else?"

"No. I swear. Neither does Vrain."

"Vrain?"

"Lucas. The other dude. The one who took off. We didn't think it would get this far. Shit, we weren't going to hurt you or anything. I guess we got a little carried away, huh? Maybe we were a little too good," he said with a hint of hope in his voice.

"First act not bad, second act not so good. You can forget about the Oscar, my friend."

I handed him back his wallet. I looked at the pistol and smiled.

"Were you the guys who tossed my room in London?"

"Huh?"

"My hotel room in London. Were you guys there?"

"I don't know anything about that."

I closed my hand into a fist. A sense of power surged through me. This threatening stuff was kind of addictive.

"I swear. It wasn't us."

"How about here?"

"Here?"

"My apartment?"

He shook his head.

"Don't shit me, Johnny."

"I'm not. Really. It wasn't us."

"What did the cop say when he rousted you the other day?"

"He reamed me out. Said I shouldn't be carrying something that looked like a weapon."

"Get in any trouble?"

"I told him I was an actor, just coming from an audition. He believed me."

"This time it might not go so easy on you."

"What are you talking about?"

"You're in River City, my friend."

"Huh?"

"As in Trouble, with a capital T."

"I'm in trouble?"

"You are."

"Like how?"

"Stalking. Threatening me with a deadly weapon," I was having trouble keeping a straight face, but let's face it, I was having fun.

"I didn't threaten . . ."

"Sure you did."

"What deadly weapon?"

"That pistol in your pocket."

"You saw. It's not real."

"I couldn't know that. I could have you arrested. Maybe I will," I said, reaching for my cell. "They catch you with that, they don't care if it's real or not. You threatened me with it. That's all they have to know. It's on your record, my friend."

"My record? I don't have a record."

"Sure you do. That cop had to write it up. It's not going to go well for you if I call this in."

"Oh, come on, man. I didn't know what was going on. I thought it was some kind of joke."

"It was no joke to me."

"Oh, please, man. I'm just a guy trying to make a living."

I tapped the pistol on the palm of my hand. "You know, I've got a soft spot for artists. So it's possible I could forget the whole thing, but you've gotta do something for me."

"What's that?"

"I want to know who's behind this."

"I already told you, I don't know."

"I know what you told me, but I want you to do your best to find out. So your next gig is playing detective, and I hope you do a better job of that than you've done playing a thug. Get in touch with your agent and get him to tell you who hired him . . ."

"Her. My agent's a woman."

"Even better. Just flirt with her a little."

"What if she doesn't know?"

"She got paid. Probably by check or credit card. Believe me, she knows, and I want you to find out and tell me." I gave him my card.

I pulled out his driver's license from his wallet. "I'm going to hold onto this until I hear back from you."

"I need that, man!"

"An actor with a car?"

"No. But it's my ID. And I was going to rent a car this weekend to take my girlfriend to the beach."

"Then I guess you'll have to work fast, won't you? Give me a call this afternoon," I said as I flipped him the fake gun. "Hold on to this. You never know when it might come in handy."

27
THE BACK PAGE

Klavan and Loomis were standing, several feet away from each other, outside Rabinowitz's building. Loomis, wearing chinos and a blue button-down shirt, untucked, was smoking a cigarette and staring out into space. Klavan, wearing a dark sport jacket over his usual T-shirt, again displaying the Rolling Stones' giant tongue, was on his BlackBerry. Neither one was paying attention to the other. Or to me, as I sidled up beside them.

"Good afternoon, boys," I said.

"Cutting it pretty close, Swann," said Klavan as he tucked his BlackBerry into his pocket. "What the hell happened to your eye?"

"A door bumped into me."

"You oughta be more careful . . . with doors. I see you forgot your umbrella. How about we get this show on the road."

Klavan led the way, with me sandwiching Loomis between us. He said the magic word, I couldn't quite hear what it was, to the doorman, and we were pointed in the direction of the proper elevator bank. Once upstairs, we were greeted with a sign that read, "No firearms allowed." Two uniformed guards greeted us, and we had to go through a metal detector before we were allowed inside.

The difference between Rabinowitz's digs and Klavan's was immediately apparent, the Motel 6 versus the Plaza Hotel. Klavan's place was very unbusiness-like, studious, with lots of clutter, but Rabinowitz's office was an opulent palace, as neat and orderly as a high-end boutique. The bookcases were elegant built-ins, painted bright white and all uniform in size. There were a number of plush easy chairs, two sofas, enough seating to hold a couple dozen people comfortably amidst a sea of glass and chrome. There was an open bar in one corner of the large room, manned by a uniformed bartendress, and scattered about the large room were uniformed waiters and waitresses carrying silver plates of hors d'oeuvres. There were several computers spread throughout the room, obviously available to anyone who needed them. Perhaps a dozen or so well-dressed men and women, holding onto catalogues describing the books that were to be auctioned, stood around, chatting with each other. It was, without doubt, a class operation.

"Shut your mouth, Swann," Klavan said as he elbowed me in the side. "Make it look like you actually belong here."

"Damn," I whispered, "this place makes me feel like I don't belong anywhere."

Klavan checked his watch. "Fifteen minutes till game time. Wanna check out some of the merchandise?"

"Sure," I said.

"I'll hang back there," said Loomis, gesturing toward the bar area.

"Suit yourself," said Klavan.

I looked at him out of the corner of my eye. "Not afraid of seeing some of your own handiwork, are you?"

He shot me an angry look. "I don't know what you're talking about." I know that look. I've seen it dozens of times from guys whose cars I've repoed, or husbands I've returned to their rightful owners. It's not a pretty look, and it's a look that's sometimes followed by violence. In this case, I knew violence wasn't going to happen, but it did give me an interesting insight into what Loomis might be capable of if given the right opportunity.

Klavan and I headed over to a series of tables with glass cases on them. "These people are a little scary," I said as we maneuvered through the well-dressed crowd, which had grown somewhat since we'd arrived.

"Don't be intimidated, Swann. They put their pants on one leg at a time, just like you and me."

"Yeah, but they look like they have someone helping them do it. This is really something. 'The show is not the show, but they that go. Menagerie to me my neighbor be. Fair play. Both came to see,' " I muttered.

"Just have fun, Swann."

We joined the line of gawkers and passed by a dozen or so books, as if we were at a buffet. "Beautiful editions, aren't they?" said Klavan, whistling softly through his teeth.

"Jealous?"

"I'd be shitting you if I didn't admit I was. Rabinowitz has the magic touch, man. I don't know how the hell he does it, but he always manages to get first shot at these things."

"Where's the guest of honor?" I asked, referring to the Hemingway book.

"Teddy's a master showman. He'll milk this thing for all it's worth. That's why the auction's here and not at Doyle's or Sotheby's or even Swann." He looked at me and smiled at his little joke. "He'll pull that baby out of a hat when it suits him."

The collectors were mostly middle-aged men, with just a smattering of women, none of them Marcy, none of them under forty-five, all of them very conservatively dressed. It was the middle of summer, yet there was very little skin showing in that room. Standing at different places throughout the room were men dressed in ill-fitting suits, with earphones discretely tucked in their ears. Guards. I looked at my watch. It was closing in on three. As if on cue, people started to move away from the exhibited books, toward places to sit.

"Let's grab a seat while we can," Klavan said.

"I don't want to sit up front."

"You'll miss all the action, man. The big bidders sit up close, and I love seeing the looks on their faces as prices skyrocket."

"I'm not here to buy books, Klavan. I need a good vantage point so I can see the room."

"Suit yourself," he said as we found seats near the back.

I looked at my watch. The second hand was nearing the twelve. I heard a door open behind me and turned my head. Two women walked through the door. One of them was Dana Simmons, who looked very different from the way she did in Boston. She was wearing a very conservative gray skirt, a white blouse and high heels, her dark hair pulled up in a bun. The other woman was much younger, in her twenties, but similarly dressed. I couldn't be sure, but she did bear a resemblance to the photo of Marcy. They walked close together, whispering to each other, and I had a strong feeling from their body language that this was a little more than just a student–teacher relationship. What's more, I didn't know. But I meant to find out.

I nudged Klavan with my elbow and whispered, "She's here."

"Who?" He started to look over his shoulder.

"Don't look," I ordered. He jerked his head back.

"Marcy Phillips."

"Holy shit." They passed to the right of us. "Who's the hot chick with her?"

"Dana Simmons. She's a professor at Syracuse."

"What's she got to do with this?"

"Not sure."

We watched them as they moved forward, finally taking a seat at the end of the second row, about as far away from us as they could have gotten, which was fine with me. I didn't want them to know I was there, and the way they were positioned, I didn't think they would.

Dana leaned over and whispered something to Marcy. She smiled. Dana patted her shoulder.

"That looks like the student–teacher relationship I have in my dreams," said Klavan, just as a man dressed in a very expensive dark designer pin-striped suit emerged from a door at the other side of the room. There was a buzz, and I figured the man had to be Rabinowitz. He was tall, over six feet, slim, and his salt and pepper hair, cut short, looked like it had been gelled into little spikes. He looked a bit like Harrison Ford. He wore wireless-rimmed glasses, the lenses so clean that when he turned a certain way, the light was reflected forward, like a laser.

He took a moment to survey the room, which was totally quiet, then headed right toward us.

"Oh, shit," said Klavan. "He's coming our way."

"Introduce us. But don't forget to lie about who I am."

"Don't worry."

"Klavan," Rabinowitz said as he stopped in front of us. "I didn't think they let you out during daylight hours."

"Only for special occasions, Teddy."

"Who's this?" He gestured with his hand, not deigning to look at me.

"Henry Swann. He's representing a Midwest consortium."

"Who would that be?" he asked, still without a glance my way.

"I'm not at liberty to divulge their identities," I said.

"I'm smelling bullshit, Klavan."

"If anyone can, it's you, Teddy. You've slung enough of it. Truth is, I don't give a fuck what you think. I'm here to enjoy myself, and if I see any bargains, I'll jump in."

"Hope you can swim, Klavan. The water's pretty deep, and I don't see a life raft in sight."

"I'll do my best, Teddy, even if it means doing the dog paddle."

Rabinowitz turned his attention to me. "So long as Klavan's willing to vouch for you, I see no harm in letting you bid." He turned to Klavan. "Because I know you wouldn't do anything to screw up the wonderful relationship we have, Klavan. Am I right?"

"Right as rain, Teddy."

"Well, Mr. Swann, I hope you've got your checkbook handy. And please don't be shy."

"I don't think you'll have to worry about that," I said.

Rabinowitz checked his watch. "I think we've kept the animals waiting long enough. As the late, great Gary Gilmore said, 'Let's do it!'"

Rabinowitz headed toward the podium, shaking a few hands along the way, as if he were running for office.

"Good afternoon, ladies and gentleman," he said in a voice so mellow, he could have fit right in on the late-night shift at a classic rock FM radio station. "I'd like to thank you for taking time out of your busy day to join us here for what promises to be a very special auction of a particularly beautiful . . . and valuable . . . collection of rare books. Now, if everyone's got their checkbook handy, why don't we begin?"

"He's so fucking slimy," said Klavan. "He's nothing more than a dressed-up used-car salesman."

"But he's good."

"Yeah, that's the fuckin' worst part."

I kept an eye on Dana and Marcy. Somehow, as far as I could tell, we'd managed to elude their sight. Given the relatively small size of the audience, I counted nineteen of us—not including the hired help—all very serious-looking bibliophiles, I didn't think that would be the case for very long. Eventually, they'd look back and see us. I looked over to Sean, who was half-hidden behind one of the bookcases. He was staring in Marcy's direction. It wasn't a loving stare. I just hoped he'd keep his cool. I considered going over to him to read him the riot act, but that would just bring unwanted attention to us.

I leaned over to Klavan and asked, "Is everyone here a serious collector?"

"There are a few agents here. They represent various collectors as well as institutions like UT. They're the ones seated closest to the computers, in case they have to check something out. There's a hell of a lot of disposable cash represented here."

"Including yours?"

"If I see something interesting and the price is right, I might just loosen the old purse strings. But I'm going to let you do some of the bidding for me, so it looks like you're legit. Just follow my lead." He looked around. "See that old gray-haired chick over there?" he pointed to the front row, farthest away from us.

"The one sitting at the end of the row?"

"Yeah. Haven't seen her in a while, but guess who one of her favorite clients is?"

"You're kidding."

"Nope. Carlton Phillips."

"You think she's working for him today?"

"It's possible. And with his kid here, that could get interesting, don't you think?"

"Very . . ."

"I'm sure all of you have had an opportunity to examine the books up for auction today," Rabinowitz intoned gently, "and can see that each and every one of them is in fine condition. And if you have any questions, please don't hesitate to ask . . . though you all know how much I hate to be the center of attention."

Laughter.

Suddenly there was a commotion in the back of the room. I turned around. Someone was trying to get in, but the guard at the door was giving him or her a little trouble.

"Dammit," a booming voice cried out, "the traffic sucks in this city. How's someone supposed to be someplace when they're supposed to be? It's not a fuckin' Broadway show, for Chrissakes. Just let me in."

Heads swiveled toward the voice—and that's when Dana Simmons spotted me. Her face reflected what I read as surprise but then, recovering quickly, she seemed to smile. She leaned toward Marcy and whispered something in her ear. Marcy turned to look in my direction.

"It's all right, George," Rabinowitz said, "you can let him in."

"Thank you," the voice boomed. "Finally, a man of reason."

In strode Richard Dubin.

"Jesus, now the gang's really all here," I muttered.

"You know him?" Klavan asked.

"I do."

"Who is he?"

"The head of the English department at Syracuse."

"What the hell's he doing here?"

"Beats me. But suddenly we're in the middle of an Agatha Christie novel with all the likely suspects in the same room."

"Suspects for what?"

"I haven't the foggiest idea, but I know something's going on that isn't on the up and up."

"I think I'm going to enjoy the hell out of this," Klavan said as he folded his arms across his massive chest and leaned back.

"Sir," Rabinowitz said, his remark aimed at Dubin, "I believe there's a seat over there. And once you're seated, we can begin."

"Sorry," Dubin said, tipping his Yankee baseball cap to the crowd. Without seeing me, he took his seat and Rabinowitz began the operation. First he went through the dozen or so books that would be auctioned, providing the provenance for each, sometimes adding an amusing anecdote or two about the author or the works, which included books by Twain, Wharton, Miller, Stein, Capote, Malamud, Mailer and Bellow. Then, he got down to business, with his assistant removing each copy carefully from beneath the glass enclosure. Rabinowitz held up each book, and the exceedingly gentlemanly bidding began. Klavan had me bid on four books and I won two of them, an inscribed first edition of Bellow's *Herzog*. "Damned good price for a Nobel Prize winner," he remarked, and a signed first edition of Roth's *Portnoy's Complaint*. "He made jacking off an art form," he said about that one. In quick succession, Rabinowitz auctioned off a copy of *Adventures of Huckleberry Finn*, which went for $30,000, Joyce's *Ulysses*, also thirty grand, and Salinger's *The Catcher in the Rye*, unsigned for $15,000. I had to admit that it was exciting, and each book really did take on the patina of a beautiful work of art.

After each book was sold, Rabinowitz smiled, made a note on a pad in front of him, and occasionally commended the folks in the room for their fine taste and for setting a new monetary record for him. When he'd finished with the books that were listed, he raised his arms over his head in a sign of victory, and the crowd applauded as if they were at a Broadway performance. Then Rabinowitz, in a gesture that reeked of showmanship, reached out his hands, palms down, in an effort to calm the crowd. Immediately, the room went quiet.

"I want to thank all of you for your cooperation, but we're not finished yet. As some of you know, we have a book that wasn't listed in the catalogue. A late arrival." He dipped his hand beneath the podium and pulled out a book that was carefully wrapped in plastic, as were all the other books sold that afternoon. "This is the jewel in the crown of our auction this afternoon. It's a collector's dream, a copy of Ernest Hemingway's *The Sun Also Rises*, with a very *special* inscription to none other than his friend and rival . . ." He paused for dramatic effect. "F. Scott Fitzgerald."

There was an audible gasp in the room, as Rabinowitz continued without missing a beat, obviously enjoying the fact that he had his audience in the palm of his hand. "I believe the inscription will be of particular interest to Hemingway and Fitzgerald scholars."

While he spoke, my eyes darted back and forth between Sean, who was still standing near the back of the room, his eyes fixed on Marcy and Dana, and on Marcy and Dana, who I noted occasionally touched each other in a way that definitely wasn't casual, but rather with the intimacy lovers have.

"The value of this book is obvious, so in an effort to save time, I'm going to start the bidding at a hundred thousand dollars."

Immediately, hands shot up and the bidding started. Within what seemed liked seconds, it reached $125,000, a bid offered by the woman Klavan had pointed out as representing Carlton Phillips, and that's when I thought it was time to shake things up a little. I stood up and said, "Excuse me, but we're now talking a lot of money here. How do we know this book is what you say it is?"

The room was suddenly hushed. All eyes on me.

"Excuse me?" said Rabinowitz, obviously taken aback by my audacity.

"This is an awful lot of money, and I was just wondering how we know that the book is authentic."

"Because I say it is," said Rabinowitz, who quickly regained his composure. "Anyone who knows me, Mr. Swann, knows that my reputation is impeccable. I do not handle books whose provenance I can't guarantee. But if you doubt my word, well then, I suggest you simply sit down, shut up, and let the others here bid."

"Just wanted to make sure," I said, "because I've heard some rumors lately as to forged associations."

"You can assume I stand solidly behind anything I sell."

"Just wanted to make sure," I said as I sat back down. I could see from the mumblings I heard around me that I'd thrown off the rhythm of the auction, which is just what I'd wanted to do.

"I'm certain we're all glad you did. Now, shall we get back to the bidding? We're at a hundred twenty-five thousand, do I hear a hundred thirty?"

A fellow in a dark suit and rep tie raised his hand.

The gray-haired woman raised hers.

Finally, when the bidding reached $220,000, the only one left was the gray-haired woman.

"I think we have a winner," Rabinowitz said, "and if I had a gavel, I'd smack it down right now. Congratulations, Sylvia, you've bought yourself a book!"

The audience applauded.

The auction was over.

28
WHO WROTE THE BOOK OF LOVE?

Those who'd purchased books were huddled around a desk at the far corner of the room, as one of Rabinowitz's aides collected checks and took pertinent information. Klavan had informed me that unless cash exchanged hands, the books were not released until checks cleared. Others, who hadn't made successful bids, stood around chatting with each other. From what I could tell, their conversations were focused on the Hemingway book, most of them wondering just what the inscription said. They might never know, since the gray-haired woman disappeared quickly, as soon as the auction ended, with the book in hand, accompanied by two burly-looking guys with bulges under their jackets who had suddenly appeared as soon as the auction ended.

When the room cleared somewhat, Marcy approached Rabinowitz, and they had a few words. Finished, she returned to Dana's side, smiling. Dana squeezed her shoulder and Marcy's smile broadened. I glanced over at Sean, who was still sulking in the corner. I knew he was dying to approach Marcy, but he was acting surprisingly sane by holding back. I didn't know how much longer he could restrain himself, so I excused myself from Klavan, who said he'd use his own check for the books he purchased through me, and approached Sean, whose eyes were tiny, black orbs.

"Easy, Sean," I said, putting my hand on his shoulder.

"Those bitches sold my fuckin' book."

"Is it real or a fake?"

He didn't answer, but kept glaring at Marcy and Dana.

"Don't worry, I'll see you get what's coming to you when this is all straightened out."

"She bitch-played me."

"You allowed yourself to be played, my friend. You're as guilty as she is. Your hands are far from clean. But don't beat yourself up. We're all guilty of something. Some of us pay for it, some of us don't."

"She'll pay, all right . . ."

I shrugged. "Maybe she will, maybe she won't. In the long run, what does it matter? I need to know what's going on, Sean. I think you can tell me."

"That damned book cost me. A lot. I trusted her. I believed her."

"She's a mixed-up kid, Sean, and you're lucky to be out of it. She's Dana Simmons's problem now."

"That dyke. You think I care about that?"

"If you care about yourself, you'll just man up and walk away. Consider yourself lucky if it ends here, like this. Why don't you just meet me downstairs, and we'll go somewhere to talk this out later."

He leered at me for several moments. I leered back at him. Finally, he turned and left. I knew he didn't want to. But he did. I wasn't sure he'd be downstairs when I finished, but it didn't matter. I found him once; I could find him again. And this time it would be a lot easier.

I looked back at Dana and Marcy, who'd by now been joined by Dubin. They were standing by the podium. Rabinowitz was over by the table, examining the checks and credit card receipts. Dana turned her head and saw me. She smiled. I smiled back. She waved me over. Klavan saw me walk toward them and followed me. "You don't mind if I tag along? I think this is going to be interesting."

"Suit yourself. I guess the gang's all here," I said as I joined them.

"Depends what you mean by gang," said Dubin.

"Take it any way you like," I said.

"You think you've figured things out?" said Dubin.

"Is there something to figure out?"

"You tell me."

"I think so. I've got some of it. But there are some loose ends."

"That's life," said Dubin. "Lots of loose ends."

"I hate loose ends," I said, turning to Marcy. "I'm Henry Swann. I'm sure you know I was hired by your father to find you."

She nodded.

"I feel as if I know you, Marcy."

"Well, you don't," she said like a petulant child. "So don't act like you do."

"I know you're a very clever young woman."

"Is that so?"

"Unless, of course, this whole thing was hatched up by the three of you."

"What whole thing?" said Dana.

"This scheme to rip off your father."

"I don't know what you're talking about," said Marcy.

"Me, either," said Dubin.

Dana kept her mouth shut.

"You all did pretty well for yourselves."

They were silent.

"What do you mean?" asked Klavan.

"They were in this together. Marcy stole the book from her father. At that point, it might just have been a fine rare edition copy. Maybe signed. Maybe not. She conned Sean into doctoring it. Adding the inscription and the association, which was probably a doozy of a story. Then, after she steals it from him, and with the help of"—I gestured toward Dana and Dubin—"these guys, she set about selling it for big bucks through Rabinowitz. Maybe he was involved, maybe not. If he was, it was probably because he got screwed over by Phillips at some point. But whatever, because everyone came out a lot richer."

"I don't know what you're talking about," said Marcy. I looked at the other two to see their reactions. They were smiling. I knew I was on the right track.

"You really stuck it to your father, didn't you? That was the real kick, wasn't it? It wasn't about the money, but now you've got it and your old man's got the book, which was his to begin with."

"Think what you want. I don't care," said Marcy as she turned away from me.

"So," said Klavan, "is it a fake or not?"

"That's the sixty-four-thousand-dollar question. The other question is, why would Phillips buy it back for so much money when it was stolen from him in the first place? Why not just report it and have the cops take it from there? But I don't think I'll get those answers here, will I, gang?"

"We didn't do anything wrong, Swann. We were just the facilitators," Dubin said. "Like I told you, I've got tenure. I don't need the money."

"To give you the benefit of the doubt, maybe you bought the sob story Marcy here was dishing out. You, too, Dana. Unless there's something else you got out of it."

"I'll let you figure that out, Swann," she said, her voice dripping with sarcasm. "After all, you're the detective."

"Skip tracer," I said, correcting her.

"Unless I read you wrong," said Dubin, "I think you're going to walk away from this as if nothing happened."

"I'm afraid you've overestimated me, Dubin. By the way, nice touch hiring Abbott and Costello to follow me."

They looked at each other quizzically. They had no idea what I was talking about.

"So you don't know anything about Mr. Smith and Mr. Jones?"

"I have no idea what you are talking about," said Dubin.

I looked at the two women. Dana seemed genuinely surprised. As for Marcy, I couldn't tell a thing. Her face was a blank sheet of paper. There was something wrong with this chick. I pegged her as a borderline at best, a sociopath at worst. There was just no way of reading her. She might have hired them; then again, maybe not. Whether she did or didn't, she certainly wasn't going to own up to it. So it was either Marcy or Phillips or Rabinowitz. Or someone else.

"Dubin, you want to help me here?"

"You know what you know, and that's all that you know," he said in a piss-poor imitation of Popeye.

"So, Marcy, what do you think I should do about your old man?"

"What do I care?"

"Do you really hate him that much, that you'd steal from him and then rip him off?"

She didn't say anything.

"What do you want me to tell him?"

"Tell him whatever you want to tell him."

"That the book's a fake?"

"Who said it's a fake?" said Dubin.

I threw up my hands. "Who gives a shit? I'm gonna go home now. I did what I was paid to do. I found you, Marcy. The rest is up to your old man. And you two," I said, turning to Dana and Dubin. "If I were you, I'd watch my back. There's something seriously wrong with this kid."

Sean was waiting for me downstairs, sitting on a bench across the street, in front of the park, smoking what I assumed was a cigarette. When I got closer, I picked up the distinctive odor of weed, which immediately took me back to my good old days in Spanish Harlem. I sat down beside him.

"Want a hit?" he asked.

"I'll pass. So Sean, between you and me, what's with that book?"

"What do you mean?"

"Is it real or isn't it?"

He shrugged and took another hit of the joint.

"What about the inscription? What did it say, and why's it so important to people?"

He exhaled slowly, a steady stream of smoke escaping from between his lips.

"Let's just say it was personal. Very personal."

"Personal how?"

"It throws a whole other light on the real relationship between Fitzgerald and Hemingway."

"What's that supposed to mean?"

"It means that maybe they were a lot closer than people think."

"They were rivals."

"Yeah. And maybe they were more than that, if you know what I mean."

"What's that supposed to mean?"

"You ever heard of the kind of love that dare not speak its name?"

"You mean the inscription shows they had a homosexual relationship?"

"Yeah."

"But is it real, Sean? Is it real?"

He took another hit, sucking back the smoke deep into his lungs. He looked at me and smiled.

"Wouldn't it be pretty to think so?"

29
CLOSING THE BOOKS

I was still reeling from Sean's revelation about Hemingway and Fitzgerald. If, and it was a big if, it were true. It certainly wasn't out of the question. There had always been rumors that Hemingway's bravado and chauvinism hid something a little darker and more taboo. Fitzgerald, too, had his own demons. But how likely was it that Hemingway would out both of them in a book's inscription?

The only thing left for me now was to pay a visit to Carlton Phillips. I wasn't sure what I was going to say to him, other than to report that I'd found his daughter. I'd just open my mouth and see what came out.

There were still plenty of questions to be answered, and maybe Phillips could answer at least some of them.

I called him at his office and told him we had to meet.

"Not here."

"Fine with me. Your office makes me nervous. Where?"

"You know the Citicorp building on Third and Fifty-fourth?"

"Yeah."

"Downstairs. In the Atrium. I'll be at a table in the middle of the room. Meet me there in twenty minutes."

It was almost seven o'clock when I got there, and the Atrium was pretty empty, except for a few homeless people camped out around the edges of the large area, waiting till closing time when they'd be kicked out. It was cool. It was safe. And nobody would bother them till then. Phillips, dressed in a suit and tie, was sitting at a table, sipping coffee and reading the *Wall Street Journal.*

I slipped into a seat opposite him. Without looking up, he said, "I'll be finished with this article in a moment."

"You think I don't have better things to do than wait for you to finish reading an article that'll be there ten minutes from now?"

He looked up. "I'm fairly confident you don't," he said.

I hated this guy, and yet I also felt sorry for him. So what if he was an asshole? His daughter was a piece of work, and she'd ripped him off for 200 grand. I could wait.

Finally, he folded the newspaper, removed his eyeglasses and put them down on the table, crossed his legs and said, "I'm all ears . . ."

"I found your daughter."

"Congratulations."

"I'm not telling you anything you don't already know, am I?"

"No. You're not. And frankly, unless there's something else, your services are no longer required."

"You didn't give a damn about finding your daughter, did you? It was all about the book."

"And what if it was?"

"Why weren't you honest with me? Why didn't you tell me the truth and just hire me to find the book? Why the charade of finding your daughter?"

"I have my reasons, and I don't feel obligated to share them with you."

"You know the book might be a fake, don't you?"

He said nothing. His expression remained unchanged.

"You don't give a fuck, do you?"

Still nothing.

"And the reason you don't give a fuck is that it really wasn't the book you were after. It really was your daughter you were out to protect, wasn't it?"

"I don't know what you're talking about."

"She's accused you of molesting her. She stole a book from you. She thinks she's conned you out of over two hundred grand, but she hasn't, has she? The fact is, you bought it back to protect her. You don't care about the money. You don't care that she's demonized you. You feel guilty for something, don't you?"

"Guilty? Of what?"

"You think you failed her as a father. You think you're responsible for what she's turned into. But it's not true. You may be a class-A sonuvabitch, but you didn't make her what she is. She was born that way."

"And that makes me not responsible?"

"You're not going to be able to clean up her messes for the rest of her life. Or yours. Do you think she's going to love you because she's got your money? Because you saved her ass by taking the book off the market, protecting her from embarrassment when it turns out the book is a fake?"

"You're sure it's a fake?"

"It doesn't matter what I'm sure of. The fact is, that book is never going to see the light of day, is it? You'll destroy it and no one will ever know if it's real or not."

"Assuming I have it."

"Oh, you have it. Or had it."

"Think what you want. Do you really think I care?"

"I know you don't care. But let me tell you something, Phillips. If I've learned anything the last few years, it's that the harder you try to control things, the more chaotic and out of control they become. If you think burying that book is going to end things, you're mistaken. Marcy's still out there, and she's not finished hurting you or anyone else around her. Sean's her victim. Dana Simmons will be next. You can count on that. So you can cover up for her as much as you want, but it's not going to change her. Chaos reigns, my friend. The center is falling apart. You can't trust anyone or anything. Because if you do, you're doomed. You think the fact that she's your daughter, your flesh and blood, means that you're connected in any real way? Because if you do, you're in for a real disappointment. You haven't heard the last of her, and when you do, prepare yourself for trouble. You think you're tough. You think you can handle things. You're in for a rude awakening," I said as I stood up. "You'll get my final bill in the mail, and I'm gonna stick it to you, my friend. Because you can afford it, and because you know I'm right about everything. Just do me one favor."

"What's that?"

"Lose my number."

I left him sitting there, staring out into space. I should have hated him, but I didn't. I didn't feel sorry for him, either. He was just another misguided casualty of life who thought that money can fix everything. I used to think that, but I know better now. Money can change life, but it can't fix it. You can make the signal come in clearer, but in the end, you're only going to see what someone wants you to see.

There were still questions to be answered—who left the notes for me in London? Who tossed my rooms? Who hired Smith and Jones? But in the end, did it really matter? Would my life be enriched by knowing everything? Would I sleep any better at night?

No. To all of it. Maybe all those things were connected to the case. Maybe not. I've learned that not everything needs to be connected. Sometimes, you're better off squinting at that out-of-focus picture and letting your mind put it together.

For now, I would cash my check and let everyone else worry about the rest of it.

I wasn't quite sure what I was going to do next. But I did know I wasn't going back to installing cable. And skip tracing . . . well, who knew what the future would bring? But the past was past, and to prove it, I pulled out my cell phone and brought up the photo I'd taken of the old neighborhood where I'd had my office. I stared at it for a few moments. Then, I hit the delete key.

The screen went dark.

ABOUT THE AUTHOR

Charles Salzberg is a freelance writer based in New York City. His work has appeared in *Esquire, New York Magazine, GQ,* and the *New York Times* and he has been a Visiting Professor of Magazine at the S.I. Newhouse School of Public Communications at Syracuse University. He now teaches writing at the Writer's Voice and the New York Writers Workshop, where he is a Founding Member. The first novel in the Swann series, *Swann's Last Song,* was nominated for a Shamus Award for Best First PI Novel, and a Swann short story appears in *Long Island Noir.*

Henryswann.com
Charlessalzberg.com